DATE DUE

#47-0108 Peel Off Pressure Sensitive

Country Wives

By Rebecca Shaw

THE BARLEYBRIDGE NOVELS

A Country Affair
Country Wives
Country Lovers

COUNTRY WIVES

A Barleybridge Novel

Rebecca Shaw

 THREE RIVERS PRESS • NEW YORK

Copyright © 2001 by Rebecca Shaw

All rights reserved.
Published in the United States by Three Rivers Press, an imprint of the
Crown Publishing Group, a division of Random House, Inc., New York.

Three Rivers Press and the Tugboat design are registered trademarks of
Random House, Inc.

Originally published in Great Britain by Orion Books, Ltd., London,
in 2001.

ISBN-13: 978-0-7394-7664-2

Printed in the United States of America

Design by Barbara Sturman

List of Characters in the Barleybridge Practice

Mungo Price .... *Orthopedic Surgeon and Senior Partner*
Colin Walker .... *Partner—large and small animal*
Zoe Savage .... *Partner—large animal*
Graham Murgatroyd .... *Small-animal vet*
Valentine Dedic .... *Small-animal vet*
Rhodri Hughes .... *Small-animal vet*
Dan Brown .... *Large-animal vet*

NURSING STAFF

Sarah Cockroft *(Sarah One)*
Sarah MacMillan *(Sarah Two)*
Bunty Page

RECEPTIONISTS

Joy Bastable *(Practice Manager)*
Lynne Seymour
Stephie Budge
Kate Howard

Miriam Price .... *Mungo's wife*
Duncan Bastable .... *Joy's husband*
Letty Walker .... *Colin's wife*
Gerry Howard .... *Kate's father*
Mia Howard .... *Kate's stepmother*

The Barleybridge Practice

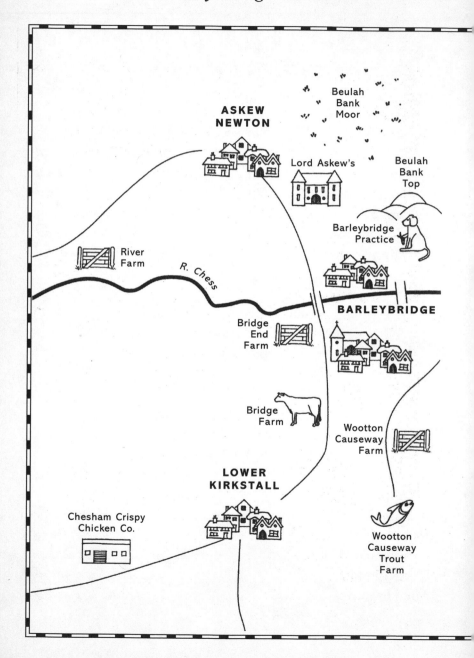

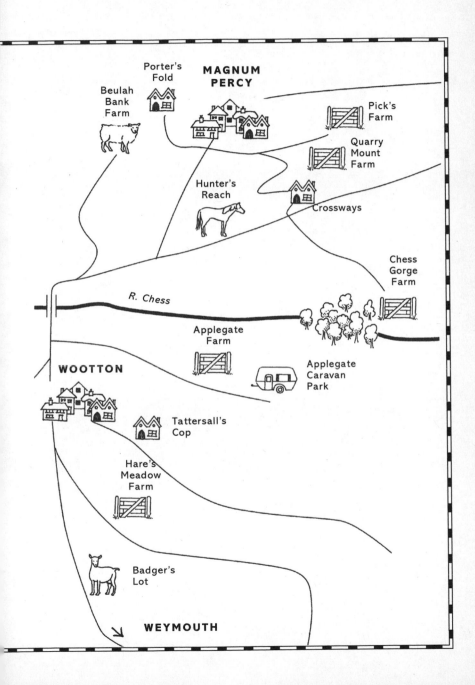

Chapter

· 1 ·

The temporary vet had been working for the practice one whole week, and Joy wasn't at all sure he should be there another day, never mind waiting until they had appointed someone permanently. It wasn't that he didn't work hard, or that he didn't know his job, because he did; his experience was extensive and his meticulous punctuality and his enthusiasm were A1. No, it was none of these things; it was his *attitude* that got up her nose and not only hers but Mungo's and everyone else's too. He'd be in shortly and she was wishing like hell he wouldn't be, and that it would be the much-lamented Scott who would be nonchalantly strolling in to collect his call list, his devastatingly blue eyes twinkling, his hands in his pockets, and be setting himself out to flirt with her. But it wasn't to be; all she could do was make sure that over her dead body would this particular temp become a regular member of the staff. Glancing at the reception clock, she saw she had only five minutes exactly before the glass doors swung open and *he* would march in, brisk and alert, eager for whatever the day would bring, good or bad.

She checked his list of calls for the fourth time to make sure he couldn't find any fault with it and wished Kate weren't on her day off because she seemed to know instinctively how to deal with him. Kate needed a break, though. She'd been looking ghastly this last week, and they all knew why but didn't dare say a word to her because Kate was endeavoring to carry on as though Scott had never existed, but it was evident from her face that he'd worked his magic on her, as he had on others, and his sudden departure had hit her hard. Joy heard the outer door open and braced herself for the arrival of Daniel Brown.

Somehow he could have been excused some of his bluntness if he'd been good-looking but he wasn't. He was a couple of inches under six feet, well built, very dark haired with a kind of craggy face that even his mother couldn't call handsome, and he had large, challenging, alert brown eyes, which missed nothing. Also, there was a sort of "in your face" energy about him which intimidated lesser mortals.

The inner glass door crashed open and there stood Dan, in his brown corduroy trousers, his checked sports jacket and matching cap; jaw jutting, his dark eyes wide awake, eager to begin his day's work. "Good morning, Joy. Got my list?"

"Good morning to you. Here it is, Dan; long list today, I'm afraid."

"Afraid? Why afraid? Isn't that what work is about? I shan't earn my keep if I'm sitting about all day twiddling my thumbs. Those results back from the laboratory?"

"The mail hasn't come yet, unfortunately."

"That isn't your fault; I'll ring in during the morning."

Joy nodded her head. Come back, Scott, all is forgiven.

"Right, I'll be away then. There's something wrong with the Land Rover. That chap who had it before me must have driven it like a maniac. Which garage do you use for servicing the vehicles?"

"Vickers."

"Where is it?"

Joy turned to the map pinned behind the reception desk and pointed it out to him. "But Mungo likes to know; I'll tell him."

"No need for that. I'll take it and see what they say. Something to do with the transmission. I can't afford for it to break down and leave me stranded with calls still to do. That's not the way to run a practice, is it?"

"Well, no, it isn't."

"Are they not serviced regularly?"

"Of course they are; but we can't repair them before they've gone wrong, can we?"

"Is it you responsible for seeing them serviced?"

"Well, yes, but . . ."

"When is the service due, then?"

"Look here . . ."

"I asked a simple question."

"I'd have to get the records out."

"Then do it now; let's find out. I can't afford to be standing around here wasting time." Dan tapped his fingers impatiently on the reception desk.

"At this time in the morning I'm busy with clients and appointments. I'll have a look later when I've a few minutes to spare."

Dan shrugged his shoulders. "Very well, but don't say I didn't warn you. I can't stand inefficiency; and if the Land Rover breaks down today, that's exactly what it will be: inefficiency, yours not mine."

"Look here . . ."

"If it's cost you're concerned about, I can assure you that if I take it to the garage myself, don't fret yourself, they won't overcharge *me*."

Joy, seething with the injustice of his opinions, thought, *No, I bet they won't. They'll do it for free just to get you off the premises.*

He studied his list for a moment. "This first call, Lord Askew's? Is it a stately home, then?"

Joy answered him as civilly as she could: "A minor one, but stately all the same. We do all his farm work, but his horses are looked after by a practice near Sherborne."

"Why don't we do *all* his veterinary work?"

"Because his horses are rather special; the Sherborne practice specializes in equine work, and he prefers to use them."

"That's enough to get my back up. However . . ."

"Be seeing you."

"Indeed." Dan nodded his head at her and dashed out through the front door.

Livid with temper and more determined than ever that he had to go, Joy listened to the roar of the Land Rover and heard it brake suddenly; and then there was the screech of brakes other than his. But there was no sound of metal on metal, so they must have missed each other. Pity.

Dan roared off, guided by the sign for Askew Newton as he was leaving the town. He'd spent a whole evening in the clinic painstakingly copying onto his own large-scale map the names of the farms and their positions from the map behind the reception desk, so now with only the briefest reference to his handiwork he could head off to the various clients. It took a while to get to know all the farmers and their own particular idiosyncrasies; but he was already getting the hang of the place, and Dan had to admit to a liking for it. It hadn't been easy coming back to England after seven years abroad, but a clean break had been the best thing. He'd done that and found this job in less than a week of returning, and he had half a mind to stay if they would have him.

He swung into the turning for Lord Askew's place, admir-

ing the beautifully sculptured parkland and enjoying the glimpse
he caught of the large stone house through the trees.

He pulled up in an immaculate cobbled courtyard surrounded
by stables. A groom was walking a horse across the yard. Dan
didn't know when he'd seen a more princely looking animal. It
was a wonderful roan, just the shade which appealed to him.
He admired it for a moment, thoroughly enjoying its beauty.

The groom called to Dan. "Morning, can I help?"

Dan got out and went across to him. "My name's Dan Brown,
from the Barleybridge Veterinary Hospital, come to see Chris?
Has a cow with mastitis."

"That'll be through the archway."

"Right." Dan paused for a moment, looked at the horse and
said, "Don't like the look of the action of his front feet." He
touched his cap to the groom, climbed back in the Land Rover
and swept away through the arch. Now this really was a well-
kept place. Just what he preferred to see. Attention to detail
meant well-cared-for animals and he liked that, did Dan. Nothing he hated more than careless husbandry. In fact, if it was
careless, *husbandry* was a misnomer.

A man he took to be Chris came out to greet him. "Where's
Scott, then?"

"Gone back to Aussie land in a hurry."

"Not surprising. Woman trouble I expect! He was a rare
womanizer, was that Scott. There wasn't a female anywhere
around these parts who hadn't fallen for his charm, including
her ladyship. Pick of the lot of 'em he could have had. So, it's
goodbye, Scott, and hello . . . ?"

"I'm Dan Brown, come to see a cow with mastitis."

"I'm Chris, nice to meet you." Chris appraised Dan with a
piercing eye as he shook his hand and said, "That Scott was a
bad lad, but he knew his job."

"You'll find no fault with me. Lead the way."

"Didn't say I would; just didn't want you to get the wrong impression of Scott."

"How big's your herd?"

"One hundred and forty-three at the moment. All pedigree Guernseys."

Dan was impressed, but he was appalled when he saw how ill the cow was.

While he took her temperature he very, very quietly asked how long she'd been like this.

"Three or four days, not bad like, just off color more than anything this morning . . ."

After checking the thermometer and feeling the affected quarter of the cow's udder, Dan straightened up and looked Chris in the eye. "You're the stockman, are you?"

Chris nodded.

"Are you sure?"

Puzzled, Chris nodded again.

"No stockman worth his salt would allow a cow to suffer like this. She's been more than "off color" as you put it for three or four days, as well you know. You ought to be ashamed of yourself. It could be almost too late to save her. Is his lordship about this morning?"

Chris took a deep breath, "Out riding. But . . ."

"There's no buts about this. How many years' experience have you had?"

"Eleven years in charge, but look here, it's not my fault."

"Kindly tell me whose fault it is, then? The gardener's or the housemaid's or someone?"

"No, of course not, but his lordship . . ."

"Oh! I see, now it's his lordship to blame, is it. What time is he usually back from his ride?"

"Any time now."

"I'll deal with the cow and then I'll deal with him."

"It's the money you see."

Dan wagged his finger at Chris, saying, "I don't expect owners to *lavish* care on their beasts, but I do expect them to be well cared for. With veterinary work, a good motto to remember is 'a stitch in time saves nine,' and you'd do well to abide by that."

"But that's what he doesn't . . ."

"I bet one of his eventers would have had quicker treatment than this, no matter the cost."

"Yes, but you see . . ."

"It may surprise you to know that cows feel pain just as much as horses."

Dan, having assessed the cow's problem, went back to his vehicle and picked out the drugs which past experience told him he would need. He returned and concentrated on treating the cow. While he waited for an injection to bring down the milk into the infected quarter to take effect, he gave the cow antibiotics into the vein. After a few minutes he was able to strip out the milk and give the cow some relief. "I would normally suggest that I leave you some antibiotics for you to give her for the next three days; but in view of your reluctance to call us in, I'll be back in the morning myself first thing. Right?"

Angered by his attitude, Chris said, "Right. Perhaps next time you might let me get a word in edgeways."

Dan turned back. "I'm so sorry, please . . . be my guest."

"His lordship gets wild if I call in a vet too early or if he considers we could have managed without. It's the money, you see. It all goes on the horses. It's more than my job's worth; I've a wife and children, and we're living in a tied house and that. If I upset him we'll all be homeless. Scott knew that and made allowances."

"I beg your pardon. I was angry; it always affects me like that when pain could have been avoided. I'll clear it with . . ." The clatter of hooves and a loud, braying voice interrupted him.

Quietly Chris said, "That's him back."

"Right. See you tomorrow." Dan, emerging from the archway, saw a splendid black horse skittering about on the cobbles; and mounted on its impressive back was a giant of a man in immaculate riding kit. From under his riding hat a thick swath of snow-white hair framed a ruddy, well-fleshed face with a prominent pulpy nose dominating it.

"Mornin' to you. Who might you be? Here, Gavin, take him for me." Lord Askew dismounted and eyed Dan up and down. He was a head taller than Dan, so the word giant was very apt. His shoulders were wide, his chest built like a barrel and his arms were thick as tree trunks.

Dan held out his hand. "I'm Dan Brown from Barleybridge."

Lord Askew ignored his outstretched hand. "Seeing that damned cow of mine, I've no doubt. Eh? More cost. Coming back tomorrow, are you, on some flimsy excuse? More money. Never ending it is."

Dan deliberately kept his voice low in sharp contrast to his lordship. "You have a herd of over a hundred cows and you can't expect them to produce milk at the rate they do without needing attention from time to time . . ."

"Eh? Speak up. Can't hear."

Dan raised the level of his voice but kept the same quiet determination in his tone. "I'm sorry to have to say this, but I should have been called earlier. In fact, to be honest, I'm annoyed your stockman has felt compelled to leave it so late."

Lord Askew began to bluster. "I damn well don't know who you are, but whoever you are you've too damn much to say for yourself. Too damn much, and I shall be having a word with Mungo Price about you. What's yer name, you say?"

"Dan Brown. You can have as many words as you like, but Mungo will agree with me that she shouldn't have been left for so long. As I have several other calls to make this morning; if you will excuse me, I must leave right now."

"Damned impertinence! There's no need to come back in the morning. My stockman can see to her."

"Either I take responsibility for her or I don't, you can't have it both ways. I shall be here tomorrow. By the way, that roan"— he nodded his head in the direction of the roan now tethered to a ring in the stable wall—"has a problem with its front feet."

Lord Askew's face registered shock bordering on horror. "Eh? Eh?"

"Good morning to you."

Dan drove away seething with temper and well aware he'd made a big mistake tackling Lord Askew in the way he had, but people like him made his blood boil. Mungo would be rather less than pleased to have that blustering idiot complaining on the phone, though. Well, if it cost him his job so what? He had his principles; and that poor stockman, tied hand and fist because of his domestic circumstances, couldn't be allowed to take the blame. Dan Brown was probably heading for the biggest apology of his life.

On his way to Tattersall's Cop he called in at the practice for the results of the specimens he'd sent to the laboratory, to be faced by an indignant Joy. She beckoned him into her office with a schoolmarmish finger. "I have had Lord Askew on the phone. What on earth have you said to him, as if I need to ask."

"I've no doubt he explained very thoroughly, Joy, and I shall make a point of apologizing to him tomorrow when I go."

"You won't be going. He refuses to have you on his land."

"Does he indeed."

"Also, what on earth were you doing examining one of his horses? It's hardly veterinary etiquette, is it?"

"I didn't. It was obvious. Only a fool could have missed it."

Joy calmed down a little and a glimmer of amusement flicked across her face. "Only a fool!"

"Yes. I must confess his lordship looked more than a little startled. I bet their so-called equine vet will be there humming and hawing this very minute. Mail come?"

"Yes. Here we are." She handed him the letter he was waiting for and watched as he opened it.

His face lit up and he raised a clenched fist into the air. "Eureka! I knew I was right! Ha!"

Briefly, Joy couldn't help but like him. "This won't cancel the appointment you have with Mungo at one. He can't see you now because he has a full list of consultations this morning, but he wants you to make sure you're here. We can't afford to lose a good customer, and Lord Askew has a lot of influence. It's not just him we'll lose; he'll tell half the county."

Dan, looking at her with a dead-straight face, replied, "You're very wrong there, very wrong; he'll tell *all* the county. Nothing I did or said was out of order, believe me. I will not tolerate neglect. Must be off. This Tattersall's Cop, is there anything I should know?"

"Beautiful, beautiful setting. Lovely people, struggling to make ends meet. We try to be economical with their bills."

Dan raised his eyebrows. "Tut-tut! That won't pay back the overdraft."

There he was again, catching her on the raw. Rather tartly she answered him with "That's Mungo's worry not yours."

"Indeed it is. Be seeing you at one." As Dan went back into reception, he glanced around the seating area, catching the eye of a few of the clients and giving them a brusque nod of greeting.

After the door had closed on his departure, one of the long-standing clients called out to Joy, "He looks a bit grim, Joy."

Between tight lips she answered, "His heart's in the right place."

"Well, he certainly wasn't in the right place when good looks were given out."

A general chortle broke out.

"Bring back Scott, I say," another client contributed to the debate.

"All these bleeding hearts he's left behind, nothing short of criminal."

"It was 'is 'ands I liked, sensitive they were."

"Did you ever see him in his shorts?" The client rolled her eyes in appreciation.

"Oops! Steady, Bridget, you'll be spinning out of control!"

They all laughed and then resettled to discussing their animals' symptoms.

Joy silently agreed with them. Despite the broken hearts among her own staff, Scott had brought laughter and delight with him to the practice every day and that couldn't be bad; added to which, the farm clients loved him for his expertise. She'd an idea they would appreciate Dan's knowledge too, but they'd never appreciate the man. And neither would she.

By a quarter to one Dan was eating his homemade sandwiches outside on the old bench by the back door. There was a powerful wind coming down from Beulah Bank Top, which seemed to slice through any clothing you chose to be wearing, but Dan preferred the peace and quiet to the banter in the staff room where most of the staff ate their lunch. Social chitchat had never appealed to him and still less now with so much on his mind. Though when he'd visited Tattersall's Cop, his own problems had been momentarily forgotten. What a beautiful, neat little farm it was, loving care in every inch of hedging, in every ditch, in every farm building but . . . it seemed to Dan that Callum Tattersall dabbled first in this and then in that, never sticking at anything long enough to get real returns on his investment. He hadn't enough acres, not enough guts and, to be honest, not enough commitment. Bad luck had played a big part in his life too, or so Callum had said as they shared a mounting block while they drank their coffee. A sick wife needing a lot of care, a one-in-a-thousand chance of disease decimating his entire turkey flock, his scheme for producing fresh farm yogurt failing, to say nothing of the race horse he had bought a share in which, after falling at the first fence, was never fit for racing again. But you dratted well couldn't help but like the man. A shadow fell across his legs, and he looked up to find Mungo standing beside him. Dan put the apple he was about to sink his teeth into in his pocket and shifted farther along the bench to make room for him.

Mungo broke the silence with, "Well?"

"I was polite, controlled and well mannered, and absolutely right. Like you, I abhor animals having to suffer because their owners are too mean to get treatment for them; and that's what it is: absolute, sod-awful meanness that makes that huge well-fed lord of the manor refuse to allow the stockman to call for help when the chap knows it's needed. I shall go tomorrow to attend the cow, in spite of being forbidden to do so, because my professional integrity is being challenged and neither you nor I can allow that. I shall, however, apologize." Dan looked at Mungo and waited for his reply.

"The big mistake was examining the horse."

"I didn't. Just watching him trot across the yard I knew his problem, without doubt." Dan grinned. "You should have seen old Askew's face when I commented on his limp. You'd have enjoyed it."

"Would I? You're not wet behind the ears—I'm well aware of that—you know what you're doing, but I've spent twenty years of my life building up this practice and I don't want to lose it all because of someone . . ."

"Yes?"

". . . someone who thinks he's a clever beggar."

Dan grunted and held back on an angry reply.

Mungo, sensing his anger, tried a more conciliatory approach. "Horses. I didn't realize."

"Worked for an Arab sheikh for a while. Learned a lot."

"Interesting work."

Dan nodded. "You'd do well to take horses on. Just that bit more money into the coffers. You see plenty hereabouts when you're driving around."

"Never had the inclination."

"Worth thinking about. There's money in it."

"Got to speak frankly, Dan. To be honest, I'm not in it for the money. Yes, I have wages to pay and drugs to buy and a building to keep up, but my main reason for being a vet is the animals; and their needs are paramount in my mind. Do well by them and you and I will get on famously; have money as your prime motivation and we won't, and you can leave."

"You're not questioning my integrity too, are you?"

"No, I am not. I'm just . . . telling you. Putting it on the line, so we both know where we stand." Mungo stood up and faced him. "Watch yourself tomorrow. I dislike Lord Askew as much as you do; there's nothing gracious or pleasing about him, but he is a client, his bills are always paid on the dot and we owe him a duty of care, and also he has a lot of influence."

"Exactly, a duty of care and that's just what I shall be doing when I go in the morning: caring."

"Good, then you and I understand each other. Dinner with us tomorrow night in the flat, Miriam says, if you've nothing better to do."

"Thanks. Yes."

"Seven-thirty."

"Fine. I look forward to it."

DAN arrived at Mungo and Miriam's at seven-twenty-nine precisely after a long, arduous day. He was the last to arrive. Waiting to greet him were Joy and her husband, Duncan; Colin and his wife, Letty; and a heavily pregnant Zoe with no husband. Something about the tension in the air made him wonder if this was to become a third-degree interrogation, because here he was, faced with all three partners.

Miriam came out of the kitchen and broke into smiles on seeing him. "Dan! How lovely!"

She gave him a great big hug as naturally as if they'd known each other for years and he responded gladly, "Miriam! Nice to see you again."

When she released him, she asked what he would like to drink. Briefly he studied her face, saw how genuine her greeting was and felt grateful. "A whiskey and water, please."

"Mungo, a whiskey and water for Dan. The food is almost ready." She crossed her fingers and laughed.

Colin introduced his wife, Letty. She was short and round and pale and blond, and had the misfortune to have chosen to wear a cream wool suit and Vaseline on her lips instead of lipstick, so she appeared to have no substance at all, but her tongue belied her appearance. "Got the practice into deep trouble and you've only been here a week."

"Letty!" Colin protested.

"Deep trouble?"

"Hadn't you heard? Lord Askew has canceled his account with us."

"No, I hadn't heard. More fool him."

"After your rudeness . . ."

Colin interrupted, "Letty! It's none of your business. Leave it."

Looking Colin directly in the face, she said, "Our income is my business. It cost an arm and a leg to set up this place. If the practice fails, so too do we." In profile Dan saw that Letty's nose was longer and sharper than any he'd seen in a long time. Unfulfilled, that was her trouble. Then he smiled inwardly at his assumption, or thought he had.

"It's amusing, is it?"

Insulted by Letty's thinking he was not taking the matter seriously enough, Dan answered her sharply, "No, it is not."

"Wait till Mungo's taken in what's happened. You'll be out on your ear in no time at all."

Dan, growing angrier by the minute, asked her, "Shall I indeed?"

She nodded her head vigorously. "If I have my way you will."

Exasperated by her rudeness, Colin said, "Please! Leave it, leave it." By his tone it was obvious he knew she would ignore his protest.

"I hadn't realized you owned the practice."

Slightly taken aback by his directness, she paused a moment and then answered him, "I do have a large say in the matter but then money talks, doesn't it?"

"Are you always so unpleasant to people you don't know?"

"I beg your pardon?"

"I said are you always so unpleasant to people you've never met before?"

"Unpleasant? I believe in calling a spade a spade and so do you, judging by what you said to Lord Askew yesterday morning."

"I hadn't realized you were there?"

"I wasn't. Colin told me."

"Ah!"

Miriam called out for help in the kitchen from Mungo and asked Joy to seat everybody.

In the general mêlée of Joy's organizing everyone, Dan deftly separated himself from Letty and managed to find a seat next to Zoe. "Hello, Zoe, how are you?"

"More to the point, how are you?" Lowering her voice, she added, "She really is the absolute limit. I don't know how Colin puts up with her."

"He seems well laid back."

"One day the worm will turn, believe me. One can put up with so much and then . . ."

"Water?"

Zoe nodded. Dan poured her a glass of water, and wishing not to become involved too deeply in practice politics, he asked, "Are you hoping to come back to work after the baby?"

"Of course."

"How will you manage?"

"My mother lives with me. Between us we shall cope."

Dan hesitated. "I hadn't . . . I didn't know . . ."

"There's no need to tiptoe delicately around the matter, I'm unmarried and intend staying so, this"—she waved vaguely in the direction of her bump—"is a momentary blip."

"I see. That's a new word for a baby. Blip."

"I hear a hint of disapproval. You can disapprove as much as you like. I don't really care."

"I'm old-fashioned enough to believe that two are better than one where babies are concerned."

"There will be two. My mother and I."

They were interrupted by the soup arriving.

Miriam came to sit down and put herself out to make him feel comfortable. She was an astute and caring hostess and a thoughtful conversationalist, and after a few minutes of her company, Dan dismissed his clashes with Zoe and Letty as more a misfortune on their part than his.

"Where were you working before you came here, Dan?"

"Here and there. In the the Gulf, the Caribbean, in the States. But now I'm home for good."

"You mean in England for good."

Dan nodded. "That's right."

"Good, I'm glad. There comes a time when gadding about all over the place is just not enough anymore, and one longs to put down one's roots. Is that how you feel?"

There was a slight hesitation, then Dan answered firmly, "It is."

"That's lovely. I am pleased. Is the flat all right? I paid a company to clean it and everything; they're usually very good. If there is anything you're short of let me know. The flat is my particular charge, you see, so any problems, see Miriam."

Dan, who had been about to reply, got beaten to it by Letty. "He won't be here long enough to know if anything's missing."

Colin touched her arm and said, "Now, Letty; now, Letty."

Miriam flushed. Dan saw her agitation and felt concerned. She was too sweet to have to suffer this kind of unpleasantness. Visibly angry, Miriam said, "Letty, I expect my guests to put themselves out to be *charming* while they are in my home, even if they're . . . not charming." She stood up and began to collect the soup plates.

Dan said loudly, "That soup was delicious, Miriam, if I might say so, some of the best I've had."

"Thank you. I shan't be long with the main course. It's all ready."

Joy bounced up to give her a hand and they both disappeared into the kitchen.

A long silence fell because those still sitting at the table had been surprised by the sharpness of Miriam's retort to Letty.

It was Duncan who saved the day. "My cat, Tiger, shall I have her spayed when the time comes? Do you advise it, Mungo?"

"Question is, do you want kittens?"

"No."

"Then have it done; it's the only way."

"Have I the right?"

"Right to what?"

"Have I the right to have her snipped? I wouldn't want to have the snipping job done, so have I the right to have the cat done. It's not as if I can ask her permission, is it?"

A wave of laughter went round the table, except for Letty, who pulled a disapproving face. *What else could the woman expect when sitting at a table dominated by members of the veterinary profession*, thought Dan.

Mungo stopped laughing long enough to say, "Look here, Duncan, it isn't very long since you mocked me at this very table for loving my Perkins and here you are treating Tiger as if she were a human being. She isn't; she has no soul, no aspirations for the future, no knowledge of what she's having done, no thinking 'God! Now I shall never be a mother; why is he doing this to me?' So blessed well get it done for her sake. Come on, man. There's no debate."

"Isn't there?"

Duncan asked Zoe and she agreed with Mungo. He asked Dan and he said, "Having litter after litter of kittens is cruelty in the extreme, and finding homes for them all even more cruel for yourself. There's no debate, like Mungo said."

"I'm not too sure."

Dan replied emphatically, "Well, I am. In fact, come to think of it, there are plenty of human beings who could do to be snipped, never mind the odd cat."

"She isn't an odd cat, she's my cat," Duncan protested.

"Your cat or not, I would have her snipped. She'll never know the difference, and the world will be dozens of unwanted cats the fewer. Two-minute job. Bring her in tomorrow and I'll do it for her."

Panicking, Duncan said quickly, "No, no, she's too young yet."

"Well, when she's old enough I'll do it and . . ."

Zoe forcefully interrupted him. "Was 'plenty of human beings' a reference to me?"

Dan laughed. "About human beings having the snip? Come to think of it, there can't be that much difference between doing a cat and a human being. If you want snipping, Zoe, after your blip has arrived, just say the word. It could be a first. You wouldn't need to wait for months; we could slip you in between ops." He pretended to look at the operations diary, using his hands as though flicking through the pages. "Let's see. Valentine has a castration at eleven-thirty, a spay at twelve, would twelve-thirty suit you? How about it, Mungo? Neutering human beings could open up a whole new world for us humble vets."

Mungo, enjoying his joke, didn't get a chance to answer because Zoe got there first. "Did you say that to illustrate yet again your disapproval of me being a single mother?"

"The manner in which you conduct your life is none of my business, though I do have a right to my opinion."

Zoe, losing her temper with him, demanded, "Well, let's hear it, then."

"I don't think it a subject for the dinner table."

"I do."

Dan looked at her, saying quietly, "Very well, I'll state my case. I think it is the height of selfishness for young women to want a baby purely for their own satisfaction, and that, unfortunately, is very often the case. I understand that some single mothers don't even tell the man they have made use of about the birth. That is appalling. Babies are not a fashion accessory, nor are they there to be born simply because their mothers need someone to love. They do not ask to be born; but when they do come, they deserve the very best from two parents. I do not know the circumstances of the conception of your blip; so I cannot judge, can I?"

By the end of his statement Dan was speaking loudly and the others couldn't help but hear. It seemed odd to everyone that he should have such strong views on the matter, and more than one seated at the table intuitively surmised that there was more to Dan's views than just an opinion aired.

They were all embarrassed into silence by his outburst. Only Zoe was distressed by it, because he had so accurately put his finger on her own feelings about becoming pregnant.

Miriam broke the spell they were under by bringing in the main course: a huge dish of beautifully presented crown of lamb surrounded by roasted vegetables, which Mungo took from her and placed at his end of the table. Joy followed with a couple of tureens and the two of them sat down. Miriam said, "I've just had a thought; you're not vegetarian, are you, Dan? I never thought to ask."

"No, I'm not and that lamb looks delicious." He watched the admirable, almost elegant way in which Mungo carved and served the lamb, and thought how much he liked the man—he was so honest and straightforward and compassionate. It hardly seemed fair that so many enviable qualities should be concentrated in one person. Dan caught Letty watching him, and he met her ice-cold gaze boldly. He smiled and raised his glass to her, but her eyes slid away from him as she completely ignored his gesture. He realized he'd made more than one enemy tonight.

The dinner party never quite recovered after the argument between Zoe and Dan, and he wasn't the only one glad when people began to leave.

Mungo called him over to his side of the room as he was about to go. "A word, please, before you disappear, Dan." He led the way back into the dining room and closed the door. "Askew has rung me to say he is not requiring our services anymore. He's going to the practice in the High Street. He claims you trespassed this morning, and he is threatening you with police action. He also says that there is nothing wrong with the horse and that what you said, you said out of malice."

Dan raised his eyebrows in surprise. "Do you believe him?"

"I don't know what to believe. You tell me."

"OK, in his opinion I did trespass, but like I said, the cow merited further attention; and in all conscience I gave it that attention this morning, nothing more, nothing less. I wasn't able to apologize because his lordship hadn't got back from his ride when I was ready to leave, but I shall do it in writing tomorrow. As for the horse, I know I am right and his vet is wrong." Dan shrugged his shoulders. "But there we are. There is the possibility of doing something about it if it is treated immediately. To ignore it will cut short its career quick smart."

"I see. Well, do not lose me any more accounts. We can't afford it."

"I'll do my best."

"We've advertised the job, by the way."

"Fair enough. I quite understand."

"Take no notice of Letty. No one else does."

"I won't. She's a bitch."

Mungo's head came up with a jerk. "She's right, though, about the practice losing money when we lose clients, and don't forget that."

"Mm. Goodnight and thank you for a lovely meal. Much appreciated."

"Thank Miriam before you go. She does all the work and it was her idea. I'm taking Perkins out. OK."

Dan found Miriam making a start on stacking the dishwasher. "I'm a whizz at stacking dishwashers. May I?"

"Lovely man, making an offer like that, but I have a strict rule: first-time guests may not help clear up."

"I doubt there'll be a second time."

"You wait and see." She took his hand and held it between both her own. "Welcome to the practice from me. Goodnight."

"Goodnight, Miriam."

Chapter

· 2 ·

Dan, heartened by Miriam's obvious approval of him, set off next morning to begin his calls with new heart. Before he'd gone to bed after the dinner party, he'd penned a groveling apology to Lord Askew, which had gone against his temperament to do but which he'd seen the necessity for. He'd taken it with him to the practice to post, with a copy to Mungo.

He was only halfway to the village of Wootton when the engine cut out and he came to a halt. Nothing he could do would make it start again, so he rang in to Barleybridge and asked Stephie to ring the garage for him and request them to come to the rescue. He cursed himself for not having called there the previous day, but it was too late now.

Dan went to sit on the fence beside the road and enjoy the early morning air. He'd forgotten how beautiful even a November morning in England could be; the sun wasn't shining but it was reasonably bright, and his view of the roofs and spires of Barleybridge to his right and the great sweep of woodland in front of him was very pleasing. There was something about the countryside here at home which fed the soul. Dry, arid plains, for all their feeling of space and freedom, didn't enrich him, but this did. He contemplated living here and decided once again that if it came about, he'd jump at the chance.

His reverie was eventually broken by the rumble of a van approaching from his left. Even before it slurred to a halt in the middle of the road, he could see it was patently almost derelict; one headlight was missing and it was difficult to ascertain its original color. All along the side nearest to Dan was a massive dent, which must have hindered the opening of the door. A head encased in a balaclava with slits in it poked out from the gap where the driver's window should have been. "I recognize that Land Rover; you must be Scott's replacement?"

Dan slid off the fence and crossed the verge to speak to him. "That's right. I'm Dan Brown."

"I'm Phil Parsons. Applegate Farm. Nice to meet you, Dan. What's up? Enjoying the air. Nought to do?"

"Plenty to do, but I've broken down."

"I'll give you a lift into Barleybridge; Blossom and me's off shopping, it being market day."

The head of the said Blossom appeared from behind Phil Parsons and gave Dan a shock. Her peroxided hair appeared to have reached the very heights of dazzle. That, combined with her lavishly applied electric-blue eye shadow, her dark plum-colored lipstick and her yard upon yard of cheap gilt jewelry, gave Dan the distinct impression that she was a lady ever on the lookout for "talent." If they were husband and wife, or partners, the two were the most incompatible pair he had ever come across: she a painted doll and he . . . well, he didn't know what Phil was because you couldn't see for his headgear, but he could smell him from where he stood.

Blossom greeted him in a slightly breathless Marilyn Monroe kind of voice. "Pleased to meet you, Dan."

Dan touched the bill of his cap in greeting. "And me you.

I'll ring the practice again and see what the state of play is. I might be glad of your offer. If you'll excuse me."

Stephie answered, saying they were about to ring him to tell him that the garage couldn't come out with the truck for at least another two hours as they were away on a job already, and if he could get a lift, then to come in to the practice and he could borrow Mungo's car to do his rounds, and the truck would tow the offending vehicle in, and they'd let them know the problem as and when. Dan clicked off his mobile and relayed the message to Phil.

"Jump in. Shove up, Blossom." He threw a pile of women's magazines and farming leaflets onto the floor by his feet to make room for Dan.

"It's very kind of you. I need a few things with me. Won't be a minute."

"Leave the keys in. Nobody'll pinch it; it's too well known."

Dan climbed up into the van, squeezed himself in beside Blossom and struggled to shut the door. Eventually, by almost sitting on Blossom's lap, he managed it.

"Here, put your things in the back behind me." She ducked her head away to make room for Dan to reach into the back. When he turned to look where to put his belongings, he found himself staring into what appeared to be a boudoir. The inside walls of the back of the van were thickly draped in pink filmy fabric, and the floor was filled with what must be a mattress covered in shiny, lurid-pink furry stuff with frilly pink and white pillows piled on top of it. Dan, without saying a word or letting his face slip, placed his things on the nearest pink and white pillow and squeezed himself back into position. Blossom wriggled delightedly, causing waves of a rich, overpowering perfume to escape and envelop him. "Well, set off then, Phil. We'll never get there set here in the middle of the road like this. Turn the key."

A vehicle behind tooted impatiently, so Phil turned the key and the engine responded with the most tremendous heave. Phil shoved it into gear and off they lurched. Dan had a nightmare ride back into the town, made worse by the constant titillating movements of Blossom. His right thigh felt her flexing and reflexing her leg muscles, his right arm was subject to a series of surreptitious nudges and rubbings, and her left hand hovered constantly within reach of his knee.

"You farm then, Phil?"

"Mm. Dairy, bit o' this, bit o' that. Few sheep."

"Perhaps I'll be round to see you one day."

"Nothing more certain. You should try the garage at Wootton, where we've just been. He charges half of that lot in the town and he doesn't use new spares either, he just . . . what's that word you use, Blossom?"

"Innovates."

"That's it, he makes his own spares; blacksmith he is, by trade. A real handy chap to have about."

"I'm sure. But Mungo has an account with the one in town, so I've no alternative."

Blossom asked, "Liking it here, are you, Dan?"

He looked at Blossom and got a provocative wink from one of her wickedly cheeky eyes. "I am."

"Well, when Phil calls you out, remember the kettle's always on and you're always welcome, isn't he, Phil?"

Phil nodded, concentrating on the traffic and taking time off to shake his fist at an innocent motorist. "Half of 'em don't know how to drive around here. I bet none of them have passed their test."

"Look who's talking!" Blossom giggled.

Immediately he realized Phil wasn't qualified to drive. Dan began to wish the journey at an end; but it was market day and the main streets in the town were packed with vehicles, and they made slow progress. "Look, if you like, I'll get out and walk the rest. It might be quicker, save you hanging about."

"Absolutely not. I said I'd give you a lift, and give you a lift I shall. We're nearly there." Phil stuck his head out of the window and called out a stream of abuse at a man on a motorbike who stuck two fingers up at him and caused Phil to abuse him even more.

Blossom giggled helplessly and lolled her head on Dan's shoulder. "You are a card, Phil Parsons! What will Dan think?" She nudged his ribs caressingly.

"I've heard worse, not much worse, but worse."

Blossom giggled again. "Ooh! You've been around, then. I can tell you're a man of action! At least he hasn't used the Aussie ones Scott taught him. They're terrible."

Phil screeched into the practice car park and, banging his boot on the brake, said, "Here we are then, safe and sound. Call anytime you're passing. Applegate Lane just out of town. If you've come to the turning for Wootton Causeway Farm, then you've missed our turning. If you've got to Applegate Caravan Park, you've gone past us. Have a care."

Blossom squeezed his knee. "And don't forget the door's always open even if we haven't called you out. Come anytime. We like company, don't we, Phil?"

Dan collected his belongings, jumped out, gave them his profuse thanks and went in through the back door.

Kate was working in her office and he paused in her doorway. She looked up to smile at him. "You look white as a sheet. What's happened?"

"I broke down and got a lift from Phil Parsons."

"Not in that dreadful van?"

Dan nodded. "The very same. He wears the most extraordinary headgear."

"Never takes it off."

"Never?"

"I've never seen him without it even on a warm day."

"How odd. Blossom. Is she his wife?"

"Apparently so. They're an odd couple."

Dan stared into space for a moment, looking as though he was wondering how to phrase what he had to say. "What does she do for a living?"

"She doesn't. She just helps him around the farm, if it could be called a farm."

"I see. Have you ever ridden in his van?"

"Never."

"I truly believed I was about to depart this life. It has no license plate; he hasn't taken a test and he'll definitely have no insurance, so don't accept a lift from him."

Kate laughed. "And don't whatever you do go in their kitchen and accept a drink or anything to eat, or you most certainly might depart this life. Coffee? Before you set off?"

"It must be time, and then I'll be off. Everyone will be wondering where I've got to."

When he'd drunk the coffee she made for him, he picked up Mungo's keys from Miriam and left.

Kate took coffee through for Lynne and Joy, and stopped to talk for a moment.

"I can't stand that man," Lynne said after she'd thanked Kate for her coffee. "I really can't. Scott was a so-and-so, but him . . . at least Scott was fun."

Joy snapped, "That will do, Lynne. Enough said."

"I disagree, I think we all have a right to have an opinion about him. After all, we do have to work with him. I say the sooner he goes, the better. He never mixes, you learn nothing about him, he isn't one little teeny-weeny bit of fun."

"I have asked you once; I shan't ask again. He is actually one of your bosses and it won't do."

Lynne put down her mug and folded her arms. "Are you telling me you like him?"

"I don't have to like any of the staff, but we do work for him in a sense and I don't approve of you criticizing him behind his back. Say no more about him, please."

"Well, I'm sorry, but someone has to speak up. The two Sarahs don't like him, and I definitely know Bunty doesn't."

"At the moment Bunty doesn't like any man, so her opinion doesn't count; and I don't particularly take to the idea of the gossiping you must have been doing to learn all this."

Lynne turned to Kate. "You're keeping quiet. What do you think?"

"To be honest, I like his attitude. He's paid to do a job and he's doing it very well indeed. I've an idea that underneath his bluntness is a first-class brain. Full stop. Just because he doesn't play the fool like . . . Scott did, doesn't mean he's no good."

"Oh yes, certainly he's doing his job well; he's already lost us one customer. Pity he didn't use his first-class brain, as you call it, when he blew it with old Askew. It's typical of you, though, you're only standing up for him because you know you're going to be a vet too. If he stays here much longer we'll all be out of a job."

Joy was furious with Lynne. "In my office. Now!"

With her office door firmly shut, Joy said, "In front of clients! Have you no sense? Every word they hear in here is listened to with avid interest. It'll be all over town before we know it that (a) staff don't like Dan, and (b) he's losing us business. You haven't even the common sense to lower your voice. I won't tolerate it, Lynne. You know my thoughts on confidentiality; you've been here three years and by now you should know what to say and what not to say."

Lynne didn't answer.

"Well?"

"It's not only me."

"Perhaps not, but the others know when to keep their mouths shut. Kate gets on with him all right. Why can't you?"

Lynne sneered, saying, "Oh yes, dear Kate, she would, wouldn't she? She's hoping to join the glorious profession, isn't she? High and mighty veterinary surgeon Kate Howard. Oh yes."

Joy didn't answer until she had forced herself to exert extreme control over her temper. "If you are dissatisfied with your work to the extent that you find it necessary to be so unkind about a member of staff, who most certainly does not deserve it, you had better do a rethink about your whole career."

"Are you asking me to leave?"

"I am not. I'm just asking you to have a think about your future. Jealousy will get you nowhere at all. You're young, bright, well set up, smart, good-looking, hardworking. If you're unhappy, what's holding you back from making a change?"

"Nothing. I suppose."

"I don't want you here if you don't want to be. But I would be sorry to lose you. Very sorry. Think about it."

"I take nothing back. Kate's a stuck-up, too-big-for-her-boots person, too clever for her own good, she is. As for Dan . . . Zoe was in here earlier. She doesn't like him either."

Joy held up her hand. There was a strong overtone of finality in her voice when she replied, "Enough said. I don't want to hear any more." She glanced at her wristwatch. "Now take an early lunch and when you come back for the evening surgery, make sure your face at least is pleasant. A Miss Vinegar Face I do not want to see."

So what with Letty taking a dislike to Dan and now Zoe—though *she* deserved all she got in Joy's opinion—and the staff, Joy felt that Dan's days were numbered. There was no way they could manage without him at the moment, though, for he did more calls in a day than any human being should be expected to do. Without him Colin would simply never go to bed.

Joy thought about Colin—thin, meek Colin with muscles of steel and a ferocious tenacity when work required it—and wondered how on earth he'd come to be married to Letty. They were exact opposites. She of the savage tongue and plump, insipid appearance and he of the build like a whippet, relaxed, kindly come day by day. Maybe his temperament was brought about as a direct reaction to Letty's. But they owed her a tremendous debt, for without her parents' money procuring Colin a partnership, they'd never have been able to be so ambitious in buying the land and purpose-building the hospital to such a high standard. No, they owed her a debt; and whatever they might think of her, she'd have to be kept sweet. Which brought her back to Lynne. The girl must be eaten up with jealousy, and what had Kate ever done to deserve such spite?

As she was thinking about her, Kate knocked and came in. "I'll hang on a bit longer, shall I? For lunch, I mean."

Joy pushed her fingers through her hair and looked up. The girl was bearing up well in the circumstances. "Leave the door open in case a client comes in. Sit down. You mustn't take what Lynne says too seriously. She's very unhappy with life at the moment, I'm afraid."

"I know. She said so a few weeks ago. Those brothers of hers have overshadowed her all her life and stopped her reaching for the stars herself, so it's left her unfulfilled."

"Well put. Yes, that's her problem, I'm sure. Very wise. We'll soon replace her if she decides to leave."

"I'd be willing to do extra days if we're in a fix. I need the money for college. I hope."

"Thanks. We'll wait and see."

. . .

WHEN Mungo came upstairs into the flat for his evening meal, he found Miriam in the kitchen making a sauce to go with the salmon she was cooking. He kissed the back of her neck and put his arms round her waist, resting his cheek against the back of her head. "Busy day?"

"This afternoon I went to the market."

"Yes."

"A client came up to me and said how sorry she was to hear that we weren't doing so well in our new premises. 'All that money you've spent,' she said."

"Who said that?"

"I can't remember her name, but she has five or six cats, and keeps a menagerie of hamsters and rabbits and the like."

Mungo let go of her and leaned against the worktop where he could see her face. "That's not very helpful, is it?"

"No. Apparently she's heard about us losing Lord Askew and says they'll be leaving in droves. He has such influence, she says."

"This is all down to Dan. Blast him."

"Actually, when you think about it, he only did what was right. He didn't put a foot wrong, and that apology of his was superb. I'd have had him back in again next day if he'd apologized to me like that. It was a masterpiece."

Mungo had to laugh. "Honestly, when will you stop seeing the world through rose-colored spectacles? Whatever he did or didn't do, he lost us a client."

"I know, but Lord Askew is the kind of client who, if there had been one single mistake, wrong diagnosis, lost calf, death of a cow, would have had us crucified. Do we really want clients like that? I reckon we're better off without him."

"Miriam!"

"It's true. I could have slapped that client's face for her. However, what's worse is she didn't hear it from anyone connected to old Askew; she heard it from someone who'd been here at the clinic this morning. They'd overheard a conversation at the desk."

"Did they indeed. Wait till I see Joy; I'll have a thing or two to say to her."

"Joy wouldn't be so careless. It was more probably the girls."

"You're right, as usual. But I can't let Dan go yet; we need him."

"I don't see why you should."

"Do I hear you working up to persuading me to let him stay?"

Before she answered him, Miriam served the food. As she carried their plates into the dining room, she said, "As you well know, I never interfere with the running of the practice."

"I detect . . . mayonnaise?" Miriam nodded. "And a hint of self-righteousness in your tone. You know full well you never say we must do this or not do that. You manage everything very competently with subtle hints here and there. I didn't realize how majestically you manipulated me until a couple of years ago."

"I don't know the first thing about running a practice."

Mungo almost choked. "That must be the understatement of the year! How I love you. I really do."

Miriam went red and fell silent.

"Darling! I didn't mean to upset you. Come on. I love you no matter what."

She still didn't answer him.

"Come on, pick up your knife and fork and finish your food. It'll be going cold. Darling?"

Miriam shook her head. "That's the first time you've said 'I love you,' and it sounded truly, truly, truly convincing to me."

Her voice was so low Mungo could scarcely hear what she'd said. "I didn't hear you properly; say it again."

She repeated it word for word without looking at him.

He was stunned. And then shattered when he heard her next words.

"When you marry someone who has lost the love of his life before you came on the scene, you're never quite sure, you see."

It was Mungo now who was lost for words.

"You feel second best. All the time."

"But you know I love you."

Miriam stopped looking at her plate and looked instead at him. "Of course you do; I know you do. You were wonderful when the children died. I don't know where you found the strength, and I wouldn't have got through it if I hadn't had you like a rock beside me; but as for that powerful, overwhelming, bewildering surge that comes with first love, I've always felt I had that but that you didn't because of how you loved Janey. Somehow I feel I've missed out; there's a kind of aching void." She placed her knife and fork together. "I envy Janey for having been your first love. I so wish it had been me."

Perkins ambled in. His bright brown Airedale eyes looked at each of them in turn. Then he came to sit beside Miriam and placed his chin on her knee. His head was jammed uncomfortably under the edge of the table, but he didn't care; he'd sensed her need for his sympathy and had come to give it to her. Perkins's simple gesture of solidarity made her tears flow.

Mungo leaped from his chair, uncomfortable at the thought of the dog having more sensitivity than he did. "Here, look, it's clean." He gave her his handkerchief. "If only you knew."

"Then tell me."

But he couldn't for her sobbing. "Come into the sitting room, and I'll get you a stiff drink. Then I'll tell you something I've never confessed to anyone else." He put his hand under her elbow, helped her up out of her chair and, closely followed by

Perkins, they made their way out of the dining room. He sat her in her favorite chair and poured her a brandy. "Here, sip this."

Mungo pulled a chair close to hers and sat in it. On the other side of her, Perkins watched and waited. "Better?"

Miriam nodded.

"Then listen. Every word is the absolute truth. I've never been able to tell anyone this because . . . well . . . you'll understand when you hear." He leaned his elbows on his thighs and stared into the fire. Perkins put his chin on Miriam's knee again and prepared to listen to what Mungo had to say.

"I met Janey when I was a student. She was a high flyer in the mathematics faculty, with everything going for her. We met at a student disco and I fell instantly in love. She was beautiful, exquisite, exciting, stimulating, amusing, highly intelligent. All the things anyone could hope for in a woman. We fell into bed together within the week. I was obsessed, totally obsessed, and I wasn't really me anymore. My work, everything, fell apart. I couldn't get enough of her, either her body or her personality; she brought fire and power into my life in a way I had never experienced before. And at twenty-two that is mind-blowing. I could not believe how lucky I was."

Mungo, so wrapped in his story, wasn't aware of the pain he was causing Miriam. The words *exquisite*, *exciting*, *beautiful* sounded to her like the tolling of her own funeral bell.

"We were the golden couple of our year. We were asked to all the parties; no function was held without an invitation to us; socially we were the seal of success everyone yearned for. Somehow I managed to pass all my exams, and the marriage we planned took place that summer. I had one friend who had uttered a word of caution when I'd first started going around with her, but I was too much in love to take note of what he said."

Seeing a glimmer of hope, Miriam asked, "What did he say?"

"He said, 'I hope you know what you're doing You're taking a grave risk.' I was so wild with him, we had a row; and it was weeks before we healed the breach."

"What did he mean?"

Mungo smiled grimly. Perkins took his head from Miriam's knee, curled up with his head on her feet and went to sleep.

"We couldn't afford a long honeymoon; so we had just a week in a seaside town in Brittany, came home and I began work immediately while she played at housekeeping for a while before finding a job. We had a fantastic sex life, Miriam, believe me. It was that satisfaction and the fact that I was working all hours like assistant vets do in their first job that meant I never had any time to suspect anything was wrong for months and months. One night we went to an evening wedding reception, and I arrived there having been on call all the previous night and spending most of it up; and I was exhausted. Maybe my view of life was jaundiced because of that, but I suddenly caught sight of Janey from across the room and saw her with new eyes. She was flirting with a friend from her tennis club, and there was something about her body language which alerted me. This wasn't the flirting of a happily contented wife; this was something very different. There was a kind of craving in the way she was behaving, and I looked away completely bewildered by what I'd recognized and caught the eye of a chap I'd never liked. He raised his glass to me with a mocking, knowing look on his face; and I thought, my God he's been to bed with Janey. I just knew it in my bones. For certain."

"Mungo!" She took his hand.

"To cut a long, sordid story short, I found out she'd been sleeping around quite often, with whoever took her fancy, all the time I'd known her."

"Mungo!" Miriam kissed his hand.

His face became almost savage as he said, "She drowned in that f-f-ferry disaster coming back from the Continent after a weekend in Amsterdam with someone unknown. I searched the list of victims to see if I could find a name I knew, but I couldn't; so presumably he's still walking around somewhere."

"Well, it could have been someone you didn't know and he could be dead, but he's of no consequence."

"No, you're right. I spent two years pining for her, hating her, loathing her, loving her, missing her. I was in a complete daze, on autopilot, terrified anyone would find out what a fool I'd been, and how nastily and shamefully my passion for her had been betrayed. I sold the house and used the money to set up my first practice, with Joy as my nurse." Mungo hesitated and wondered whether he should tell her about Joy—was this the moment? But he felt the warmth of Miriam's hand so sympathetically clasping his and knew Joy's secret was best kept to himself.

"Then one day this lovely woman walked into my surgery with a sick cat, which unfortunately I had to put to sleep—not the best of situations in which to meet your future wife—and I looked into her eyes and saw my salvation, and found new hope. And since that day I have never looked back. Her name was Miriam and I love her." Mungo gripped her hand. "I'm unbelievably sorry for not telling you that my silence about Janey was hiding my shame and not my love."

"You were very badly hurt. I expect you felt that as long as you didn't talk about it, it had never happened."

Mungo nodded. "I felt as though I would soil our love for each other if I told you and that if I did, you'd think less of me. No one knows, Miriam, only you and the other men, I suppose."

"I shan't tell a living soul."

They sat silently for a few minutes, then Miriam said, "You

see, Dan's so like you. Firm as a rock, with tremendous integrity, professional beyond compare and yet with such hurt in him."

"How can you say that? You haven't known him five minutes!"

She ignored his surprise at her intuitive understanding of Dan. "It's his dependability that makes me want him to stay. He'll do so well for us. Whatever Letty with her money or Zoe with her bigoted opinions says about him, he must stay."

"We'll see. We're stuck with him anyhow for a few more weeks till we find someone else. Has he confided in you, then?"

"About what hurts him? No, of course not. I just sense it. Like you, the hurt lies so very deep." She bent down to stroke Perkins. "I'm just so deeply grateful I needn't fear Janey anymore."

"I've been a fool not to have told you before, but I'd no idea you felt second best like you do."

"I didn't intend you should; no second wife wants to dwell on her predecessor. You see, I believed for you to have loved her so much Janey must have been perfect. But she wasn't. So I shan't feel like I did anymore."

"You've no need to at all. You're everything to me, since the day we met."

"Thank you. Me too. I loved you that first day and have worshipped you ever since."

Mungo tenderly placed his hands either side of her face and kissed her lips. "I am forever in your debt."

"And I in yours for rescuing me from such a lonely life and for loving me with a love I don't deserve." Miriam gently released herself from his grasp and leaned back in her chair. Staring into the fire, she said, "We'll get over this problem with old Askew. You'll see. I'm so pleased we made the move and got this place built. It not only gave me something to fill my mind after the children died, but businesswise it was the right thing to do. Everything works so well. Rhodri and Graham and Valentine and you and Colin and now Dan. With Zoe back we shall make a good team. Where we would be without Joy I don't know, and she is such a good friend to me. We shall miss Kate when she goes, though. She'll make a good vet. Kate will be like you and Dan: dependable, strong, clever, caring."

He thought of how it pained him when he first realized that Kate's face reminded him so much of Janey's; but having shared his anguish with Miriam, he felt it no longer seemed to matter. "Nice girl. I hope she makes it."

"So do I. I'm sure she will."

"We've had the most horrendous day at the practice. I'm shattered; but I've chemistry to do for tomorrow night, and I've got to press on with it." Kate leaned her elbows on the kitchen table and waited for some sympathy from her father.

Gerry thumped his fist on the table. "Think of the rewards! I'll be so proud." He reached across and patted her arm. "There's no father could be prouder of his daughter than me. When you go to college I shall tell everyone I meet."

"Dad! Please, you won't say a word, will you, till we know for certain?"

"I'm not daft. I can bide my time. I never thought when you were born that you'd grow up to be a vet."

"What did you think I'd be?"

"I never gave it a thought, I was too busy being amazed at what I had produced. A miracle you were to me. An utter miracle!"

Watching his face glowing with his memories, Kate wondered about asking him what her mother had felt on that day. The subject had been taboo all her life, but there came a time . . . "And my mother, what did she think of me when she saw me?" Kate knew she was in uncharted waters with her question, but she had to ask it; she had to know. For the first time in her life she saw her father's eyes fill with tears. She watched him take out his handkerchief and blow his nose, saw when he'd finished that he was too filled with emotion to answer. "Sorry, Dad, it doesn't matter if you can't . . ."

Gerry shook his head. He got up from the table and went upstairs. Kate could hear his footsteps climbing right up to the attic and then the whirr of his train set starting up, and she knew that certainly tonight she wasn't going to hear about that elusive mother of hers. She shrugged her shoulders.

Mia came in from the supermarket loaded with shopping. "Give me a hand, love, will you?" Mia gave her a couple of bags. "Thanks. Where's your dad?"

Kate put the bags down and pointed to the ceiling.

Mia looked resigned. "Train set? Do men ever grow up? Just think if I were still playing with a doll's pram. They'd be taking me away!"

"I've never thought about it like that. I wouldn't let them, though. I'd look after you."

"Thank you, that's a relief to know. I suppose we have to be thankful he isn't a train-spotter! I couldn't be married to a train-spotter, could you?" Mia wrinkled her nose in disgust, half laughing, half serious.

"Certainly not." Kate had to laugh. "Do you know that's the first time I've laughed today."

"Why's that?" Mia finished putting things away in the fridge and sat down to listen.

"It's not the same without Scott: no jokes, no pulling silly faces at the windows, no flirting."

"I'm sorry you miss him so." Mia laid a hand on Kate's cheek, with a loving look on her thin face, her eyes kindly and full of sympathy. "This Dan Brown's a miserable so-and-so, is he?"

"Oh! No. He's not, but nobody but me likes him. They all think he's too blunt, too up front with his opinions, and what none of them likes is he's lost us a good client, and that is bad news."

"It must be."

"But worst of all it seems Lynne's abandoned us. She was sent home to lunch early because of a row with Joy about Dan Brown and didn't come back—no phone call, no nothing. What makes matters even worse is that Colin's wife, Letty, has insisted she'll come in tomorrow to help out if Lynne doesn't turn up."

"What's happened to Stephie, then?"

"On holiday for three weeks, a family wedding in New Zealand. We are grateful for Letty's help."

"So what's the problem?"

"You should have seen Joy's face when Colin told her. I didn't need to ask what she thought of the idea. She tried hard to sound enthusiastic, but it rang very hollow. She said afterward to me that she'd be praying like mad tonight for Lynne to come in because she couldn't stand Letty. She must be difficult, because Joy is always so loyal about people. It's not like her to talk about someone that way."

"I like Joy; she's nice. She might do better, might this Letty, than you think. Keep an open mind."

"I will." Kate idly rearranged the tiny flowers Mia had put in a bowl in the middle of the table and then said, "I've upset Dad. He said it seemed like a miracle to him when I was born, so I asked him what my mother thought of me, and he couldn't answer. That's why he's upstairs with his trains."

Mia sighed. She spotted a flower in danger of falling out of the bowl and pushed it back in. "I'd better go see. Put the kettle on; I'm parched. He never speaks of her to me, so . . ." She got up from the table and began to climb to the attic.

She found Gerry engrossed in rearranging the figures standing on the main platform. With a Q-tip he was meticulously cleaning a porter pushing a trolley, intense concentration on his face, not noticing her arrival. It was a magnificent layout, with trees and station buildings, sidings and signal boxes, passengers and rolling stock, parcels waiting to be loaded, ticket office open, sandwich board announcing a day trip to the sea next Saturday—minute detail lovingly and painstakingly worked upon by a real enthusiast. Zooming round a wide curve at the far edge of the layout was the Flying Scotsman hurtling toward the station.

"It's me."

Gerry looked up, startled. "Sorry. Didn't hear you. What do you want?"

"In the best of all possible worlds your wife would like you to come clean with Kate about her mother. There. I've said it."

Gerry didn't answer.

"I mean it, Gerry."

He bent to replace the porter, and his knuckles collided with the Flying Scotsman as it dashed by. It shot up in the air and crashed down on the signal box farther down the line.

"Damn and blast! Now look what you've made me do. It's all your fault."

"No, Gerry, it's yours. You should have told her years ago. She's reached an age when she needs to know; and I can't tell her because I never met the woman, did I?"

Gerry tenderly picked up the engine and examined it. He appeared engrossed and Mia thought she'd lost the initiative, but suddenly he answered her. "How can I tell her that her mother walked out on her, a defenseless, helpless babe? What's that going to do to her?"

"Sometimes, however hard it is, it's better to face the truth. After all, it isn't as if she's been in an orphanage somewhere, is it? She's had you all her life and then me since before she can remember. She's never been without family."

He pleaded with her, "You tell her, Mia, for me. Please."

"I'm sorry. I've done all that for her myself over the years, all the birds and the bees stuff and the like. But this time, Gerry, it's you who has to stand up and be counted." She wetted the corner of her handkerchief on her tongue and rubbed at a mark on the roof of the signal box. "Hiding in here won't make the problem go away; and I can't tell her, can I? I wasn't here. Please, Gerry, explain to her." A bush had got crushed by the accident, and she plumped it straight. "If you don't, she could well go looking for her; and you wouldn't like that, now would you?"

Gerry's head came up with a jerk. "She wouldn't, would she?"

"Why shouldn't she? You couldn't stop her if she did decide to."

Gerry placed the Flying Scotsman gently back on the rails beside the platform, pressed the "go" button and off it went, with his eyes following it anxiously. "No damage done."

Mia deliberately misunderstood him. "There will be if you don't speak up."

"I'll think about it."

"You'll do more than think because if you don't do it voluntarily, one day I shall broach the subject myself in front of her; and then you'll have to tell, and you won't be prepared and you'll make a mess of it. I mean it."

Gerry looked shocked. "You wouldn't."

"I would. And when you tell her, you tell her *everything*."

"You wouldn't go against my wishes."

"Try me. It will be painful for me, and I know it will be very painful for you, but she has a right."

"She hasn't. It happened to me, not Kate; she was too young to know."

"That's nonsense and you know it. You're burying your head in the sand." Mia put an arm round his shoulders. "Kate's made a pot of tea. Come down."

"In a bit."

"I love the pair of you, you know. Not just Kate. I do understand, but it has to be faced. She's not to blame."

Gerry finished dusting the passengers and regrouped them on the platform. Mia pointed to a dog laid on its back between the rails. "Look! The dog's fallen on the line, the poor thing."

"So it has." He dusted it off and stood it beside a little girl. "When I made this little girl, I thought of her as Kate."

"Well, unlike that girl, Kate has grown up; remember that when next you play with all this." She waved an arm at the layout.

"*Play? Play!* I don't play, I *operate*."

Mia laughed. Standing at the top of the attic stairs she said, "Cup of tea ready if you want it." From the third step she paused to add, "I meant what I said." She went down, looking forward to a cup of tea and watching television with Kate; but Mia drank her tea alone, for Kate had gone to her room to work.

THE next day began badly for Kate. The everlasting roadworks which appeared to have been disrupting Barleybridge for the last decade had caused even more chaos than usual, in consequence of which she was fifteen minutes late for work. Gratefully she saw that Letty's little Mini wasn't in the car park and heaved a sigh of relief; at least that meant she wouldn't have her wrath to face, though it also meant there'd been no one on the desk for the first fifteen minutes of the morning.

Leaping out of her car, she raced through the back door, flung off her coat and gloves, grabbed her uniform, put it on in record time and dashed into reception.

"You're late!" Letty glanced at the clock behind her. "Fifteen minutes late. It's not good enough when we're shorthanded. You'll have to work an extra fifteen before you go for lunch."

Kate held up her hands in a conciliatory gesture. "Fine, it's the blessed roadworks still. One day I expect they'll have all the new sewer pipes laid, and then I shan't be late. It was worse than ever this morning. I thought you hadn't come; I didn't see your car."

"Colin gave me a lift. Then you should take that into account and leave earlier." Two phones began ringing at the same time. As Kate reached out to pick up the receiver of one of them, Letty said, "Hurry up! Answer it!"

When they'd both attended to the phones, she went on, "You know we leave the phones ringing no longer than three rings. You'll have to smarten up. It's no way to run a practice."

Kate put up with Letty's bullying tactics with as much patience as she could and was just reaching the end of her tolerance when Dan came in. He burst in through the door at his accustomed speed, gave a brief nod to the waiting clients and went to the reception desk. "Good morning, girls. My list please, Kate."

"Good morning to you, Dan. Here we are. Your first call is at Applegate Farm; I don't know what for. Sounds urgent, but then Mrs. Parsons always does make it sound as if their entire stock is about to expire the first chance they get, and—"

Letty brusquely interrupted their conversation by saying, "Might I ask, Mr. Brown, why you consider it fit to arrive to begin your day's work one and a half hours after you are expected? And unshaven, too."

Dan glanced at Kate and she saw a spark of anger in his eyes. She knew why he was late; he'd come straight to the practice without breakfast, having been called out to the other side of town at five past six that morning. She was going to speak in Dan's defense before Letty put her foot in it any further, but she was too late.

Dan answered first. "And a very good morning to you too, Letty." He turned his back to her and spoke to Kate. "Yes, you were saying?"

Letty gasped with anger. "I asked you a question. You might have the courtesy to reply."

Patiently he faced her and said softly, "I was called out at five past six this morning to a cow with a twisted gut. I have just finished. I have had no breakfast, and I am here to start my day's work. Do you have a problem with that?"

Letty had the grace to blush. "I see. I beg your pardon."

"So I should think."

Kate said, "Look, if you've missed your breakfast, Miriam will be only too delighted to find you cereal and toast. Let me go and ask her. If she finds out you've not eaten . . ."

"Colin has to manage without many times."

Dan retorted, "Having you to live with, I must assume he has a stronger constitution than me. I should be most grateful, Kate, if Miriam doesn't mind. I didn't get a real meal last night either because I was called out; so yes, that would be great."

"I'll go and ask her. You can use the shower if you like."

Dan gave a broad grin. "Do I need to?"

It was Kate's turn to blush. "No. I thought it might make you feel better, that's all."

"Thank you, I will. Won't be long. I want to get started on that list." He gave Letty a mocking Nazi salute, clicked his heels and disappeared toward the shower room.

"That man is insolent."

"That man is working his socks off, Mrs. Walker. I'll leave you in charge while I get his breakfast."

"How long have you worked here? Three months, is it?"

"About that."

"You've far too much to say for yourself, far too much. I can see it's not a moment too soon that I've come here to work. The whole place is falling apart. Joy needs to smarten things up. Wait till she's in tomorrow. I'm making a list for her."

"I'm going for Dan's breakfast."

Miriam was only too delighted to make breakfast for Dan. "Of course I will, the poor man. Toast and cereal. Right. Tea or coffee?"

"Well, I didn't ask. I imagine he's a coffee man, actually."

Miriam got busy in the kitchen. "I do like him."

"So do I, but I'm afraid he's caught Mrs. Walker on the wrong foot this morning."

"Does anyone ever do any other? Sorry, I shouldn't have said that. Still, I rather imagine Dan is perfectly capable of getting the better of her. No word from Lynne?"

"Joy rang her first thing, and she'll be back next week. A cold, her mother said."

"Mm. That came on rather suddenly. There, just the toast to wait for." Miriam leaned against the kitchen worktop and said, "Don't let Letty get you down. She goes at four and then I shall be in. Just sorry I've this dental appointment, but I daren't miss it. Toothache, you know. Thanks for working all day. At least it means Joy gets her day off."

The toast popped up and shot from the toaster with such vigor that both slices hit the window, just missing a plant on the sill. Miriam rescued them, gave them a brisk dusting off and wrapped them in a napkin to keep them warm for Dan. "Sorry! I keep meaning to buy a new toaster, but it's such fun when it does that, I keep putting it off." She smiled as she handed Kate the tray. "Take care. Say to Dan he's welcome to breakfast any time."

Kate felt she should warn Dan about the dreadful conditions at Applegate Farm. "It's filthy. Absolutely filthy. You must put your boots on before you get out of the Land Rover."

"Why?"

"Why? Because of the mud and filth."

"No. Why is it so filthy?"

"Well, you've seen Phil Parsons. His farm takes after him."

"I see."

"Scott tried to get him to clear up, but he never did."

"Right. Well, I won't tolerate it. I shall certainly have a word. The animals must take priority. It's sheer idleness leaving a farm mucky. I'll sort him out."

Letty heard him say this as she was going past with a message for Mungo. Putting her head round the door she said, "You'll do no such thing. We can't afford to lose any more clients. Who is it you're referring to?"

"Phil Parsons."

"Oh! Well, he'll be no great loss. It's like getting blood out of a stone getting him to pay."

"I have your permission, then, to have a word?"

Letty looked uncomfortable. "Well, no, I didn't mean that exactly."

"Then kindly leave me to decide, Letty. I am the vet."

Letty's face registered very real annoyance almost as though she hated the idea that Dan was the professional and she wasn't. Angrily she snapped, "The sooner we can manage without you the better."

Dan raised his eyes to the ceiling in despair.

On her way back from seeing Mungo, Letty came in to say Mungo wanted her to remind him about attending that charity auction, and had he accepted? Dan, his mouth full of toast, nodded. He emptied his cup and fled to begin his calls.

Applegate Farm proved to be as Kate had said. Dan surveyed it from his driving seat and shook his head in disbelief. The actual buildings were in quite good nick, he thought; it was the muck and mess around the whole place which shocked him. Even the farmhouse looked chronically neglected. Torn curtains at the dirty windows, doors and window frames seriously in need of a lick of paint, old farm machinery rusting in the yard and shrouds of cobwebs clinging everywhere.

He twisted round, picked up his Wellingtons from the big washing-up bowl he kept them in to avoid mud inside his vehicle, put them on—which was difficult in the confines of the driver's seat—then jumped out.

Phil Parsons leaped out from a doorway on the far right of the yard. "You're here. For God's sake, where have you been? Blossom said it was urgent. Come on!"

Dan paddled his way across the yard and went into the darkest, grimiest stall he'd ever seen, to be confronted by Phil's bull in deep distress. His head was hanging low and loud rasping noises filled the air. His flanks were heaving each time he breathed, and Phil began hopping from one foot to the other shouting, "Do something! Do something! What's up with 'im. Pneumonia, is it? Or what?"

Dan studied him for a moment and said, "Has he been off color?"

Phil shook his head.

Out of the gloom came Blossom. "Right as a trivet when Phil came in to say goodnight before we went to bed. Just stop that awful noise, please; Phil can't stand it. Nearly out of his mind, he is."

"Find him like it just this morning? No signs of it last night?"

Phil shook his head.

"I wonder. He's beginning to bloat; look, there's a lot of gas in there. He might have swallowed something, and it's jammed in his throat." With his eyes still on his patient, Dan observed the saliva pouring from the bull's mouth. Obviously, his throat was completely blocked. He asked, "His temper. What's it like?"

"Like a baby. Sweet as a nut."

Through the gloom Dan thought he saw Blossom look a mite skeptical; but whatever, he had to do something about it, and now. "Has he a name you use for him?"

Filled with consternation that Dan didn't know his name, Phil said, with reproach in every syllable, "It's Sunny Boy. That's his name."

Very calmly Dan opened the stout gate to the stall and slipped in quietly. He laid a hand on Sunny Boy's neck and said, "Well then, Sunny Boy. You're not too good this morning, are you?" Sunny Boy shuffled from one foot to the other in apprehension; strangers weren't welcome, he was saying. Over half a ton of bull not taking a liking to him made Dan excessively careful. He let his hands slide down Sunny Boy's neck and throat, feeling gently as he went.

Phil watched his every move.

Aware he was being expected to work miracles, Dan tried again, feeling with sensitive hands for an obstruction in the massive throat. "I've an idea I'm right. Not sure, but it's worth a try. I'm going for a gag to hold his jaws open while I feel down inside. You secure his head with a rope through his nose ring and I want two ropes, not just the one, from his halter to hold him firmly."

"He's not used to being tethered."

"Well, if you want him cured, you'd better tether him. I can't put my arm down his throat with him free to move about. Anchor him good and proper, if you please."

But the whole exercise was fraught with problems: Sunny

Boy, despite his kinship with Phil, refused to respond and tossed his great head this way and that trying to avoid the ropes. In his struggles he briefly stood on Phil's foot, which brought a halt to Phil's efforts. When Dan came back, he was still only tethered by one rope through a ring in the wall; and his breathing was growing worse.

Dan joined Phil in the stall, equipped with a gag, a powerful torch and a meter-long piece of fence wire bent into a narrow U-shape. "Give me the rope." Phil hobbled back a few steps, leaving Dan with the rope. "Now, see here, my lad, that will do." He said this in a loud authoritative tone and, to his surprise and Phil's, Sunny Boy stopped tossing his head and allowed Dan to slip a rope through the ring in his nose. "Now, Phil, tie him up. Both sides."

With Sunny Boy's head virtually immobilized, Dan, inch by inch, got his jaws open and fixed the metal gag in place. Sunny Boy was now a model patient, though sweat was pouring off Dan. This warm, moist mouth edged with those great yellowing teeth and with half a ton of restless bull behind it was no place even for a vet to be hanging about in, and with Blossom holding the torch and Phil positioned ready to push on Sunny Boy's neck below the obstruction, Dan swift as light slipped the wire down his throat, slowly guiding the loop over and behind whatever it was jammed in Sunny Boy's throat. "Now, Phil, start pressing upward from behind as I pull."

He manipulated and fiddled and twisted and lost his grip and tried again, and slowly he began to get a real grip on whatever it was; and against a background of Sunny Boy's labored breathing, he got the wire right behind, dislodged the object and brought it out. He threw it out of the stall, removed the gag and left Phil to release his patient. "I'll hang about to make sure all that gas which has accumulated in his rumen does come up, just in case."

Blossom picked up the object and examined it in the light of Dan's torch. "Why, good heavens, it's a kiddie's ball. Where did he get that from?"

But Phil wasn't listening to her. His Sunny Boy, the pride of his life, had been saved. Had Dan been able to see Phil's eyes, he would have seen tears of joy. As it was, they soaked unseen into his balaclava. He came out of the stall, bolted the gate behind him and, taking Dan's grossly slimy, dripping hand in his, shook it vigorously. "Brilliant. You've saved his life. Brilliant! I can't thank you enough. Blossom, get that kettle on; we'll have a coffee." Phil wiped his hand on his jumper.

Dan said, "That sounds good. I'll wash up first. Where's the tap?"

Tremulously Blossom breathed, "You were so masterful with him, Dan. 'That will do,' you said; and he did just as he was told. It was like a miracle." She clung to his arm. "Thank you. Thank you. I don't know what Phil would have done if Sunny Boy had died. Kettle, right. Milk and sugar? No, we'll have cream today. Yes. Celebrate, that's what we'll do."

Dan washed his arms under the outside tap using the bar of soap he always carried with him. "You'll have to warn your children about leaving balls near your beasts, Phil."

"Ain't got none. It's them damn kids from the trailer park. There was a load of 'em here yesterday buying milk. It'd be one of them." He went to lean his arms on the wall of Sunny Boy's stall and wallow in admiration. Dan joined him. "I have to say this, Phil, he's a grand beast. Beautiful creature. Where did you get him from?"

"Born right here in this stall. Absolute fluke. His mother was Christabel. I bought her as a heifer and found she was in calf, and it was this great beggar. Few weeks back Scott had to put her to sleep—old age, really. Poor Sunny Boy was right upset when I told him. Off his food he was."

Dan realized there was a great deal of good, sensitive heart in Phil and that he needed careful handling. Instructing him to clean up the place could be counterproductive. While they both gazed in admiration at Sunny Boy, now cheerfully munching his hay, a cat slipped under the bars of the gate and entered the stall.

"Get out, you daft beggar, I've told you before. Come on. Puss, puss, puss."

"Nice cat. Good-looking."

"Come on, see what your Phil's got in his pocket for you. Come on. Puss. Puss." The cat changed her mind and squeezed out under the gate again. Phil gave her a jelly bean. "Them's her favorites. Blossom calls her Scott and reckons she's hers, but she isn't. She belongs to me. Her and me's mates. Bit older and she'll be clearing this place of rats."

"Problem, is it?"

Phil nodded.

"They're always a problem on any farm." Still looking at Sunny Boy, Dan continued to pursue his point: "Secret is to limit the number of places they have to hide in and not leave any animal feed available." He eyed the sacks leaning haphazardly against the far wall.

Phil nodded, not really listening.

"You know—clearing up rubbish, sealing up holes. While your beasts might flourish, they'd do even better with more light and air."

Phil nodded again, but this time he was listening.

"Dumpster. Large Dumpster, that's what's needed."

Phil stirred.

"Placed outside in the yard, a couple of hours' work would make a big difference."

Blossom came with three mugs on a tray. She rested the tray on top of the wall and handed out the mugs. Dan took his first sip before he remembered Kate's warning. Too late now. Blossom joined them, squeezing in next to Dan, resting her arm on the wall. "Isn't it lovely now he's breathing all right?"

Dan continued, "Then the next thing would be to sweep down every wall, every window; get rid of all the muck and cobwebs; then a bag of sand and cement, and fill all the holes, replace the stones that have fallen out. Then paint." He gave a broad sweep with his arm and his imagination full rein. "Everywhere. Just imagine a snow-white barn, with the beams picked out in black and Sunny Boy in pride of place with the light shining in from that window above his head. A wonderful setting for a magnificent beast. What a picture! And no more than a beast of his caliber deserves." He paused to let the picture sink into Phil's brain. "I can see three or four wheelie bins lined up against that far wall with the feed in. Blue, I think, would look good against the white. Imagine, Blossom. Why, you could hold tea parties in here."

He drank down the last of the coffee, put the empty mug on the tray, said, "Thanks. Be seeing you" and left to shouts of gratitude from Blossom and Phil.

As he drove to his next call, he thought about the charity auction Mungo had asked him to attend in his place. He was obliged to go but would have preferred someone to go with. High-profile animal charity event, lots of country people there, no doubt, so whom should he ask? It would have to be someone from the practice because he didn't know anyone else. If only Rose were here . . . ; but she wasn't and wouldn't be, and he'd better close his mind to her because wishing would achieve nothing at all. Unbidden, a picture came into his mind of her striding beside him along that magnificent beach, very early one morning, almost before the sun was up . . . the fine, silvery sand filtering up between his bare toes . . . her slender fingers entwined in his, swimming naked in the sea, the chill water rippling against his skin . . . breakfasting on the beach afterward. He could still smell the ripeness of the peaches she'd brought with her, and even now his forearms could feel the roughness of the sun-dried towel she lay on . . . pain shot through him at the thought of her. He quickly closed the door on Rose and bent his mind to solving his problem.

Whom to ask to go with him? Not Bunty, nor Sarah One or Two, no, he'd ask Kate. Yes, Kate. He liked Kate, liked her straightforwardness and her no-nonsense manner; and he knew she liked him, which was more than could be said for any of the others.

He pulled into the yard at Tattersall's Cop with his mind made up. Definitely Kate. He was sure she'd say yes, if only for the chance to see the wealthy at play, and he guessed they'd derive the same kind of amusement from it too.

THE auction was to be held in the newly named Lord Henry Askew Hall, a splendid edifice built at the height of the Arts and Crafts movement, with wonderfully ornate decoration, richly painted walls and dramatic paneling that required none of the specially installed lighting or the drapes with which someone had seen fit to embellish it. Vast flower displays burgeoned in every corner; and the general impression was of an overdressed, very rich, stately old lady. Originally it had been the town hall, and out of a kind of ingrained stubbornness the majority of the inhabitants still called it that. Lord Askew, however, was inordinately pleased to have the hall named after himself and made a point of attending every possible event ever held in it.

Dan and Kate arrived just after seven. They each left their overcoats in the cloakroom and emerged into the hall to find a receiving line awaiting them.

Out of the corner of his mouth, Dan murmured, "I bet Mungo never thought Lord Askew might be here."

"Oh no! I've never met him. Where is he?"

"The last in the receiving line."

"That's him? He doesn't look much like I imagine a lord should."

"But he is. Here goes."

They shook hands and introduced themselves as they went down the line, meeting the chairman of the charity and his wife and various other officials. Then finally came the moment for Dan to face Lord Askew. He took the bull by the horns saying, "Dan Brown, my lord, Barleybridge Veterinary Hospital. May I introduce my friend Kate Howard."

Kate shook his hand saying, "Good evening, my lord."

But he wasn't taking any notice of her; he was bristling with indignation at Dan. His great voice boomed out, "Still here, then? Thought you'd have been gone long since."

"Indeed not. Hopefully, I'm here to stay."

"Mungo Price has written to me as well as you, but it's not enough, no, not enough. I shan't come back to you, not after your behavior. Damned insolent. Damned insolent."

His face flushed redly but with a hint of blue about his nose and lips.

Dan played his humility card. "It was a most unfortunate occurrence, my lord, one which I very much regret, but I cannot have my professional decisions overridden."

"Can you not! I pay the piper so I call the tune, don't you know."

Dan couldn't resist taunting him. "And the roan. How is he?"

"Fine, fine . . ." He opened his mouth to add something else but changed his mind.

"If you will excuse us, my lord, we're holding up the line. Perhaps there will be an opportunity to speak later."

"Yes, yes."

As they moved away, Dan said, "I think he's having doubts about that horse. See his hesitation? You watch, before the night is out he'll have found a reason to speak to me about it."

"He's not going to ask your advice, though, is he; do you think?"

"No, I expect not. His trouble is he's gone too far down the line to find it easy. Let's get a drink. What would you like?"

"Orange juice, please."

He made no comment about Kate wanting a soft drink, took a gin and tonic for himself and found them a corner where they could stand, watching the elite of Barleybridge enjoying themselves. On a huge balcony built out over the entrance hall an orchestra was playing tunes from well-known musicals, and the whole room buzzed with pleasurable excitement.

"So, Kate Howard, this is how Barleybridge enjoys itself."

"Only from time to time and most especially because Lord Askew is footing a large part of the bill. He's terribly keen on hunting and can't abide this new legislation, you see."

"So the profits go to the campaign, do they?"

Kate nodded.

"The sad part is having to put down all the hounds."

"They can't be rehomed, I expect."

Dan shook his head. "Absolutely not. They haven't a cat in hell's chance of being domesticated. They're a savage lot underneath, having been brought up as pack animals. If you watch them for a while, you see which are the leaders and which are the lowest of the low, and the consequences of stepping out of line can be terminal."

Kate felt sad and it showed in her face. Dan glanced at her, taking in her almost classical profile, and he wondered where she had got that from. "What does your father do?"

"He's sales manager for the biscuit factory the other side of town."

"And your mother?"

Kate corrected him. "My stepmother, Mia, she's a miniaturist."

"Wonderful talent."

"It is. She's becoming quite well known. Never without work."

"That's good. How long has she been your stepmother?"

"Since I was eighteen months old, or thereabouts."

"Your mother? Where is she?"

Kate looked up at him. "I've no idea. She walked out on us."

Dan replied, "I'm so sorry; I didn't mean to hurt you."

"How could I be hurt when I've never set eyes on her and don't even know her name. My dad finds it all too hard to talk about. Thinks it doesn't concern me, that only he has the right to suffer; but everyone needs to know their origins, don't they? I know I wish I did."

Kate was appalled by the change which came over Dan. Whatever had she said to have brought such an anguished look to his face? She'd always thought of him as having emotion tightly under control, if indeed he had any at all; but here, surprisingly, there appeared to be a totally unsuspected secret, which obviously lay painfully deep.

To give him space, Kate remained silent, watching people and observing the very differing fashions the women guests had chosen to wear. She looked down at her own black number, which Mia had run up for her after she'd got Dan's invitation. It was elegantly simple and just sufficiently detailed to bring it way up from downright ordinary without being ostentatious, and she knew she looked good in it. Hang not knowing her birth mother; Mia more than compensated.

Dan tossed down his G&T and abruptly said, "Another orange? Then we'll take a look at the buffet. Eh? Should be time for the auction soon."

"Right."

"You buying anything?"

Kate had to laugh. She looked at the auction catalogue. "Well, I certainly haven't enough money to buy anything at all and, what's more, I don't want corporate entertaining at Formula One in Monaco with last year's championship winner no matter who he is, or a ghastly weekend in Scotland shooting grouse on Lord Askew's estate, or an evening with a third-rate pop star at the Café de Paris, or a day as an extra on a film set no matter how prestigious the stars." She paused for a moment while she thought of the worst thing possible and came up with "And I definitely do not want the cricket bat signed by the entire English team."

She managed to bring a smile to Dan's face. "What *do* you want, then?"

"That's easy to answer. To be a student at the Royal Veterinary College next October, that's all." She checked the catalogue again. "But I don't see that here, or have I missed something?"

"You a vet! I'd no idea. What do you need to get in?"

"They'll have me if I get a grade A in chemistry. That's all I need now." She clenched her fist and struck the air. "I've got biology and physics, so it's only one small hurdle and I'll be there. Well, not so small, actually."

"That's brilliant. I'm so pleased. It's five years' hard work, believe me, but you'll never regret it."

Kate risked another look at his face. It had regained its normal inscrutability. "It's worth it, isn't it?"

Dan nodded. "Wouldn't be doing anything else on earth. Constant challenge, ever changing work, out in the open air in wonderful countryside. What more can a man ask? Or a woman for that matter." He laughed and added, "And the best of it is the patients can't argue about the treatment."

The orchestra played a great flourish, and the chairman made his speech and the auction began. Dan found them each a chair in the back row, and they prepared themselves to be entertained. Halfway through, Dan felt a touch on the back of his chair. He half glanced round and saw it was Lord Askew's great hand resting there. Tactically he knew it was good sense to ignore it. But they'd just reached the exciting part where the auctioneer announced the big prize of the evening, the weekend in Monaco at the Grand Prix. The noise mounted and the auctioneer had difficulty in getting silence.

"I say, Brown, come out. I need to talk." Lord Askew was incapable of speaking quietly, and his request boomed out just as silence had fallen. The auctioneer gathered everyone's eye yet again and began the bidding.

Dan stood up and followed his lordship, who took him to a quiet corner on the balcony where the orchestra had been playing. "I say, where did you learn about horses?"

"In Dubai."

Lord Askew raised his eyebrows in surprise. "With a sheikh?"

"Yes."

"Price has never had a proper equine vet, you know."

"He told me."

"Plenty of experience, then?"

"Some experience mixed with a lot of instinct."

"Instinct. Hm." Lord Askew pushed his hands in his pockets. The noise from the auction couldn't be ignored. He raised his voice a little. "That roan, my daughter's, don't you know. Stickler for the horse being in tip-top condition." He raised his voice a few more decibels. "Don't suppose you would come to take a look? Private, don't you know. Nothing to do with the practice."

"I am surprised, my lord, that a man of principle like yourself would make such a request."

Lord Askew edged nearer and in a loud stage whisper said close to Dan's ear, "Don't push *me*. I don't bargain. But I would pay twice the going rate for your opinion."

"I'm sorry. I am going to pretend this conversation never took place. Please excuse me." Dan walked away back to Kate and took his seat again, a grin on his face like that on the proverbial Cheshire cat.

Chapter

· 4 ·

Joy called out from her office, "It's the first Monday. Have we got the fire bucket ready?" She got no answer and wondered why. It was five minutes past eight, so Kate should be on the desk. "Hello! Anyone there?"

Getting no reply, Joy went to see why. She couldn't believe her eyes when she saw that Stephie was back from New Zealand. But where had her long, lank brown hair; her sallow skin; her expressionless face gone? In their place was short, bouncy hair with blond highlights, a tanned face and a bright, bubbly expression. "Stephie! You're back!"

Kate said, "I'm speechless. I didn't recognize her when she came in."

"I can't believe this. My dear. Welcome back. So this is what New Zealand has done for you. I think I'll be on the next flight. Book me a ticket, quick."

Kate nodded in agreement. "Me too. God! What a change. You look fabulous."

"You like my new look, then?"

"Like it! We're dead envious, aren't we, Kate?"

"We most certainly are."

Stephie explained. "It was my cousin; she persuaded me. I feel a fool, really." She looked at Kate for reassurance.

"You don't look it. You look great."

Joy asked her if the wedding went off all right.

"Well, apart from a massive rainstorm while we were in church—thunder, lightning, the works—it went off fine. Except the best man couldn't find the ring, and the prawn cocktails were off so we couldn't eat them, and the bride's father got the worse for drink and gave a hilarious speech. Yes, it all went well."

Kate asked her what the best man was like.

"He was superb! In fact . . ."

Joy and Kate prompted her to continue. "Yes?"

"He'll be over here at Christmas."

"Will he indeed!" Joy wagged her finger at Stephie. "Coming to see you, is he?"

"Well, I might see him; might, you know. But he is writing."

Joy gave her a hug. "I'm so glad you had such a wonderful time. Sorry to bring you back down to earth, but we must press on." She retreated to her office, smiling to herself, thinking what an amazing effect an interesting man can have on a girl.

Stephie filled Kate in on the details between dealing with clients and answering the phone. They had a busy morning ahead of them with a full appointment list for the general clinic and a full one for Mungo's orthopedic clinic too.

Stephie put down the receiver after battling to fit in yet another client for the small animal clinic and said, "Don't you think we're busier than ever?"

"I'm certain we are. I've been working whole days while you've been away because of Lynne."

"What's the matter with her?"

"Virus." A man was standing at the desk, a long-haired ginger cat in his arms. "Good morning. How can I help?"

"I've found this cat by the side of the road, laid in the gutter. I think it's been run over."

Kate felt Stephie give her a slight kick with her foot. "I see. Where?"

"Near the precinct, by the parking garage. It was crying; that was why I noticed it."

Kate leaned forward to look more closely at the cat. "Poor thing. Lucky you found it. It looks very unkempt, as if it's a stray. Look, put it in this box and I'll get one of our vets to attend to it. I can't take it in unless I have a name and address. Really, the RSPCA would be the best place."

Quickly the man said, "Can't get there; no car. Too far out."

Kate nodded. "I see." Stephie passed her the clipboard, and Kate picked up her pen. "Right, sir. You're Mr. . . . ?"

". . . Thomas."

"And your address?"

The man hesitated, then said, "This cat's not mine, you know, not mine no, no."

"But surely you'd be interested to know how it gets on?"

"Oh yes, yes. It's . . . 43 Oakroyd . . . Gardens."

"And your phone number?"

"Not on the phone."

"Perhaps you have a phone number at work?"

"No, that wouldn't do. They don't encourage private calls."

Stephie asked, "Just a minute. Where did you say you found it?"

"Like I said, on the slope up to the parking garage."

Kate, intent on the cat's suffering, said, "It's very good of you to bring it in."

Stephie said, "We'd really prefer a phone number, Mr. Thomas. Perhaps a neighbor's? Or a friend's?"

Mr. Thomas turned on his heel and left before they could

stop him. Stephie dashed into the laundry room to watch the car park and was in time to see him get into a little Ford parked as close to the exit as he could get, start up, back out and drive away at high speed.

She raced back into reception and wrote down his registration number. Kate, smoothing the cat's head with a gentle finger, asked, "What are you doing?"

"I wasn't born yesterday; that chap *has* got a car, and I've written down his number. I was suspicious of him right from the start."

"What do you mean?"

"Honestly, you're too good to be true, you are. That's his own cat."

"No, it's not. He said he found it in the gutter. Obviously, it's been run over, or at least collided with a car or something."

"Kate Howard! You're not fit to be let out. I'd bet a million dollars on it being his own cat."

"Well, why didn't he say so, then?"

"Because he's too mean to pay for it."

"Well, honestly! I don't believe it. Anyway, I'd better get some help. It looks in a bad way."

"I've come back not a moment too soon. Gullible, that's what you are."

"OK, OK. Come on, sweetheart, let's get you looked at."

"Mungo's free for half an hour; his last client didn't get here."

"Right."

Kate watched Mungo's sensitive hands delicately examining the cat. She marveled at the way they appeared to be "reading" the cat's injuries. "Broken left hind leg—make a note—fairly certain a crushed pelvis." The cat yowled. "Sorry, old chap. Fleas—look here—several ticks. God, what a state it's in. Look at this!" Mungo held the fur of its throat between his fingers exposing the flesh. He carried on parting the fur all the way round its neck and found a nasty red weal encircling it, with raw flesh and dried blood in several places. "Goes all the way round. It's a wonder its throat hasn't been severed it's so deep in places. As if someone's tried to throttle it with a cord. That's not a car accident, is it?"

Kate felt sick. "The chap, Mr. Thomas, left an address."

"Did he? Got all this down?"

"Yes."

"Look at his pads. As if he's been dragged along the road and had the skin seared off. I've seen that before with a car accident."

The door opened and in came Dan. "Mungo I . . . Oh! Sorry!"

"Come and look at this, Dan. What do you think?" Together they reexamined the cat.

Dan straightened up and asked Kate who'd brought him in. She explained.

"Check to see if his address is genuine. Please."

Mungo asked him what he thought. "It all appears consistent with a car accident, but the neck injury. . . We both have been vets long enough to know how cruel people can be. I wonder if this cat has been tied by the neck to a car bumper, or a bike possibly, and dragged along the road. See his claws, almost pulled from their beds; friction burns on his pads and they're bleeding in places. This isn't a normal car accident, is it? I reckon this is a cruelty case. But the cat could have been dumped, and he genuinely has picked it up."

"So why run off?"

"Frightened he might get blamed?"

"But it's unlikely he would know what we've found out about the cord round its neck. Its fur is so thick he'd never notice it without close examination. If he was innocent, what has he to be afraid of?"

Kate, feeling even more sick than she had been when listing the injuries, came back in and said, "Must be a false address. I've looked in the street directory, and there's no such road in Barleybridge."

Mungo shrugged his shoulders. "We shouldn't be surprised. Right. He needs a painkiller, rest and quiet, and a drip and antibiotic. We'll leave him to sleep and get some strength back, then we'll X-ray later today. He's too bloody thin as well. Get Bunty for me, Kate, please."

When she'd left his consulting room, Mungo said, "I'm not letting this go. I'll get him for this, so help me."

As Mungo washed his hands, Dan commented, "I thought I'd seen everything there was to see out in the Caribbean and in Dubai, but this . . . in a country which prides itself on being compassionate, it takes some beating. But we've nothing to go on. False address, wrong name too, I suspect."

"Obviously. I've another client in ten minutes. Did you want to see me?"

They were interrupted by Bunty coming in to attend to the cat. Mungo gave her instructions for its care, asking her also to photograph him, especially the neck injury, and by then his next client had arrived; so Dan said he'd see him later, that it wasn't important. He'd been going to tell Mungo about Lord Askew at the charity auction but in the circumstances decided it could wait.

At the reception desk Stephie was comforting Kate. "Look, you weren't to know; the chap seemed genuine enough. It was something to do with his shifty eyes. Did you notice he never really looked us in the face?"

"That poor cat. Mungo thinks it's a cruelty case."

"Really? Not a road accident, then?"

Kate shook her head.

Dan came out of the consulting room to have a word with

them. "Don't you go blaming yourselves, girls, just one of those things."

Kate answered him almost before he'd finished speaking. "I *am* blaming myself. I'm far too trusting of people."

"Look, write down a description of him while he's fresh in your mind. It could help the police."

"Police!"

"Yes. Mungo is livid and so am I. A disgrace. But don't you girls feel guilty, please. You weren't to know. Write down his description and as much of the conversation you had as you can remember."

"I've got his car registration number." Triumphantly Stephie held up the notepad she'd scribbled it on.

Dan leaned across the desk and gave her a kiss on both cheeks. "Clever girl. You should be in the police. Hang on to that; it could be our only link."

Stephie blushed.

"Bunty's taken charge of him now."

Stephie approved. "He'll pull through, then. She's brilliant with hopeless cases, is Bunty."

"We know now why he didn't go to the RSPCA—too afraid of prosecution. Well, bad luck. Thought we'd be a soft option. We'll get him yet. Quiet day. Finished my calls. I'll have lunch and hope something comes in meanwhile." He gave them half a salute, but not the Nazi one he reserved especially for Letty, and disappeared into the back.

THE police arrived later in the afternoon in the shape of Sergeant Bird. Only his uniform made him recognizable as a police officer, because true to his name he was a thin, birdlike little man. At some time he must have had the height qualification necessary to join the force, but since then he'd shrunk. The peak of his cap almost engulfed his face and shaded a pair of piercing, almost black eyes, which viewed one with the apparent intention of taking one into custody immediately.

Placing his cap on the top of the reception desk, he said, "Sergeant Bird. Where's his nibs, then?"

Kate asked, "His nibs?"

"Mungo. He thinks he has a cruelty case. A cat."

"That's right. He's operating all afternoon, so he can't be interrupted I'm afraid, but—"

"Understandable. Mustn't disturb the great man at his work, of which I am his warmest admirer." Sergeant Bird settled his forearms on the top of the desk. "Five years ago my German shepherd, Duke, was within an ace of having to be put down, all hope lost. I brought him to Mungo. He operated on his hips when the practice was down the town in the old premises, and he's never looked back. Since then I've had the greatest of respect for him. He said on the phone there's no evidence of identification."

"All we have is a description of the man we wrote down as soon as he left and . . . his car registration number." Kate brought out the notepad like a magician bringing a rabbit out of a hat.

"Ex-ce-llent. Quick thinking, that. Photographs too, I understand."

"They're here and Bunty's done a list of his injuries for you."

"Now that Bunty is a treasure. If she's in charge, he'll pull through. I've great faith in her too."

"Hope so. He'll look like a nice cat when he gets better and puts on some weight. He's terribly thin."

"I'll have a look, if I may."

Before Kate could say she thought it inadvisable as they were so busy, Sergeant Bird had disappeared into the intensive care room and hadn't come out when Stephie came back on at four.

Stephie giggled when Kate told her Sergeant Bird had come. "I bet he's hanging about to see Bunty. Fancies her like nobody's business. Keeps asking her out and she won't go."

"I'm not surprised. He's a lot older than her."

"Exactly. It's been going on since I joined the practice, and I've been here three years. He's round here like a shot on the flimsiest of excuses."

"And he's smaller."

Stephie giggled again. "I know, I know . . . sh! He's coming back."

Sergeant Bird came to the desk, saying "I'll be off now. Tell Mungo I'll be on to this straightaway." He picked up his cap and disappeared out of the door, some of the spring having gone out of his step.

After the door closed, Stephie said, "She's turned him down again, you can see. Nice chap, but he's not marriage material, is he now? You wouldn't even fancy him enough to live with him, never mind marry him."

Kate had to agree.

HE was back the following day. "It came to me after I'd left. Was your security camera switched on yesterday?"

Joy clapped a hand to her forehead. "Of course! Of course! Aren't we fools! It's so unnatural, all this modern technology, you don't think to refer to it. He'll be on there. You're not just a pretty face, are you?"

Sergeant Bird grew a whole inch. "No, I'm not."

"What about the car number? Got anything from that?"

"Not registered. So that's another thing I can get him for, once I catch up with him. Where's the film, then?"

"Just a minute. I've got to think about this. Where is yesterday's film? It should be in my office safe. Hold on."

Sergeant Bird leaned his back against the desk while he waited for Joy and surveyed the waiting clients. He recognized one or two of them and said good morning to them.

"Morning, Dickie. How's things?"

Sergeant Bird hated it when people called him Dickie. He'd always thought Aubrey was such a distinguished name, but no one ever called him by it. "Fine. Thanks."

"I see your lot haven't solved this stolen car racket in the parking garage we've all read about in the paper. Front page in the local paper again this morning."

"No." He turned to face the desk to put an end to the ribbing he knew he was going to get.

Joy returned with the video in her hand. "All is not lost. We'll run it through, shall we?"

Eager to get away, Sergeant Bird took the video, saying "I won't put you to any more trouble. I'll do it at the station."

"I need a receipt for it. Sorry, but you know, must follow the rules."

"Of course."

Named Copperfield by Bunty, who always went in for distinguished names for any animal without one, the cat in question had been operated on that morning. It had been long and difficult, but Mungo, when he finally stripped off his gloves, was very satisfied with the cat's condition. "I'm handing him over to you, Bunty. Make sure the two Sarahs know what to do. He seems in good heart, and he must be a fighter to have survived what he's gone through. All he needs now is careful nursing."

"He'll get that. We'll have him up and about in no time."

"I know you will. We shan't get paid for it, but what the hell; the poor thing deserves the best after what I suspect he's been through. I just hope Dickie Bird finds that chap before I do."

Bunty carefully picked up the still unconscious Copperfield and took him to the recovery room, where loving care and constant monitoring had him eating and trying to get on his feet in no time at all.

They were gathered to watch him try to walk outside his cage one afternoon when the phone rang, and it was Zoe's mother calling to say that Zoe had had her baby boy, six pounds ten ounces and fighting fit, and yes, Zoe was fine and would be out of hospital tomorrow, and she'd be bringing baby Oscar in for them to see in a few days.

Kate went out to buy a card for them all to sign. Dan came in at about half past six, having finished his calls, so Kate asked him if he'd like to add his name to it.

"She's had her blip, then? What is it?"

"A boy. She's calling him Oscar."

"My God! What does she think she's had, a dog? The poor child."

"I know you always speak your mind, but really . . ."

Dan sat down to sign his name. "Oscar Savage! Has quite a ring to it, I suppose. But he still sounds like a dog to me."

"Well, you'll be able to see for yourself when she brings him in."

"So long as I'm not expected to do the billing and cooing."

"You sound as though you don't approve."

Dan stood up and handed Kate the card. "Frankly, I don't. It occurs to me that she's having this baby as some kind of statement about making use of a man to give her the baby she wants, intending deliberately to deny him all knowledge of it just for the hell of it. One musn't have children simply to make statements; they're not pawns in the game of life. There's five pounds toward a present for him. I expect we're clubbing together, are we? The boss, is he in?"

Kate nodded.

He smiled at her and strode off to find Mungo.

Kate stood looking at his signature. A great flourish of a signature it was: *Congratulations!!! Daniel J. F. Brown.* Such confidence in every stroke of his pen—big, sharply pointed letters in a stylish, authoritative hand. He must have more insight than people gave him credit for, though, because Zoe had used very similar words to her about making use of men when they'd been discussing Oscar's arrival some weeks before. She hoped he wouldn't show his disapproval of the baby in front of everyone. He'd already made enough enemies in the practice without making matters any worse; he hadn't a cat in hell's chance of staying permanently if he did. The interviews for his job began on Monday, and then it would be goodbye Dan; and she couldn't help feeling it would be a mistake to rid the practice of such a good vet.

DAN had found Mungo working at his desk. He tapped on the open door and said, "Time for a word?"

"Of course. Sit down." Mungo took off his glasses and prepared to listen.

"When Kate and I went to the charity auction, I don't suppose you gave it a thought that Lord Askew would be there?"

"I did not! You didn't have a showdown?"

"No." Dan had to smile. "He took me to one side and asked me if I would see that roan privately."

Mungo's eyebrows shot up his forehead. "Did he?"

"I told him that I wouldn't and haven't heard from him since."

"I see."

"Thought I'd better tell you just in case something was said."

"Thank you. He's obviously worried, then?"

"He is. If he should ask me again, what would you like me to say? I wouldn't go privately for obvious reasons, but would you be interested if he asked me to go as your employee?"

"I've never bothered with equine, not the slightest interest. It's not the horses themselves; it's their owners."

"They can be the very devil; you just have to know how to get along with them. But I would do it if you gave me the go-ahead. He may never ask me again. However, I must have the position clear, in case he does. He's very influential; his approval could bring in many more equine clients, and it would be another string to your bow. I know I'm not here to stay, but it might influence your choice of a permanent vet if I got Lord Askew's account."

Mungo tapped the end of his pen on the desk while he thought. *Tap. Tap. Tap. Tap.* "I'll consult with Colin and Zoe. Thanks for being so straightforward about it. Do you enjoy it?"

"Wouldn't want to be wholly equine. I like variety, you see."

Mungo put his glasses back on and said, "I'll let you know. Young Copperfield has been walking about today. Good news, eh?"

He rang Colin that same night, and they had a long conversation about the pros and cons of the situation. The upshot of it was that Colin thought it was highly unlikely Dan would get asked again; but if he did, why not? After all, the fellow wasn't going to be there for long, was he? These new applicants seemed promising and one of them did have horse experience, so why not let Dan lead the way if it so happened?

Ten minutes after he'd spoken to Colin the telephone rang, and Mungo found himself on the receiving end of Letty's bile. "Colin's told me. You said yourself you weren't keen on him when he first came, and I've seen nothing of him to endear him to *me*. Giving him this opening is nothing short of ridiculous. He'll be thinking he's here to stay, and I'm not having it."

"*You're* not having it?"

"No, I am not. The man is insolent and arrogant, and what's more it seems to me he's too keen on making the practice pay and not enough on the animals."

"May I remind you that Colin is the decision maker and as he has gone along with the idea . . ."

"Colin is the decision maker only because I put him there and money talks."

Mungo held a bitter retort in check. "Anyway, I haven't spoken to Zoe yet, so if we all agree then that's final; and even if it's two out of three, namely Colin and me, it's still final. Goodnight, Letty. Thanks for ringing."

"I haven't finished."

"Well, I have."

"Now look here. Colin has some rights, you know."

"He has, and he's exercised them and he's agreed with me."

"Just how much influence does this man have on you? He isn't in the place two minutes and he's persuading you to take on equine, something you have set your face against all the time you've been in practice. Think carefully, Mungo. The man's a devious beggar, believe me. He's carving a niche for himself."

"If it weren't for Dan, with no Zoe available so we're a vet down, Colin would be working day and night, *every* night at the moment. So think on that, Letty. Goodnight." He was usually too well mannered to put the receiver down on someone, but this time he did. As he lowered it to the cradle, he could hear Letty still furiously expostulating. Damn and blast the woman. Was she right? Was he being manipulated? Miriam would put him straight. Mungo found her reading in the sitting room and laid his problem on her shoulders.

"No, you're not being manipulated. He's not that kind of person. Dan is as straight as a die. I know it in my bones. Since when have you taken notice of Letty's opinions, anyway? Never to my knowledge."

"If we hadn't needed her money so desperately to enable us to move here, I would never have had Colin for a partner. Letty's money put the icing on the cake, so to speak, but I didn't realize we'd be taking on Mrs. Moneybags too. Is Dan all bad?"

"No. But ask Joy; she has to work with him."

"I will." Mungo left Miriam reading her book and went to speak to Joy. When he came back, he said, "She says Dan's abrupt and speaks his mind no matter what, and gets her dander up occasionally because he expects everyone to work at the same pace as he does and won't tolerate inefficiency. But she says she's getting more used to him; and she's had a couple of clients ask specifically for him, and you can't do better than that. In her weaker moments she wishes Scott were back and then remembers all the trouble he caused. Says Dan's outspoken and doesn't get on with Letty when she comes in. Bring back Lynne is all Joy will say on that score."

He grinned and Miriam asked him why. "Apparently, Dan gives Letty a Nazi salute when he sees her . . . and clicks his heels."

"The devil he does! Oh, dear." Miriam closed her book. "Just let things ride for the time being. See what the interviews on Monday bring. You can't expect Zoe to give you an answer at the moment anyway. Her answer will be no, though, seeing as she and Dan don't hit it off."

"After our ill-fated dinner party?"

Miriam nodded. "He struck out rather forcibly at her, didn't he? I wonder why? All very personal, I thought."

"Don't ask me. I'll leave that to your woman's intuition."

"On his résumé, does it say single or divorced or married?"

"No idea. So long as they do a good job it doesn't bother

me. But all this opposition to Dan . . . it makes me wonder if inviting him to stay would be a good thing. Zoe, Letty and inevitably Colin, Joy—all against him. We have to work so closely together all day, every day; maybe we'd be inviting disaster if he stayed."

When Zoe came in to show off the one-week-old Oscar, it so happened that Dan had called in with some samples to be posted. He was in Joy's office explaining to her about them when he recognized the thin wail of a newborn baby. "That sounds like Zoe."

Joy's face lit up. "Really? Leave them there; I'll see to them. Got to look at the baby. Are you coming?"

"They're urgent; I want them off in today's mail."

"So they shall be." Joy squeezed past him, then turned back and said quietly, "You must come."

"I am."

Expecting a crumpled red little thing in whom only a mother could see any beauty, they were all stunned by how gorgeous he was. Oscar had a smooth pink-and-white complexion with a covering of very blond hair all over his head and the dark-blue eyes of the new infant. His delicate starlike hands waved impatiently from inside his crocheted shawl; one of his fingers became entangled in a hole and Joy gently unhooked him. "Why, Zoe, he's beautiful. Really beautiful." She smoothed a fingertip across his cheek. "Isn't he, Dan?"

"How are you, Zoe? Well?"

"Thank you, yes, I am. What do you think of my blip then, Dan?"

"He's a wonder. Very beautiful. You must be proud of him."

"I am. Very proud. For a blip he's not too bad, is he?"

"He most certainly isn't. He didn't get his fair skin and hair from you, did he?"

Zoe's dark eyes glared at him and while she thought of a

tart reply, Joy intervened. "Come and sit in my office, and we'll have a cup of tea. I'll ring the flat and see if Miriam's in. I'm sure she'd love to see him."

Stephie made the tea while Joy rang up to the flat, and in a moment Miriam was down the stairs and begging to hold Oscar. "Why, he's lovely, Zoe, really lovely." Taking him in her arms, she gently rocked him, placed a kiss on his forehead and stood silently admiring him.

They all crowded together in Joy's office, drinking tea and talking, till Joy clapped her hands and said, "Sorry, everyone back to work." Reluctantly Stephie and the two Sarahs left, Miriam handed back the baby to Zoe and she too left, but she didn't go back up to the flat. Instead, she went to stand outside by the back door to pull herself together. Looking up at the hills rising immediately from the edge of the car park she strove to control her longings.

She couldn't see the summit of Beulah Bank Top for the heavy looming cloud. This was the kind of day she didn't like. Sunshine and blue skies suited her personality best, but maybe the mood she was in matched up better to the dark clouds. The agonizing physical pain she was feeling became unbearable. She knew she shouldn't have taken hold of the baby, that it would bring back all her dreadful memories, but she hadn't been able to help herself; so now she suffered the appalling pains all over again as bad as ever they had been. The empty arms, that was the worst. Empty arms aching to cradle . . . Gripping her hands together, Miriam put her knuckles to her mouth to stop herself from openly weeping.

The back door opened: it was Dan coming out to continue his calls. "Why, Miriam! It's too cold to be out here without a coat."

Miriam didn't answer. Then Dan saw her anguish and, not knowing the cause, didn't know what to say.

The shuddering, almost animal-like groan Miriam gave as she tried to gain control struck Dan's heart like a hammer blow. In his concern all he could think to say was, "Can I help?"

She shook her head. Dan put his arm round her shoulders and gave her a comforting squeeze. "If there's anything I can do . . ."

Miriam replied, "There's nothing anyone can do for me. I should never have held the baby. I was a fool."

Thinking it was because she was childless Dan said, "I see."

"No, Dan, you don't. It's my children, you see. We had two, Mungo and I, and they both died. A genetic disease, so we didn't dare have any more."

"I'm so sorry. So very sorry."

"The pain never leaves me."

Still gripping her shoulders, Dan looked up at the hills as he said, "There are things which happen to us on which we ourselves have to close the door. I know it's quite dreadfully hard to do, but it has to be done. We need to turn our faces to the light when we've suffered as you have and let the pain go; otherwise we're only leading half a life, and life is so very short. Doing that doesn't mean we've forgotten, or that we care any less."

Miriam blew her nose and cleared her throat. Looking at him, she found his eyes still focused on the hills. Shakily she murmured, "You speak as if you know how I feel."

He came back from wherever he'd been, saying, "No, no, not at all. I just feel for you, that's all. Better now?"

She nodded. Dan took his arm from her shoulders. "You'd best go inside. It's too cold. I'll be off. Think about turning your face to the light and enjoying all the good things life has to offer."

She watched him rev up, reverse and swing off out of the car park at his usual breakneck speed. Miriam went to the staff washroom and splashed her face with water, found a comb someone had left behind, tidied her hair and then, hearing angry voices, went to seek them out.

Joy and Zoe were talking with Mungo in his office. Mungo sounded as though he was striving hard to keep a check on his temper. "I had to ask what you thought, Zoe. You are a partner, after all."

"Exactly, and this partner is saying no."

Miriam stood listening in the doorway because the room wasn't big enough for four of them.

"That's all very well, but we've interviewed. Two have refused the job, one wasn't suitable, one has said he'll think about it and, meanwhile, good temps do not grow on trees. We are short-handed and we can't expect you back just yet, can we? That wouldn't be fair to you or Oscar."

"I still say he isn't for one minute to think he's being taken on permanently. He's a bloody pain, he is. He's an arrogant, abrupt and bloody rude male chauvinist pig."

Mungo began to lose his temper; Miriam saw it in the way his shoulders straightened and his good looks became pinched. "All this is becoming very personal. Your decision isn't professional at all. I shall excuse you because you've a new baby, and all your hormones have got their knickers in a twist; consequently, you're not thinking straight."

"How dare you patronize me? Just because I've had a baby, it doesn't mean I've gone soft in the head."

"It bloody sounds like it to me. Anyway, Colin and I agree, so that's two out of three. So I'm afraid he'll be here for some time yet, like it or not."

"Letty rang me last night . . ."

"Did she?" The tone of Mungo's voice left Zoe in no doubt what he thought about that.

"Yes, she doesn't want him to stay either."

"According to my paperwork, Colin is the partner not Letty. Much as she might like to think she is, she *isn't*; so her opinion damned well doesn't count."

"She's determined to persuade Colin. They're having lunch together tomorrow to discuss it."

"She'd damn well better not. We can't manage without Dan, and that's the end of the bloody matter." Mungo banged his fist on the edge of the desk to emphasize his determination.

Joy said, "Mungo's absolutely right; none of us likes him, but we can't manage without him."

Zoe looked across at Joy with spiteful eyes. "Since when was Joy Bastable made a partner? It's not for you to put your penny-worth in, either for or against."

Joy, affronted by Zoe's savage retort, opened her mouth to shout, "I've a right to an opinion; I have to work with him too."

But Miriam thought things had gone quite far enough. Very quietly but firmly she said, "Zoe! Take your baby home. It isn't right for him to be hearing all this anger."

Zoe sneered at Miriam, finding her sentiment laughable.

Almost inaudibly, Miriam continued, "Take him home and leave the management of the practice to Mungo. He's never let you down in the past, and he isn't going to let you down now. So go home, take your three months off and enjoy that baby you've been *privileged* to be given. Mungo's decision about Dan is absolutely right. The man's a gem and this practice needs him. Now go home." She stood away from the door to allow room for Zoe to pass her.

Zoe gave the three of them in turn a defiant stare, but when she saw the unaccustomed determination in Miriam's sweet face, she stood up to go, suddenly wearied by it all.

"Drive carefully; he's precious."

After Zoe had left, Miriam turned to Joy. "You are my dear

friend, Joy, and always will be, but you must understand this. I don't want to hear any more from you about not liking Dan, because I want him to stay. You're making a serious misjudgment of his character, I'm afraid."

She left Mungo and Joy staring at each other, nonplussed by her out-of-character interference.

Chapter

·5·

Kate heard the entire story about the row in Mungo's office the previous afternoon from Stephie. Listening was unavoidable, Stephie said, because the door was open. The only part she'd missed was what Miriam said to settle the matter. "Good thing the afternoon clinic hadn't started, or else it would have been all over the town by last night. They really shouted at one another. I know Mungo has a temper, but this was above and beyond anything I've heard before. They were swearing, and you know what he thinks about that. I only got this job because he sacked the previous receptionist for using bad language to him once too often. Anyway, Mrs. Price sorted them out without so much as raising her voice. For the rest of the day Joy was very subdued, so I reckon she'd had a telling off from Mrs. Price too."

"So is Dan staying, then?"

"That's what I heard Mungo say. But we can't manage without him at the moment anyway, can we?"

Graham Murgatroyd's client came to the desk to pay, and from then on the morning got busier; so Stephie and Kate had no more time for discussing the events of the previous day.

Just as Mungo's morning consultations were finished and he'd gone up to the flat for his lunch, Letty pushed her way through the glass door and came striding in. "Colin? Is he back yet, Stephie?"

"No, Mrs. Walker, he's right out at Pick's Farm doing TB testing. I doubt he'll be back until the middle of the afternoon."

"He knew I was coming in."

"Oh, I didn't know that. He volunteered to go, actually, because Dan was down for going and . . ."

"Did he indeed. I'll have something to say about that. Mungo in?"

Stephie lied through her teeth, her fingers crossed behind her back. "Gone out to see a client who is too ill to bring his dog in for a consultation. Right the other side of Shrewsbury."

"There must be a conspiracy. I'll call Colin on his mobile."

Letty marched through into Joy's empty office and commandeered the telephone.

The two of them waited for her to return, which she did in no time at all. "His mobile must need recharging." Her pale lips settled into a thin line. "I'll go for lunch and make a definite appointment for tomorrow. Goodbye, Stephie."

Stephie waited until Letty had shut the inner glass door and then said, "Thank my lucky stars Mungo didn't come down while she was here."

"Why did you lie?"

"Because anyone in her bad books deserves help. Poor Colin, he won't half catch it in the neck. It's all to do with Dan staying permanently. Apparently, Letty's dead against it. I'm so glad he wasn't back in time. Fancy having to lunch with her! God, it'd be like dining with a fiend."

They both laughed, only to find when they'd sobered up that Colin was standing listening to them. Kate went bright red, but Stephie, having gotten herself in the mood for telling lies, was unfazed by his unexpected arrival. "Oh, Colin! You've just missed Mrs. Walker. If you hurry you might catch her."

But Colin didn't hurry out. Instead, he looked pointedly at Stephie, raised an eyebrow and said, "If Mungo's gone to see that dog, he'll be awhile before he's back; won't he?" From the way he phrased his question, they knew he'd been hiding in the back from Letty while they'd been talking to her. Otherwise, how would he have known what lie Stephie had told?

It was Stephie's turn to feel embarrassed. "Actually, Mungo is upstairs having lunch. He's operating all afternoon, so he shouldn't be long."

Colin nodded. "Is that the truth or another lie?"

Stephie had no way out but to say, "It's the truth this time. I'm sorry."

Colin stood with his elbow resting on the desk, apparently needing to talk. Stephie recognized a conspiratorial look in his eye, and she wondered what he was about to say.

"Tonight. Dan's on call."

Kate checked the rota. "Yes, he is."

"Well, he's got a bad cold, hasn't he, and the best thing for him is a good night's sleep with a couple of whiskeys inside him. Isn't it? So I'd better fill in for him tonight, hadn't I?"

Kate couldn't get to grips with what Colin meant. "He was all right this morning. I'm quite sure he hasn't . . ."

Colin looked at her with eyes full of meaning. "Oh no, he wasn't. He looked so bad I suspect it could be flu starting."

"Flu? I don't think . . ."

Stephie nudged her. "You're right, Colin, Dan was looking white as a sheet first thing." To emphasize that she wasn't the only one being deceitful, Stephie put a lot of meaning into her next question. "Seeing as your mobile phone isn't *working*, I'll ring Mrs. Walker for you, shall I? Let her know you've swapped."

Colin nodded. "That's right. Thanks, Stephie. Wouldn't want her to arrange something and me not be able to go, would I?"

"Of course not."

Colin disappeared into the back to see if anyone had left any of their lunch so he could help himself to it. He'd found before that it was best to keep out of Letty's way for a while till the wind had gone out of her sails. She'd been so adamant about Dan not staying. He'd suffered all the previous evening from her bitterness about Dan. He, Colin, was the partner, after all. He knew how many hours he'd have to work if Dan left. He was the best judge of practice matters, not Letty. Now, having rearranged the rota, he'd be able to avoid her a while longer because she insisted he sleep in the spare bedroom when he was on call so he wouldn't disturb her beauty sleep if he got called out. Beauty sleep! Huh! It was a bit late for that. He found Stephie's unopened packet of crisps and munched his way through it while he waited for the kettle to boil. It struck him that he, a grown man, was *hiding* and *lying* to escape the wrath of his wife. *It really shouldn't be like this*, he thought. What was worse, he'd implicated the staff in his deception, and that was unworthy of him. Colin classified himself as a silly fool, and he didn't like it.

Truth to tell, he'd been a fool for most of his married life. What Letty had needed most was a strong man. Someone who wanted the last word as much as she did. Someone who took the initiative, who simply would not allow her to have her own way all of the time, and now, by his being overconsiderate toward her all these years, she despised him. Question was, was he enough of a man to be able to assert himself in a way that would make a better person of Letty? Always it was money, money, money, as if that was all that counted in life. Well, it did, to an extent, but . . .

He put the very last half crisp from the corner of the packet

in his mouth, dropped the empty packet on the worktop
and caught a glimpse of the name of the maker of the crisps.
It appeared frighteningly symbolic to him that the maker's
name was Walker; it could have been him lying there. The
packet looked just like he felt: emptied of absolutely everything. And now that it was empty, there was nothing on earth
more useful . . . just like he was after fifteen years of marriage
to Letty. He realized it was only because he was good at his job
that his sanity had been saved.

Somewhere in the very far distance a bugle sounded the call
to battle. It was faint; but Colin Walker definitely heard it and,
accordingly, he laid his plans to regain the ground he'd lost with
Letty. A bit of romance was called for, and he'd begin with
flowers. The biggest bouquet she'd ever seen, and then . . .

HALFWAY through the afternoon Stephie declared to Kate,
"It's no good; I'll have to give in."

"Give in?"

"Yes. I've been resisting temptation for the last ten minutes,
and I can't go on any longer. I'm eating those crisps."

"Honestly, Stephie, you'll regret it. Just think how pleased
you'll be with yourself if you leave them till tomorrow."

Stephie groaned at the thought of waiting till the next day.
"I know I will, but I'm desperate. I've got terrible rumbles in
my stomach, and if I don't eat something soon . . ."

"Cashing up will take your mind off it. Do that and you'll
forget."

"Nothing will make me forget. Sorry."

Leaving Kate on the desk, she went to open her crisps and
enjoy five minutes of completely loathsome self-indulgence.
She knew she was being weak, but she couldn't help herself.

Stephie was horrified to find the packet empty, lying where

Colin had left it. Storming back into reception she said, "He's done it again!"

"Who has?"

"Colin. In my hour of need, desperate, I am. I'll kill him for this."

"What's he done?"

"Eaten my crisps. He helps himself to anything left lying about; it really isn't good. I'm sure she doesn't feed him properly." Stephie stamped about behind the desk, flushed and angry.

"Look at it this way: he must have needed them, and he's saved you from breaking your diet."

"That has nothing to do with it. I'm starving. I saved them specially. My stomach is raw with hunger."

"In my bag I have a Mars bar. You can have that, if you like."

Stephie's eyes lit up and she disappeared into the back to return five minutes later complaining of feeling sick because she'd eaten it too quickly. "I should never have had it. I feel terrible."

"I did say."

"I know. I know."

As the afternoon progressed, Stephie became more ill and had to go home early because she felt so terribly sick and looked as white as she had described Dan had looked that morning. There was no possibility that she would be in to work the following day. So, as Joy had a hospital appointment tomorrow, Kate rang Letty and asked her to come in. Letty agreed with surprising alacrity.

THE first surprise Letty had was Dan bursting in through the door at eight in his usual hale and hearty manner. "Good morning, Kate." He saw Letty and treated her to his Nazi salute plus an exaggerated click of his heels. "Good morning, Letty. Lovely isn't it?"

Through tight lips Letty managed to say good morning, followed by an inquiry after his health.

Dan's eyes sparkled. "I'm fine, thank you, yes, very fine."

"I see. I was told you had flu."

"Flu? I haven't got flu. Fit as a fiddle am I."

"I see. Then why did Colin have to do your night on call last night?"

"He asked if he could. So we swapped."

"I see."

"As things appear to be transparently clear to you today, you must be on top of everything; so have you got my list?"

Letty whipped the list across the top of the desk in a trice with a triumphant, "There you are. Colin's already left."

"Hope you have a good time tonight."

"I'm not going anywhere tonight."

"Oh! Right. I'll be off, then." Dan gave Kate a wink and dashed away.

"So what do you know about all this?"

Kate saw a great big hole waiting for her to fall into and decided to know nothing whatsoever about the situation. "Stephie dealt with it." Luckily for her, the phone rang.

The morning clinic began with Valentine and Rhodri on duty with a full list of consultations, so Letty had no more time to discuss the mysterious fact of Dan's good health. At about twelve a bouquet of flowers was delivered. Letty took them from the van driver and curiously examined the card. In neat handwriting, which she didn't recognize, it read *Mrs. Letty Walker.* Flowers for her? "Kate, do you recognize this handwriting?"

Kate looked at the envelope and shook her head. "No, I don't. It'll be the florist's, I expect. They're beautiful. I adore roses. They smell lovely."

Curious to know who they were from, but assuming it must surely be Colin, Kate tried hard not to look while Letty slid the card out of its tiny envelope. Letty flushed all over her face and right down her neck. The ugly flush enhanced her appearance not one iota, and Kate looked away in embarrassment. What on earth was written on the card? The phone rang, but Letty didn't answer it; so it was Kate who had a protracted conversation with a drug company rep trying to engineer an appointment with Mungo. When she'd finished, she saw that Letty appeared to be still in a state of shock.

"I'll fill the fire bucket so they can have a drink. Aren't they wonderful?"

But Letty didn't answer. She handed the bouquet to Kate and stood staring into the distance.

"I'll save the wrapping and the ribbon."

Kate couldn't help but see the card. All that was written on it was *With all my love*. No signature. Kate stood looking at it, unable to believe that anyone would send Letty such a card. She reexamined the envelope, and it clearly said Letty's name on it; so there was no mistake about that. Kate stood the bouquet in the bucket, pushing it against the wall so it wouldn't be in the way, leaving the card on the worktop above with the wrapping and the bow. Red roses. At this time of year. They must have cost a packet. Who on earth could have sent them?

Bunty came in to prepare a feed for Copperfield, who was still in intensive care. "Are those yours, Kate?"

"Would that they were."

"They're beautiful. Who are they for?"

"Letty."

Bunty's round, homely face registered total amazement. "Letty! I don't believe it! Who're they from?"

Kate showed her the card.

"My God, what a laugh! Whoever sent them must be mad. *'With all my love!'* Wait till I tell the two Sarahs."

To Letty's total embarrassment, there was a positive stream of staff after that making the pilgrimage to view the flowers and tell her how lovely they were.

"Secret admirer, that's what," said Sarah One.

"You're a dark horse, Letty," said Sarah Two.

"Does Colin know?" asked Valentine.

"No, he does not."

Rhodri suggested it might be a grateful client, which made them all laugh.

"It must be a joke." This last from Graham, who had never been noted for his tact.

Finally, Letty said, "Kate! I'm going home with that bouquet. It is my lunch hour, and I can't take any more of it."

"You should be flattered."

"I'm not. Far from it."

"Have you really no idea who can have sent it?"

"No. I'll be back within the hour, don't worry."

Letty found a plastic carrier bag with which she enclosed the wet stems of the bouquet and disappeared through the back door as fast as she could.

Kate stood sucking the end of her pen, wondering who on earth it could be who would send someone like Letty such a hugely expensive bouquet. She began with Colin. No. Then Dan. No, though he might as an apology for his bad behavior toward her, but he wouldn't put *With all my love* now, would he? There wasn't anyone else who would. So maybe Graham was right; it was a joke on someone's part. But it was cruel if so. Not even Letty deserved that kind of meanness, Kate thought.

• • •

THAT night at home, Kate was wondering why her dad had been so quiet all evening. She'd told them the story of Letty's flowers; and Mia had speculated as to who might have sent them, but the tale hadn't raised the slightest response from her father.

"Tired, Dad?"

"Just thinking." He caught Mia's eye and saw from her look that he had no escape tonight. He'd have to say it. The time had come; he couldn't avoid it. He'd thought and thought, and come to the conclusion that Kate had a right to know about her mother despite his reluctance to excavate his painful past. "Kate."

"Mm?"

Losing confidence, he sidestepped his problem and asked feebly, "Are you happy at work?"

"You know I am. Why do you ask?"

Gerry shrugged his shoulders. "Just thought I would inquire, to make sure."

Mia coughed significantly to remind him of his promise to her. It was no good; he'd have to press on. "Kate, now you're nineteen and a young woman we . . . wouldn't mind—in fact, we'd be glad—for you to go on holiday with someone from work. Young people's holiday, you know the kind of thing. Mia and I have always been happy to have you with us; but we wouldn't want you to feel obliged, would we, Mia?"

"No." Mia stared at him meaningfully, knowing full well why he'd diverted to talking about holidays.

"The other thing is now you're older . . . well . . . I wondered if you'd like to hear something about your mother." Quickly Gerry followed that with "Of course, if you don't want to, that's very much all right by me."

Immediately Kate blushed from her hairline right down to

her throat. She'd never been redder in her life. Dad! Dad! Her throat constricted and her voice seemed to have gone. At last he was going to tell her. At last. Struggling, she got out, "Yes, please, I'd like to hear."

Gerry clenched his hands and laid them on the cloth. In a voice quite unlike his own and secretly hoping she would still say no, he told her, "Mia said I must, so I will, if that's what you want."

Kate nodded. "Why now?"

"Because I should have told you years ago, but there was Mia to think of and I . . . couldn't. But I will now. What do you want to know?"

"It would be nice if I knew her name."

"Tessa Fenton."

In her mind Kate rolled the name around several times to get accustomed to it. Startled to realize it wasn't Tessa Howard, Kate said, "I had expected you'd be married."

Gerry shook his head. "I wanted to be, but she wouldn't."

"Oh!"

"Truth to tell, she thought herself a cut above me. Bit of rough, I think she would have described me as."

Mia looked pained and reached out her hand to hold his.

Kate, feeling affronted that anyone, let alone her own mother, would categorize her father like that, said sharply, "But you're not. Dad! You're not anyone's bit of rough."

"I was to her. To her I was the artisan she fancied for a while. What she hadn't bargained for was that your old dad had more vigor than she gave me credit for; and after she moved in with me, she was pregnant almost immediately. But she wouldn't have an abortion, thank God."

Mia's heart almost broke in two. She clutched hold of Kate's hand and sat like a link in a chain, connecting the pair of them.

Kate, horrified, had to ask, "Did you want her to?"

"No, of course not. But if she had wanted one, there wasn't much I could have done about it, was there?"

"No. So what did she say when she found out?"

"Not repeatable in present company. She was as sick as a dog for weeks. You had to admire her pluck—went to work every day feeling like death warmed up."

"Work? What did she do?"

"Solicitor."

"Solicitor!"

Gerry nodded.

"Dad, were you glad? About me?"

"Glad. The bells of heaven must have been ringing their clappers to a standstill. Glad! Was I? I was. Glad and proud and delighted and thrilled. So was she when the sickness stopped, and she could feel you moving about inside her. I used to put my hand on her stomach and feel for you moving. What joy."

Mia controlled her tears; she mustn't be seen to weep. This was Kate's night, not hers.

Kate felt peculiar. Primitive. Basic. Earthier than before. Suddenly her mother became real for her. Her dad was turned in on his memories; she could see that from the look in his eyes. He cleared his throat, saying "Wonderful days. You gave her a hell of a time when you were born, though. Day and a half, it took. Then you came in a rush, shot out almost. I remember the sun was shining into the delivery room; and it seemed to me that you were charmed, very special, a kind of chosen one. And you were so beautiful, screaming to the heavens, but beautiful. I remember the midwife said, 'She's here to stay.'"

"My mother"—it felt odd saying that—"how did she feel?"

Gerry didn't seem to want to answer.

She asked again, "How did she feel about me?" There was an almost pathetic eagerness to know in Kate's voice, a need to hear about her mother's approval or acceptance, or, heaven forbid, rejection.

Mia heard the slight change in Gerry's voice and guessed he was saying what he knew Kate wanted to hear. "Well, once they'd attended to her and washed you and sorted you out and given you to her to hold, she was thrilled. Very thrilled. You must understand she was exhausted. It had been a long time."

Mia stood up. "I'll make a cup of tea." While she busied herself with that, Gerry went on reminiscing about Kate's first week at home. "My, you were demanding. The midwife said she'd never seen a baby as hungry as you."

"What did I weigh, Dad? Do you remember?"

"Engraved on my heart. Katrina Howard, seven pounds exactly. Here, look, I found this the other day; it's the identification band they put round your wrist."

Gerry dug in the top pocket of his jacket and handed her the small plastic band. "Oh, look, Mia! Isn't that lovely. You've kept it all this time. That's so lovely; I can't believe it. Can I keep it?"

Gerry nodded.

Mia put her hand on Kate's shoulder and loved her joy as she turned the tiny plastic band round and round with such endearing care. Mia had no idea Gerry had it hidden away. It seemed today there was a lot she didn't know about him. Tessa. Hm.

"So, Kate, that was how it all started."

"That's not all, though, is it Dad? What happened then? Why did she leave me?"

Understandably, Gerry found this part of the story even harder to face than the beginning had been. He fidgeted with the cruet, placing it straight and smoothing the tablecloth; he found a crumb, picked it up and put it on his side plate; he looked up into Mia's sympathetic, encouraging eyes and finally gained the strength to say "She found motherhood wasn't all it was cracked up to be, and she couldn't cope."

"You mean she had postnatal depression."

Gerry shifted his feet uneasily. "Something like that."

"Well, that is hard to cope with, isn't it. Sometimes it can drive a mother to suicide." Immediately panicking about what she'd said, Kate asked, "She didn't, did she? Is that why I've never known her?"

"No, she didn't." Gerry stood up. "There, I've said enough for one night. Can't talk about it anymore." He headed for the stairs.

Mia called out, "Your tea! I've poured it."

"No, thanks." Gerry left them and went upstairs, and shortly they heard the Flying Scotsman hurtling along its tracks.

Kate sat silently, either fingering the plastic band or picking up her cup and sipping her scalding hot tea. Mia was silent too. In this situation there wasn't a great deal a stepmother could find to say except "More tea?"

"No, thanks. He can't leave it like this. I'm going up to find out more. He was being kind, wasn't he? Saying she might have had postnatal depression?"

Mia shook her head. "I honestly don't know. I've learned more tonight than ever before. It's a closed book as far as your dad is concerned. It's all so painful for him."

Kate drew in a deep breath, so deep her shoulders heaved as she took it. "It hurts me badly too. How could she leave me? How could she? I can't forgive that. I just cannot. Two weeks old. She can't have had much maternal feeling for me, can she?"

"We're all different, Kate. I couldn't leave you at nineteen years, never mind two weeks. But that's me. Soft old Mia."

Kate's arms were round Mia in a second, and they hugged each other tightly.

"Oh, Mia! I love you!"

"And I love you."

They hugged a moment longer, then Kate sat down and wiped her eyes on a tissue borrowed from Mia. "He can't leave it like this. He's got to tell me more. I know he hurts, but it might be better to bring it all out now, while he's in the mood. You know, Mia, he must have been devastated when she left. Imagine being dumped like that and with a baby too, when he loved her. I think he did love her, don't you? Otherwise it wouldn't be quite so hard for him. I wonder if they've communicated at all since?"

Mia shook her head again. "Not to my knowledge."

"I'm going to ask."

Kate stood up and was at the foot of the stairs before Mia could stop her. She protested, "No, don't, love, he's had enough." But she was too late.

Gerry was hunched over, watching his goods train as it pulled into the station siding. He switched it off, and as Kate looked on he pulled out his handkerchief and blew his nose.

"Thanks for telling me, Dad."

"Oh! It's you." As though he'd never broken off the conversation he continued by saying, "She was lovely looking, was your mum. That's where you get it from, certainly not from me."

Trying to keep it light, Kate joked, "Oh! I don't know. You're not that bad looking. I think I've got your nose."

"For your sake I hope you haven't. She made a big mistake, did your mum. She should never have taken up with me."

"Don't underrate yourself."

"I'm not. I'm speaking the truth. I don't like to say too much in front of Mia; it wouldn't be right. But your mother, though full of good intentions, should never have taken up with me. I was blessedly grateful for her, but more so because she gave me you. At least I had you to cling to when she'd gone. You to get up for, you to bathe, you to feed, you to support. Without you

I'd have gone under. There'd have been no point in living but for you."

"She didn't like me, did she?"

Quickly Gerry denied this. "It wasn't like that at all. She couldn't cope with being tied every hour of the day."

"But she could have found someone to care for me while she went to work. She would be earning enough to do that as a solicitor. But she didn't."

Gerry hadn't an answer to that. "Don't let it get to you what she did. You've got Mia and she's been worth twenty of your mum to you." Her dad took her hand in both his and muttered, "Worth twenty, she's been. A real lifesaver, for you and for me. So don't you go upsetting her talking to her about your mum, wanting to see her and that." He looked up at Kate to see how she'd taken what he'd said.

"I shan't. I'm not daft. It's just that it's important to me to *know who I am*. You haven't got a photo of her, have you?"

Gerry dropped her hand abruptly, swung back to his train layout and said emphatically, "No. I have not. I burned it all. Every last bit."

Kate went to the window to look out. "You know Zoe at the practice? Well, she's got her baby, like I said, and she isn't ever going to tell the father about the baby, nor the baby about his father. To me that's terribly wrong. You *need to know*. You really do. Believe me."

"Well, now you do know. So that's that. Go downstairs and keep Mia company, because she cherishes you more than life itself and that's something for anyone, rich or poor, to be very, very grateful for."

It was on the tip of Kate's tongue to ask if her dad loved Mia as he'd loved her own mother, but she changed her mind. Perhaps it would be best not to know the answer to that.

Chapter

·6·

Kate was glad she wasn't working the following morning, because she was still feeling confused by all she'd learned from her father the previous night. She lay in bed, staring at the chinks of light creeping round the edges of her curtains and thinking about her mother. It would have been so good to have seen a photograph of her. Even a faded one, just to have some idea of what one half of Kate Howard actually came from. It seemed odd that fifty percent of herself was derived from someone she'd never seen or really known anything about.

She took a hand out from under the duvet and examined it in the half-light, and wondered if she'd inherited her mother's hands because they certainly weren't the square, solid hands of her dad. A solicitor. Just think, she could have wanted to be one and not realized she was being led by her genes. Or did it work that way? Whatever. Tessa. Tessa Fenton. Kate flung herself on her other side and contemplated leaving her own two-week-old baby, and knew she couldn't, not even if they'd had to go and live together in a cardboard box somewhere. A baby was part of you. How could any mother have walked away and never bothered again? But Tessa had done just that, and for the callousness that illustrated Kate decided she wouldn't want to know her, ever, and she wasn't going to waste any more of her time thinking about her and what she was and what she looked like. And she'd never search for her. Never ever.

Mia shouted from downstairs, "Kate, phone for you."

"OK." Kate ran downstairs and took the receiver. "Hello, Kate Howard speaking."

"Dan here, Kate. Sorry for interrupting your day off."

"That's all right."

"Kate, I've had a rather surprising card this morning inviting me and your good self to afternoon tea at Applegate Farm, today. At four."

"Afternoon tea! Are you sure?"

"I am. As you know them, I thought you wouldn't say no. I'm going anyway. I've an idea there's a surprise in store for us."

"I bet there is. Food poisoning."

"Well, that too. Do you fancy going?"

"I suppose I do."

"If you've nothing else on."

"OK. But if I'm off work tomorrow, I shall blame you. What on earth can it be about?"

"I've said I think they might have a surprise in store."

"What kind of a surprise?"

"Wait and see. I don't want to let them down."

"Of course not. Yes, I'll go. Curiosity is getting the better of me."

"I'll pick you up if I may; would that be all right?"

"Yes." Kate gave him instructions about how to find her house and saying "See you at half past three, then. Bye," put down the receiver.

· · ·

THEY were halfway to Applegate Farm when Kate burst out with "Do you remember me saying I wished I knew about my mother?"

Dan nodded.

"Well, my dad told me last night. About me being born and that."

"I'm glad. Are you glad?"

"Yes, I am. He didn't tell me much, but enough. Last night I wanted to see a picture of her, but this morning I don't."

"Why not?"

"Because I can't forgive her for abandoning me."

"Oh."

"You don't think I'm right."

"It's not up to me."

"I'd like to know if you think I'm right, Dan."

Keeping his eyes on the road, Dan said tentatively, "What you mustn't do is harbor resentment toward her, because it will fester. Either forget all about her and get on with your life, or forgive her. But don't have resentment hovering about in your mind, niggling away."

"It's a very hard thing to forgive anyone for."

"It is, I agree."

"Mia's worth twenty of her, like Dad said, and I wouldn't do anything to hurt her."

"We're almost there. Prepare yourself, my child."

Kate had to laugh. "You know what this is all about, don't you?" A suspicion gathered in her mind. "Did you really get an invitation?"

He applied the brake and dipped his hand into his top pocket. "See for yourself." Dan gave her a piece of bright pink card. On it was written:

Blossom and Phil Parsons Cordaly invite Dan Brown and
Cate To Afternone Tea In the Barn Tea room At four on
Thursday (today). Pleas come.

"In the barn tearoom? Oh, God! What have we let ourselves in for? I don't know which is worse, the house or the barn."

Dan looked across at the farm buildings and said, "Take a look."

There was red, white and blue bunting, dusty and crumpled, strung over the door to Sunny Boy's stall. Sitting in the doorway was little Scott with a small Union Jack tied round her neck. Then Kate saw Blossom appear in the doorway, waving.

"Here goes." Dan waved enthusiastically through the open window. Still smiling at Blossom, he muttered to Kate that he had stomach tubing with him if need be.

He put on his boots, waited for Kate to do the same, then they both got out and marched cheerfully toward Sunny Boy's stall. The bunting appeared grubbier the nearer they got, but the welcome was enthusiastic and they cheered up enormously.

Blossom had decked herself out in the skimpiest of leather skirts. Despite the winter wind blowing, her top half was clothed in a short-sleeved pink sweater the color of the invitation card and in her hair was silver tinsel, a precursor of Christmas. "Come in! Come in!" She placed a goose-pimpled arm through Dan's and hastened him in. Kate followed.

The transformation of the barn was breathtaking. Dan looked round with amazement.

"It was all Phil's idea. Isn't it great?" Blossom squeezed his arm and waited eagerly for his reaction. "Phil's heard your car and he's gone to get the champagne from the dairy. It's cold in there. Well?"

"Mrs. Parsons . . ."

Blossom giggled. "Not Mrs. Parsons! It's Blossom to you. You're a friend. Isn't he, Kate?"

Kate nodded. "Such a transformation! It's splendid."

Dan looked at the glowing black beams, the horse brasses nailed like guardsmen on parade along the length of each beam, at the burnished brass catch on the door to Sunny Boy's stall, the newly painted feeding trough, the snow-white walls and the purple wheelie bins lined up against the far wall.

"I can see you like the bins. It was my idea to paint them purple, royal purple for a royal bull, and do you like the silver stars? That was Hamish's idea. He stuck them on."

"I am just gobsmacked. Truly gobsmacked. It is magnificent."

"Phil's thrilled to bits."

"It's so tidy, so smart, so different. Even the loose stones cemented in."

Phil came in carrying a chrome tray with glasses and champagne on it, followed by a tall, gangling teenage boy with a head of the reddest hair either Kate or Dan had ever seen. He had the pale-blue eyes and the fair, heavily freckled skin which so often go with real red hair; even his eyelashes were red.

Phil put the tray down carefully on a small side table they'd brought in from the house, saying, "This is Hamish. Come to live with us. He's helped with this, haven't you, Hamish?"

Blossom beamed at Hamish and added, "If it hadn't been for him, we'd never have got finished, would we, Hamish?"

Hamish simply grinned in agreement. But it was a beautiful grin, which lit up the whole of his face and was expressive of his pleasure at their approval.

Behind his back Blossom silently mouthed, "He can't talk."

Dan released himself from Blossom's clutching arm and went to shake Hamish's hand. "This is a big thank you from me to you for getting all this done. Wonderful job. No one could be more pleased." He clapped Hamish on the shoulder and smiled at him. "Brilliant!" Hamish grinned his appreciation.

"Now!" Phil took the champagne bottle and began the removal of the cork. "I've left Sunny Boy out of here until we're ready to drink the toast. Thought the cork shooting out might upset him."

The cork shot out, hitting the window with a loud ping.

Blossom dissolved into laughter. "God, Phil! Don't break that bloody window. It took ages to get it clean and painted."

"Right, Hamish, bring him in. He's got to be here when we drink the toast." Phil put down the bottle and proudly opened the newly painted gate to the stall.

"Will Sunny Boy let . . ." Dan nodded his head toward the open door.

"Of course. They're buddies, they are."

"Where's he from?"

"Tell yer later. Here he comes."

They stood aside to make space for Hamish to lead Sunny Boy into the stall. Round the bull's neck was tied a Union Jack ten sizes larger than Scott's; he was brushed and combed, and spruced up well enough to compete at the Royal Show. The restraint of the rope through his nose ring made him anxious and caused him to toss his head from side to side, and Kate shrank back against the wall, fearful of those great hooves of his. Hamish calmly secured his head rope to a ring in the wall and carefully shut the gate behind him. If Phil had declared he was a champion pedigree bull, no one would have challenged him. He looked magnificent in his newly refurbished quarters.

"A toast!" called Phil. He refilled all their glasses and raised his, saying "To Sunny Boy, to his new quarters and to Hamish, who did all the work!"

They all clinked glasses and drank the toast. Kate studied

Hamish for a moment and wondered about him. It was obvious Phil Parsons didn't want to explain while he was there. But why couldn't he talk? Didn't he want to or couldn't he talk at all?

"Right then. Tea. Come on, Hamish, go and give Blossom a hand, if you please."

Hamish shuffled off after Blossom, she small and dainty, he large and shambling. Phil dipped his fingers in his champagne and, leaning over into the stall, pushed them into Sunny Boy's great mouth. "He's got to share in the celebrations, hasn't he? Come on then, have a drop more."

Dan had to ask: "Who is he, Phil? That Hamish."

"He's the one who left the ball that day, the one that Sunny Boy tried to swallow. From the caravan site, he is, been staying there with a group of lads from a home. Came back to get it after you'd gone and wouldn't leave. Just hung about, not saying anything. I tried to get him to go, but he wouldn't. Blossom thought he was hungry so she gave him some food and then told him to go, but he wouldn't and it's a bit difficult making a big chap like him scat. He just wouldn't. So, desperate, Blossom said go down and tell 'em. So I did. Well, he went back to the site when they came to get him. They left the next day, and two days later he was back here. He'd hopped it at a motorway service station and walked till he got 'ere."

"How could he tell you that?"

"Showed me a receipt from a place on the M4 and waved his arms about a bit. That's what Blossom says happened anyway. He won't go. I've tried, so I thought I'd put him to good use. Blossom's made a bed up for him and, well, here he is."

"Shouldn't someone be told?" Kate asked.

"And send him back to where he doesn't want to be? He's no trouble and it does Blossom good to have someone to fuss over. She says love is all he wants, someone who cares, and she's good at that. We asked about his mum and dad, and he started shaking and went to bed, and wouldn't come out for a day and a night. Not till Blossom sat on his bed and told him he could stay and we wouldn't say a word to the authorities. Terrified, he was." Phil shrugged his shoulders. "Perhaps one day he'll speak and tell us. He eats like he's never eaten in years, straight down, whatever it is, and never has an ache or a pain, even though he reg'lar has two full plates of dinner at a sitting."

Phil's last sentence reminded Kate about food poisoning and she sent up a little prayer that she'd have as strong a stomach as Hamish apparently had. They heard Blossom's heels tapping along the yard, accompanied by the solid tread of Hamish's big feet, and through the door she came with a heavily loaded tray that she placed on the table Hamish had carried in for her.

"Hasn't she done us proud?"

Dan ate heartily, Kate sparingly, but enough not to give offense. Blossom had certainly done them proud, as Phil had said. Hamish ate as much as the four of them put together with an enthusiasm none of them could match.

They shook hands with Blossom, Phil and Hamish, and thanked them profusely for their hospitality as they left, especially Hamish for all his help with the improvements. He grinned and gave them a thumbs-up.

As Dan turned the Land Rover round in the lane Kate said, "There appear to be a lot of people around with either no parents or only one original one. Me and Oscar and now Hamish. It's not right, is it, for no one to know where Hamish is?"

Dan thought for a moment and didn't answer until they were well down the lane close to the main road. "He wouldn't have done a runner if he'd been happy where he was, and he is happy with Blossom and Phil, isn't he?"

Kate had to admit he was.

"So I think that adds up to you and me keeping quiet about him and leaving him in peace. He obviously knows exactly what's being said to him and understands perfectly, so perhaps the talking will come if he has a chance to feel safe."

"Mm. You're wiser than you look. It's funny this thing about one's roots. When he told me about my mother, my dad gave me the identification band I'd had round my wrist in the hospital, you know, when I was newborn, and suddenly I felt real, as though I'd come from somewhere and hadn't simply materialized. I felt I had roots, and identity, kind of. Silly isn't it?"

"No, it isn't."

The answer had come crisply and with a finality in the tone of his voice that brooked no further mention of the subject, leaving Kate wondering what lay at the heart of Dan—so full of wisdom and understanding one minute and then up went a blank wall and he'd gone behind it.

In truth, one half of his mind was controlling his driving and the other half was far away on the U.S. eastern seaboard, and he was lying on his back on the sand, watching seabirds swirling in the breeze below a shimmering blue sky, unsuccessfully trying to come to terms with the idea of never seeing Rose again in this life. His world had splintered into a thousand myriad pieces. He'd spoken, then, to himself of his roots. His roots and his need for home. That was when he'd decided to come home to England. Rose. Rose.

He braked heavily as a red traffic light brought him back to reality. "Sorry about that."

Kate lurched forward, saved only by the tug of her seat belt.

"Very sorry. Won't happen again."

"That's all right, happens to the best of us." While they waited for the lights to change, she said, "Have you ever wondered how Phil Parsons makes a living from that farm? Because for the life of me I can't see how he can."

"Neither can I."

"He must have some other source of income, mustn't he?"

His lips twitched as he replied, "One would imagine he must. You can't help but like them both, can you?"

Kate smiled to herself. "No, you can't. The food appeared beyond reproach, didn't it?"

"I shall pass judgment on that tomorrow. Who knows what the night might bring." Dan glanced at her and laughed. For one bright moment he appeared to her handsome. She thought of Scott when she thought of handsome and for some strange reason had difficulty remembering what he looked like. Then, like a flash, his laughing face focused in her mind and she grinned.

"What's so amusing?"

"Just thinking of Scott who was before you. You're braver than him. He refused to eat or drink there. Only whiskey we had once. And he never let Blossom get anywhere near him if he could help it. She was always after his body, he said."

"The conceit of the man! I fancy she's after any body, even half presentable, in trousers. I can't help wondering about his balaclava. It's there to hide something, isn't it?"

Kate looked out of the window. "It's left here after the roadworks. It must be. Maybe he's an escapee from a home somewhere, and he's still hiding his identity. Perhaps that's why he has so much sympathy with Hamish."

"I've an idea it's deeper than that. Here we are. Thanks for coming, Kate. They would have been affronted if you hadn't."

"That's OK. Thank you for taking me."

Dan got out and went round to open her door for her.

"Bye. See you tomorrow. Thanks again for the lift."

"See you."

Before she had got the front door open, Dan was already charging off down the street.

. . .

WEDNESDAY was market day in Barleybridge, so not only was there a street market but a cattle market too. Dan, having a morning free because of being on call all night, decided to mingle in the cattle market for an hour, before going to the supermarket to replenish his depleted food stocks.

The sheds and pens at the market were teaming with animals of all kinds: goats and sheep, cows and pigs, chickens and geese. The hustle and bustle, the sights and sounds, were energizing, and he spent a happy hour wandering about looking at the condition of the animals, some good, some poor. He listened to the auctioneer to see what prices were being achieved at the moment and winced when he heard how low the selling prices were.

Here and there the odd farmer acknowledged him, and he them, with a nod or a touch of his cap and a friendly "Good morning." Some stayed for a chat, mostly to bemoan the low prices that day. He inspected the pigs, checked out the goats— especially some pygmy goats, which at one time he had rather fancied breeding—then went to view the chickens. They were a motley collection of fancy and workaday, and he paused for a while, looking them over with a practiced eye.

Then the rain came down. Not in a drizzle, which a stout heart could ignore, but a thundering, pelting downpour. Dan hastily retreated under the porch over the front door of the Askew Arms, the oldest and most prestigious hotel in the town. As it was twelve o'clock, he decided to take an early lunch and not bother with his supermarket shopping until the following day.

He'd ordered steak and kidney pie with a half bottle of house wine and was awaiting its arrival when he heard the loud voice of Lord Askew in the dining-room entrance. Immediately the manager rushed forward to greet him. To Dan's eye the man would have done better to have genuflected and have done with it, for his obsequious bowing and scraping was embarrassing to watch. Lord Askew ignored him and surveyed the dining room with a haughty eye, which wavered over Dan and then came back to him. The manager pointed to a table in the window slightly withdrawn from the others, obviously intending to direct his lordship toward it.

But Lord Askew had other ideas. "This will do!" He headed for Dan's table and asked if the other chair was free for him to use.

Thinking a bit of courtesy on his behalf would go a long way with a man like Lord Askew, Dan stood up. "I shall be delighted to have your company, my lord. I dislike eating alone."

Lord Askew ordered steak and kidney pie too, cancelled Dan's half bottle of house wine and ordered a whole bottle of the most expensive red wine on the list.

They chatted about the state of the market, the need to keep a finger on the pulse, how farmers could survive in the current economic climate and the value of diversifying.

"Callum Tattersall has come up with another hare-brained scheme. Mushrooms this time. The man's a fool. Tenant farmer of mine, you know, keeps the land and buildings in good trim, better than some, but he's never going to be rich."

"I have sympathy for him. His wife is very ill."

"Yes, yes, that's as may be. Drag on a man is that. My lady wife has always been a great support. You haven't met her?" Dan shook his head. "Wonderful woman. Like you, speaks straight from the shoulder, always." Lord Askew fell silent, a smile twitching at his lips.

Their food came and was expertly served to them by the manager himself. Lord Askew downed the wine in less time than it took to say thank you for having it poured. He'd swallowed a second glass before Dan had got halfway through his first, and Dan's plate was still half full when Lord Askew placed his knife and fork together and sat back to unfasten his waist-coat buttons. "Excellent! Not exactly top-notch, this place, bed-rooms are damned ghastly, but they do know about food. You're always safe with a good old-fashioned English menu. 'Spect they've been serving steak and kidney pie for three hundred years or more."

"You're right, it is excellent."

"You won't mind if I smoke?"

"Well, yes, I do."

Lord Askew stopped halfway through removing the top of his cigar case. "You do?"

"I'm sorry, yes, and it does say no smoking in this section. That's why I'm sitting at this table."

"Never bother about things like that. Not me. However . . ." He put away the cigar case and leaned his elbows on the edge of the table, watching Dan finish his meal. "I recommend the treacle sponge and custard to finish, and we'll have our coffee and brandy in the lounge."

"I hadn't intended to have pudding."

"Well, I'm footing your bill, so you will."

"That's most kind of you."

"One hundred and fifty-two thousand pounds we got with the charity auction. Good night, eh?"

"It certainly was."

"Terribly keen, I am, to keep the hunt going. Shambles it all is. Complete shambles. All these job losses. Damned inter-fering." When they'd eaten their excellent treacle sponge, the manager appeared again to ask if everything was to their sat-isfaction. "Coffee and brandy in the lounge, Firth, please. For two."

"Certainly, my lord, whenever you're ready."

Dan followed him to a quiet corner, though it was difficult because the hotel was rapidly filling up, but not surprisingly the quietest table was free and Lord Askew took possession of it. As soon as the coffee had been poured for them, he said, "Now, Dan Brown, will you come to see that roan. My daughter's got great hopes for him, and I don't want her spending hours of time on it only to be disappointed."

"On the understanding that I come as an employee of the practice."

Lord Askew gave a satisfied sigh. "I'm willing to accept that."

"So long as you have finished with your own equine practice. I can't attend a client of theirs when they're still officially your vets."

"Come, come, you can't expect me to . . ."

"I'm sorry. I *might* come if you tell them I'm being called in as a second opinion, though."

Lord Askew gave another sigh of satisfaction. "Ah! That's more like it."

Dan sat back in his armchair, rested his elbows on the arms, placed the tips of his fingers together and said, "But I would expect to have all your other veterinary work restored to us."

Lord Askew spluttered into his cup, replaced it in its saucer and wiped his lips on his handkerchief. "That's asking a damn sight too much. You're too cocky by half."

"I'm not prepared to be made use of, to reassure you about that roan without some assurance that it's not just a one-off. Making use of my skills to save your skin isn't on."

"Bet you didn't treat that Arab sheikh like this, else your head would've been off."

"He knew a good vet when he saw one, my lord, so I was treated with the utmost courtesy, both professionally and personally."

"Hmph." Lord Askew shifted impatiently in his chair. "Well, that's it then. Can't have your expertise, since you're not willing even to put the horse's welfare first."

He stood, his face flushed bright red with, again, that tinge of blue about his lips. "Shan't ask again."

Dan felt concern that matters between them were to be left even worse than before. "Of course the horse's welfare is my concern, but you must understand I am not here to be picked up and put down at will. It's either all or nothing. I can assure you, you won't regret doing as I ask. In the circumstances I'll pay for my own lunch."

"No, no. A gentleman's word's his bond. I shall pay and be damned annoyed if you persist."

"In that case, thank you again. It has been a pleasure to lunch with you, Lord Askew. Please feel free to contact me at any time, should you change your mind."

"Hmph."

"So I got the free lunch, but, unfortunately, I am no nearer getting his veterinary work back."

Mungo shook his head. "One day you will, I'm sure. Are you certain of your diagnosis? After all, you only saw the roan briefly."

"One hundred percent."

"You can be a cocky beggar, you know. Still, if he calls you in for a second opinion . . ."

"He's terribly tempted, I can see that. Let's hope he asks me before he drops down dead."

"Heart?"

Dan nodded. "Seems so to me. There's something very likeable about him, you know. A softness that's almost childlike."

"I suspect you must be the first to think that. He's a hard landlord and a worse father, I understand."

"He desperately wants to be liked, but he's not sure how to go about it."

"Honestly, Dan, you're as bad as Miriam. She sees deep hurt where other people see arrogance. She includes you in that category."

Dan had been getting up ready to leave, but sat down again when Mungo said that. "Is that how you think of me? Arrogant?"

"Well, let's face it, you are. They all think you are."

"I might be blunt but I hope never arrogant."

Mungo laughed. "Well, perhaps arrogant is too strong a word. But you will have your say. Look at Letty. Look at Zoe. Even Joy feels she's taken a battering. They would all cheer if you left."

"Is that what *you* want? Because I'll leave tomorrow. Or today even." Dan eyed Mungo with a bleak look.

"Look here, Miriam would have me strung up if I so much as mentioned the idea of you leaving and, between you and me, I want you to stay too. But for heaven's sake, man, try to be a bit more easy with us all. Right?"

"Right. Off the record, I'd like to stay if you want me. Nothing I'd like better."

Mungo waved an impatient hand. "Let's leave it for now. I'm still waiting for a definite answer from the chap we interviewed. See how things work out. OK?"

"OK." He made to leave Mungo's office and then turned back. "Thank you for your support. Perhaps it's more than I deserve, having lost you such a good client."

Mungo retorted, "Well, yes, it bloody well is more than you deserve, but there you are." He grinned to soften his harsh words and Dan laughed.

"Your wife is a gem and very perceptive. I didn't know it showed. I'll be more careful in the future."

But he wasn't and he stirred up trouble the very next day.

Chapter

· 7 ·

Joy slammed the door of Mungo's flat behind her and flung herself down in his favorite chair. "Miriam? Are you there?"

"That you, Joy?"

"Yes."

Miriam entered the sitting room in her dressing gown, rubbing her wet hair with a towel. "What's the matter? Excuse the garb; I've just got out of the bath."

"I wouldn't notice if you were starkers."

"Why? What's happened?"

"Happened? It's what's going to happen if a certain person doesn't mind his Ps and Qs. I'm so blazing mad. Just when I think everything's going with a swing he . . ."

"Yes?"

"He upsets everyone. Who does he think he is?"

"That doesn't sound like Mungo."

Joy looked up at her, surprised. "It's not Mungo, it's . . ."

"Dan?"

"Yes, Dan." Joy's lips tightened into a thin line as she said this.

"Oh, Joy! What's it all about?" Miriam sat herself down and waited.

"It's only a little thing, really . . ."

"Well?"

"Well, no, it isn't a little thing, it's a big thing. You know we have a three-day roster worked out? Start at eight one day and finish at four. Next day work eight till seven with a three-hour break in the afternoon and the next, one till eight?"

Miriam nodded.

"Well, Dan wants us to change the times of the clinics and make it as the girls work, eight hours starting at eight in the morning and finishing at four, or start at one and finish at eight in the evening. Week about."

"Yes?"

"Yes? What do you mean, 'yes'? Why should we change our working practices just because he fancies putting his oar in?"

"It's worth consideration."

Joy stood up. " 'Worth consideration'? I don't believe you. I'm the practice manager, not him, and we've worked this system for years. No one's ever complained."

"So?"

"So? What do you mean, 'so'?"

Miriam placed a hand on Joy's arm, hoping to placate her. "He may have hit on a good idea. Have you asked the girls?"

"No point in stirring up a hornet's nest unnecessarily, now is there?"

"Doing this means you'd have an afternoon clinic from, say, two until three and then four-thirty till seven-thirty, doesn't it? Might be very popular. More clinic time equals more clients, doesn't it, surely?"

Joy nodded reluctantly. "Possibly. But it all depends what Rhodri and Graham and Valentine feel, doesn't it?"

"Of course. Think about it."

"You're only saying this because you want Dan to stay. Well, Miriam, you'll be pleased to hear that the chap who came for the interview hasn't yet made up his mind. Rang him up an hour ago."

"Ah!"

"So that's not good news, is it? Dan may be here far longer than any of us wants him to be."

"I'm very, very sorry to hear that. I have said before, Joy, that you're making a serious error of judgment about him. Why you're getting so wild about him when you now know he'll be leaving eventually I don't really know."

"But he won't if you have your way. It's his attitude; it riles me. Interfering busybody, he is, and he thinks everyone can work at the same pace as he does. Well, we can't."

"Perhaps you all should."

"Are you saying we don't work hard enough?"

"Well, no, not really but . . ."

"You don't have to work with him. Letty agrees with me. She can't wait to see the back of him."

Miriam couldn't believe her ears. "You agree with Letty? I thought you were sworn enemies."

"That Nazi salute he gives her—well, it's a disgrace."

"There was a time when you thought it appropriate and very funny."

"On the matter of him going we are as one."

"Name one thing he does wrong."

"One?" Joy laughed, unaccustomed mockery in her tone. "He lost us Lord Askew's account his first week. Have you got the rest of the afternoon free?" She turned on her heel and stormed out.

But it wasn't the last that Miriam heard about it, for when Mungo came up after an intense and exhausting afternoon operating it was the first thing he mentioned. "You're not going to bring up the subject of Dan, are you?"

"Not if you don't want me to."

"I don't. I've had my fill."

"But . . ."

"I'm sick of women with nothing better to do than trump up excuses to put a spoke in the wheels." He counted them off on his fingers. "Letty, because she's angry at the way he treats her, but it's nothing more than she deserves. Joy, because as practice manager she feels her nose has been put out of joint. Zoe, because a mole has rung her and informed her of the argument."

"Well, Zoe is a partner and should know what's happening."

"And now you, because you want him to stay. I understand Joy has been up and said her piece."

Miriam nodded. "For what it's worth, I didn't agree with her."

"I know you didn't; she told me. Out of sheer cussedness I've a mind to ring this chap and tell him it's all off, and then they'll be stuck with Dan. Serve 'em all right."

"Well, you would be justified. He has taken much longer than need be to be accepted. It's quite a good idea, actually, what Dan says."

"That's what I thought. They've not enough to do, that's the trouble."

"I shouldn't say that to Joy. I got my head bitten off for mentioning that perhaps they all needed to work as hard as Dan. A longer afternoon clinic might be a good idea, but it might mean the same number of appointments spread over a longer time with extra hours for Graham et al."

"It's bitchiness, really personal, you know."

"Frankly . . . here's a whiskey for you . . . I don't know what's wrong with him. If he were a time waster and disappeared for hours on end keeping clients waiting, I could understand it. Remember that one we had—I forget his name—we never knew where he was from one hour to the next, terrible chap. You should have heard Joy go on about *him*."

"Thanks. I remember only too well." Mungo took a sip of his whisky, leaned back in his chair with his eyes shut and said, "If he got old Askew's account back . . ."

"Plus the equine . . ."

Mungo smiled ruefully. "They'd still complain."

Miriam studied his face and thought about how much she loved him—he could still walk into a room and set her pulse racing. She went to stand beside him and trailed her fingers across his eyebrows. "You are a lovely man and I love you very much. Never worry, the dust will settle and they'll all calm down."

But Miriam was wrong. Graham, Valentine and Rhodri were agreeable to changes, though they doubted if the client list would increase, but the female side of the practice were vociferous in their objections.

Squeezed into Joy's office, the lay staff had a protest meeting on their lunch hour, with Joy in the chair. The discussion grew heated almost immediately.

"I like my afternoons in the precinct," Stephie said.

Letty agreed. "Makes a nice break and you get things done."

"I'd like having a morning free. No need to get up early and you could still go to the mall before you started at one." This from Kate, who, for some reason she couldn't explain, felt she needed to support Dan's idea.

Stephie boiled over. "Well, you would say that, wouldn't you, just to be different."

"Not just to be different. I think you're only angry because it was Dan who suggested it. If it had been Mr. Price or Rhodri, you'd have given it some merit and not blown a gasket like this."

"You're an item, then, are you, you two?"

Before Joy could put a stop to the personal turn the comments were taking, Kate snapped, "No, we are not. For a start, he's years older than me."

"That didn't stop you with Scott. You were panting after him, and he was ten years older than you."

Kate, squeezed between the filing cabinet and Letty, flushed but remained silent.

Joy rapped on the desk with her pen. "This won't do. You'll apologize to Kate for that remark, please. Before we go any further."

Stephie didn't reply.

"Well?"

"I only spoke the truth."

"That particular truth is none of your business. I'm waiting."

Stephie mumbled her apology, but they knew she didn't mean a word of it. Matters went from bad to worse when Letty said her piece and inferred she couldn't wait for Dan to leave. She highlighted his arrogance, his offhandedness, his insolence.

Joy, endeavoring to be fair-minded, said, "It is not Dan who is on trial here. We're here to discuss the proposal he has about our hours. Let's keep to the subject, please."

Letty was about to speak when Kate broke in, "With all due respect, Mrs. Walker, you are only standing in. It will be us left with the new hours, not you."

This innocent remark triggered Letty's acid tongue into action, and they were treated to a tirade about the running of the practice and the amount of effort everyone put in, and the inefficiency of—

Joy had to shout to get herself heard. "Just a minute. I'm not putting up with this from anyone. This meeting is closed, and we'll reconvene when we've all had time to think. Meanwhile, I'll get out a draft roster and circulate it. We might all find ourselves surprised about how nicely it works out." She stood up and looked at them each in turn, daring them to say another word and, seeing her eyes sparking with temper and her generous mouth pinched tight, they got the message and departed.

Except for Letty. "Not putting up with this from anyone? I'm not *anyone*. I would have thought you of all people would have acknowledged that I have a right to a say about anything to do with the smooth running of the practice. After all, I did put a lot of money . . ."

"Why don't you just for once allow Colin to wear the trousers?" Joy stormed out and went to spend five minutes with young Copperfield to soothe her frayed nerves. He welcomed her attentions. He was due to have his framework of pins and screws removed the following day, and as Joy sat on the floor to play with him, she wondered what his future would hold. He couldn't stay with them forever.

He purred like an old steam engine, and with his huge amber eyes staring up at her in adoration, she continued to scratch him gently behind his ears, a thing she knew from experience he liked. With good food and lots of attention he was growing into a beautiful cat, with apparently no resentment about the human race for all he'd been through. She examined his feet one by one and saw how well they'd healed. He got off her knee and found a table tennis ball he liked to play with. She bounced it for him and as best he could, lumbering with his hardware, he chased after it.

It was warm and comforting in the care room, and Joy stayed far longer than she had intended because as she played, she sensed her anger melting away, and she felt more like the real Joy, the Joy she preferred. Damn Letty for her acid tongue. Damn

Colin for not standing up to her. Damn her money too. Root of all evil when you didn't know how to use it graciously, and Letty certainly didn't. Damn them all for their animosity. She'd make the roster so attractive they'd be begging to agree to it.

Joy scrambled to her feet, gently lifted Copperfield into her arms, kissed his lovely ginger head, admired those expressive amber eyes of his and placed him in his cage, giving him a treat as compensation. He badly needed a home, did Copperfield. He mewed at her through the bars, and she left a small piece of her heart behind as she carefully closed the care room door behind her.

The row caused by Dan's suggestion rumbled on for days. To alleviate some of the aggravation, Joy rang Lynne to see if she would be returning soon, but her mother answered and said Lynne was still under the care of her doctor, who declared she was far too frail mentally to be able to come back to work just yet. Joy brought up the question of keeping her job open for her and did her mother think that perhaps she wouldn't want to return. "I'll talk to her about it. I think a complete change of lifestyle would do her more good, but I promise to have an answer for you before the end of the week."

Joy replaced the receiver and groaned. Facing further weeks with Letty on the desk was almost more than she could bear to contemplate. How could she ever have sided with her about Dan? She must have been mad. She'd talked to Duncan about the situation, and he'd agreed with Miriam. Perhaps they did have long periods when there was very little to do, and the sooner she drew up a new roster and got them all sorted, the better. Did they really need her and two more *all* the time?

Together she and Duncan had set about the new roster and, with his logical mind and her knowledge, they'd done a very good job on it. Today she'd be circulating it to one and all for their approval. There wasn't a single thing on it that they could quibble about, she was sure. Though come to think of it, no doubt Letty would find a few faults. She'd give it out and then depart for lunch with Duncan quick smart.

Duncan came to collect her early because the rain was coming down and he'd cut short his walk. He wandered into the care room and looked at the animals in various stages of recovery. He read their notes in turn and finally came to stand in front of Copperfield. At that moment he was asleep, stretched out full length on his cozy blanket. His notes made Duncan shudder. Copperfield must have become aware he was being watched, for his huge eyes opened and stared straight at Duncan. Lazily he got up, stretched and went to the bars. They looked solemnly at each other, long and hard. They both reached out, Copperfield with his paw and Duncan with a finger through the bars and, having made contact, Duncan . . . No, he musn't. They already had Tiger, and Tiger might get very upset about an intruder, and two cats were ridiculous, but . . .

Over lunch, Joy and Duncan talked animatedly about a holiday they proposed taking in the spring. It suddenly occurred to Duncan. Holiday? Two cats? Impossible. What a to-do. No, he mustn't even think about it.

Then out of the blue, Joy herself mentioned Copperfield, without any prompting. "He's a gorgeous cat. A soul mate kind of cat. Pins are out now. He'll always have a slight limp, Mungo says, but it doesn't seem to bother him."

"I don't think there's a white hair on him."

Joy looked up surprised. "You've seen him?"

Duncan nodded.

"He's lovely, isn't he?" Joy's voice had a hint of longing in it when she said this.

"He is. Soul mate, like you said."

"Like Tiger."

"Somebody will want him." Duncan looked at her, eyes

twinkling. Joy was cutting herself some cheese when he said this, and she looked up at him, knife poised above the Cheddar, and tried to read his mind. "You glorious creature you! You fancy having him too, don't you? Am I right?"

"And you?"

Joy nodded emphatically. "I do."

"So do I."

"Let's."

"Let's."

"Oh, Duncan! I love you for it. You won't regret it. He's gorgeous, absolutely gorgeous, and I love him."

"And me too?"

"And you too," Joy said without thinking.

"Do I have to keep on adopting cats to make you say that?" He had a strange, pleading expression on his face when she finally looked at him.

Seeing where this was leading, Joy took stock and then quietly replied, "I'm not sure. Perhaps two might be enough."

"I'll make do with that for now. Eat up and we'll go and declare our intentions."

"The police haven't found out who did it to him."

"There aren't any words to describe them, are there? And yet he still loves people. A human being would find it difficult to forgive and yet a cat . . ."

"Could be cupboard love. I'm never sure about cats."

"I am. Done? I'll go and pay."

"Mungo would laugh."

"Laugh?"

"Yes. After all you've said about how could anyone love an animal."

"Why mention *him* just now?"

"It was only about the cat, not about . . ." She looked up at him and wished she hadn't caused his anguish; she'd spoiled the moment for him without intending to. Maybe after all she did love Duncan but wouldn't allow herself to admit it, after all the years of loving Mungo. Joy kissed his cheek and took his hand. "Copperfield, here we come!"

They walked back into a full-scale row. Letty had come in specially to see the new roster, and she and Stephie and Kate were arguing in the accounts office. Joy could hear their raised voices as soon as she opened the glass door.

"It doesn't matter what you say, Kate; if we give in to this, we're done for. They'll think we'll do anything and everything they decide without a thought for how we feel. We've got to put up a protest even if it's only a token one. Alter something somewhere to show we're making a stand." This was Letty.

Joy put a restraining hand on Duncan's arm. With a finger to her lips she stood listening a little longer and heard Kate say, "It's for Stephie and me to agree, Mrs. Walker."

"I'm coming out on your side for your sakes."

"Well, there's no need. Stephie and I quite like the ideas behind this. Don't we?"

Stephie must have nodded because they didn't hear a reply.

Letty declared they were both fools for accepting it so easily and "what's more, that Dan will see it as a triumph."

Joy called out, "We're back!"

Stephie and Letty came out of the accounts office and took their places at the desk. Stephie embarrassed, Letty brazening it out.

"Has Mungo begun operating, Stephie?"

"Not yet, he's talking to Bunty and Sarah One in intensive care." Stephie looked as though she wished she weren't there, and no wonder, with Letty in that mood.

Duncan remembered to be polite. "Good afternoon, girls. How's things?"

"Fine, thank you."

"Good. We're hoping to adopt Copperfield."

Stephie's face lit up. "What a brilliant idea. He's a lovely cat. I shall miss him."

"That sounds like a good résumé for a cat."

Stephie smiled, but Letty merely pursed her lips and it didn't flatter her.

Mungo agreed they could take Copperfield. Joy found a carrying cage and decided to accompany Duncan home. "I shan't be long, but things are quiet and there's two of you. If you get into a panic, give me a buzz and I'll come straight back, but I just want to be there to introduce him to Tiger."

"Oh! We'll hold the fort, won't we, Stephie?" Letty said this with such sarcasm in her voice that Joy vowed there and then to put a stop to Letty's helping out. Either Lynne came back or they got someone new. She couldn't take much more of the woman, she really couldn't.

THEY placed Copperfield on the kitchen floor still in his cage. Tiger, who had come to greet them when she heard their key in the door, stood in the doorway contemplating this change of events. Copperfield peered at her through the bars.

"I think we should feed the two of them right now to let Tiger know he's here to stay. Put Tiger's bowl down first because that's how it's always been for her, and then put Copperfield's down a moment after. That way Tiger will feel like number one."

"Good thinking. It won't harm them to have three meals today will it?"

"Of course not. Make sure Tiger gets her own bowl, not the new one."

As soon as Tiger realized that food was coming up, she decided while she waited for it to have a look at Copperfield.

Advancing across the floor in silly prancing steps, she arrived at the cage and they met nose to nose between the bars. Spitefully Tiger got her claws out and tried to scratch Copperfield's nose, but he jumped back and she missed. She spat at him and yowled her annoyance at his intrusion, lashing out with unsheathed claws, swiftly and menacingly.

Joy was horrified. "Hell's bells! Have we done the right thing do you think?"

"She's only establishing some ground rules. They'll be OK soon enough."

But when they cautiously released Copperfield from the cage, Tiger, despite being not yet fully grown, went for him tooth and claw. It's difficult, however, to fight an opponent who won't respond, and Copperfield didn't. He was submissive and evasive and noncombative. When she let up for a moment, he walked away from her with complete disdain, leaving her nonplussed. Tiger got scent of the dinner waiting, so she went to eat hers while she thought out her next move. But Copperfield took himself off as though she didn't exist and went on a tour of his new home, came back and, ignoring Tiger completely, went to eat from his bowl.

Joy went back to the practice and Duncan stayed in to act as referee. He found a cardboard box which, with a little help from a sharp kitchen knife, he converted into a temporary bed for Copperfield. He lined it with a blanket and placed it on the opposite side of the fire to Tiger's and waited to see the turn of events. Tiger wasn't the only one to be ignored because Copperfield took no notice of Duncan either, and the afternoon was spent with all three disregarding each other. *We'll have to call him Copper*, Duncan concluded. His full name was too much for everyday use, and anyway Copper suited him, for his particular shade of ginger was very dark, and Copper described it very well indeed. Copper and Tiger. Yes. Yes. He longed for them to make friends, but it was many days before there was harmony between the two.

HARMONY was the last word Joy would have used about the lay staff at the practice. She wished she could put them all in a sack and give them a good shake. Letty was the problem, but the thought of the arguing that would ensue if she asked her to stop helping out before she'd found a replacement was more than Joy could bear to think of. By the end of the week she learned that Lynne had definitely decided not to return because she had chosen to register at college and improve her qualifications, so now the way was wide open for recruiting a new member of staff. Within a few days a well-qualified girl had been found, and with scarcely concealed delight Joy informed Letty that her services would no longer be required. "Her name's Annette and she's done veterinary work before. She's newly married, and they've just moved to Barleybridge and she can start immediately, so you can heave a sigh of relief, Letty."

"I've quite enjoyed myself, actually. I'll be sorry to go. But then Colin does take a lot of looking after. He's very demanding with the hours he has to keep."

"Thanks for all your help; it's been much appreciated."

"Any time you have a problem you can rely on me."

Over my dead body, thought Joy.

So just when Joy thought Christmas was going to be a complete nightmare because of Letty, it looked to be plain sailing once more. They began the new regime when Annette started work, and Stephie and Kate agreed they liked it better. Annette proved to be a pleasant person to work with, and Joy found herself with a happy team, well integrated and working with a will, though the hoped-for increase in clients had not yet materialized.

Then Dan came up with another idea. He broached it one

afternoon when only Joy and Kate were on duty, and he'd finished his list and was waiting around in reception in the hope of a call. Eyeing the space between the main door and the chairs in the waiting area, he said, "That piece of wall there is a waste."

"Is it?"

"Yes. I have an idea."

Joy pointed the pen she was holding in his direction. "Look! The last time you had an idea all hell broke loose in here."

Dan smiled. "But you have to admit it all turned out well, didn't it, in the end."

"After a lot of suffering, I admit it did."

"Well, I was thinking the other day, more revenue needed, more ideas. So how about . . ."

"Kate, are we ready for this?"

"Not really, but let him tell us."

"Selling approved things for small animals."

"Approved *things?*"

"Items we as a veterinary practice approve of. The right kind of tinned food, or dry if preferred. The right kind of collars and leads for dogs. The right kind of grooming products . . ."

"Stop right there!"

"The right kind of bedding, treats, toys for budgies, toys for hamsters, the list is endless."

"But my patience isn't. There is no way I'm going to be involved in that kind of thing."

"But we're supposed to be really into this business of keeping animals usefully occupied so they don't develop behavioral problems through boredom. We should be leading the way. I can just see Barleybridge Veterinary Hospital at the forefront in the field of animal behaviorist knickknacks—"

Joy banged her fist on the desk. "*Go away!* Go on, wait somewhere else. I mean it."

Dan winked at Kate and made his escape into the back,

deliberately pausing to study the space beside the main door before he finally disappeared.

"He could be right, you know. It could be a nice little earner. We're always getting asked if we sell things, or for advice, and we've nothing to show people. It might be an idea," said Kate.

"On the grounds that the work and the accounting for it all would far outweigh the profit, I have nothing more to say on the matter." Joy did a final flourish on the computer and left Kate on her own.

Kate's mind raced through all manner of notions in support of Dan's idea and came to the conclusion that it was a very worthwhile scheme. She mentioned it in passing to Stephie, who immediately took the idea on board and couldn't wait to get it all set up.

"Joy disapproves, though."

Stephie's face fell. "Aw! Does she? I just fancied having a go at selling those dinky budgie bells and mirrors and things. It's all the rage now, isn't it, activities to stop the poor things from going stir crazy? I reckon we'd be doing them a good turn. Things for hamsters and gerbils, toys for dogs and cats."

"So do I. But—"

"Course, it would mean we'd be approving of Dan." Stephie turned down the corners of her mouth to show her reluctance to give him credit for anything.

"So . . . why not, for heaven's sake? He works so hard for this practice, and you have to admit you're getting to like him just a little teeny bit." Kate measured about half a centimeter between her thumb and forefinger, and made Stephie laugh.

"OK. OK. Yes, I am. He's kind of growing on me, I admit. We'll make our plans tonight over a meal, shall we?"

"Right. We could have a look around the pet shop in the mall and see what's on the market." They gave each other the thumbs-up.

Deviousness wasn't in Kate's makeup really, but it occurred to her that getting Miriam on their side might be a good thing and, when she broached the idea to her one afternoon while she was helping to put up the Christmas decorations in reception, she found Miriam was entirely enthusiastic. "Is it your idea?"

"No, Dan's."

Miriam raised an eyebrow. "Oh, dear. We could be stirring things up again. But I'll talk to Mungo."

"Thank you. I'm sure it would be a good move."

"So do I. It will be storage of the stock that will be the problem and making sure people don't slip things into their bags on the way out."

"Exactly. Well, Stephie and I think just by the door isn't quite the best place."

"Pass me those red balloons; they'll look good in this corner." Miriam had climbed to the top of the ladder and was balancing precariously, waiting with outstretched hand for the bundle of balloons. "I think it's a brilliant plan, and if someone is needed to take charge of ordering and checking the stock, I'll take that on board. Thank you, Kate." She took the bundle and secured it into the corner of the reception ceiling, climbed down, folded the ladder and said, "So if I do that, no one can complain about the extra work, can they?"

"Absolutely not."

They stood together, admiring their hard work: the heavily decorated real Christmas tree with its beautiful fairy lights; the paper bells and silver balls strung across the ceiling; the nativity scene Miriam had bought in Germany for her children and which she insisted must be on view for their sakes on the central windowsill; the silver tinsel bordering the desk and, best of all, the artificial snow on the window panes, which Mungo always mocked, but which Miriam loved because it made her feel all Dickensian. She squeezed Kate's arm. "Thank you. You've been such a help."

"It's been a pleasure."

"I shall miss you next Christmas."

"If I've finished college—that is, if I get there—I could come in and give you a hand."

"You could. That would be lovely. Never fear, you'll get in if I have to throw myself on the admissions tutor's floor and offer myself to him."

"Miriam!"

"You'll see. And about selling things, leave that with me."

Chapter

· 8 ·

Joy, incensed by the maneuvering which had been going on behind her back, complained bitterly to Duncan. "I mean, who is in charge of the practice? Tell me that. Am I the manager or not?"

"Joy, for goodness sake, calm down."

"They've even worked out how to alter the chairs round to make space for the shelves." She pointed angrily to herself. "Ask me? Consult me? Oh, no! I'm very upset."

"When it was first broached, what did you say?"

"I said . . . all right . . . I said to Mungo 'over my dead body.'"

"Did he try to persuade you?"

"Yes, he did. He turned on his charm as only he can, and I refused to listen. He said how much he wanted to go along with Dan's suggestion—more money in the coffers, you know. Then he smiled and that did it. I thought not again, Mungo, you're not getting your own way any more with that celebrated smile of yours." Her eyes went dreamy and Duncan sighed within himself.

"Ask yourself why?"

She came back from musing on Mungo's charm. "Why? Why what?"

"Why you have set your mind against it."

Joy thought for a moment. "Because I can't stand any more controversy."

"Who's objecting?"

"Letty for starters, despite it being none of her business now."

"Well, you can forget her."

"Miriam for jumping in when she shouldn't. Mungo because he thinks he only has to smile at me and he'll get his own way. Dan because he's Dan."

"You're being petty."

"I am?"

Duncan nodded. "Yes. But thanks for resisting Mungo's charm . . . at last." He reached toward her with a gentle hand and stroked her cheek. "Why don't you go in tomorrow and start straight in planning everything as if you've never objected. Give them all a shock."

"Think so?"

Duncan's hand cupped her chin and turned her face toward him. "With Christmas coming on we don't want trouble, do we? Spirit of goodwill and all that." He smiled at her with such tenderness that it brought tears to her eyes.

"I don't deserve you loving me."

"You do."

Joy shook her head. "No, I don't. Though by resisting Mungo's charm I could have made my first major step forward, couldn't I?"

"Indeed."

"I wish you wouldn't get more computer work. You're so much more *here* when you're not totally absorbed in it. I don't even exist for you when you're working. Do you know that? It is hard."

"For you I won't, then. The next project which comes in I shall send straight back by return mail."

"Oh yes, I bet!"

"I will if it means so much to you."

"What would we live on?"

"Love?"

They both laughed, Joy with abandon, Duncan with a sad guardedness that hurt. Joy's glance slipped past him to come to rest on the flames dancing in the hearth. She began to despise herself for so lightly dismissing Duncan's love and, instead, snatching at morsels of Mungo's, which in reality didn't belong to her and never would. How much longer would she keep chasing shadows? Joy reached out and touched his lips with her fingers. "I'll take your advice and go in tomorrow and begin to plan."

He kissed her fingers as they lingered on his mouth. "I love you," he said, but she didn't respond in kind.

DAN was delighted to find his idea had been taken up with such enthusiasm, mainly because he'd decided, yet again, that if he possibly could, he'd definitely stay. He liked the people, he liked the clients, he liked the countryside and Barleybridge and . . . well, for the first time in years he felt "at home." Before he put his things into the Land Rover, he shaded his eyes and looked up at Beulah Bank Top. One day soon he'd walk up there, right to the very top, and survey his kingdom. He turned round and looked down into the town, a town unspoiled by twentieth-century buildings and looking as it must have done for centuries. The spires, the colorful roofs, the lovely mellow stone buildings, the shining band of river wending its way through and the beautiful arching trees, devoid of their summer plumage but still beautiful, made his heart sing. He'd buy a house and settle into the bustling life of Barleybridge.

Superimposed on his view of the town, without warning, came Rose, with her long fair hair hanging loose, inviting him to touch it, love in her eyes and on her lips, that teasing grin of hers, teasing him into making love, giving him everything there was of her . . . the thought of her wrenched at his heart so viciously he almost doubled up with the pain, and his life turned to ashes in that moment.

He flung his bag and telephone onto the passenger seat, stuck his list on the dashboard and drove wildly out of the car park, missing the bench at the back door by a cat's whisker.

His first call was Porter's Fold, so he took the steep road to Magnum Percy, turning left before he reached the village itself. This was scarcely more than a narrow cart track with tarmac, which had fallen away at the edges, leaving great water-filled hollows on either side. The only passing places were where a field gate happened to be and Dan hoped he wouldn't meet another vehicle coming the other way. The landscape became increasingly harsh the farther he drove, till he finally saw the house and the farm buildings. The land looked barely fit to support even sheep.

Hanging lopsidedly at the top of an old post was a sign saying PORTER'S FOLD. It actually said POTER OLD, the other letters having been obliterated by years of weather. The gate was open, propped back by two stones taken from the wall. He drove in, parked, put on his boots, picked up his bag and wandered toward the farm buildings, in no mood this morning to tolerate anyone at all.

Tad Porter came out to greet him. He was an exceptionally tall gray man, sparse of flesh, with a big hooked nose emphasized by his overhanging forehead and abnormally thick, bushy gray eyebrows shading a pair of morose gray eyes. He wore an old bowler hat on his gray hair, completely at odds with the corduroys and layers of holey sweaters on his body. All Dan got as a greeting was a jerk of his head toward an open stable door; it suited his mood, so he didn't even try to make conversation. There were two heifers in the stable, one looking well, though her eyes lacked sparkle, the other looking as though death was snapping at her heels. Tad pointed with his boot toe at the sick one. "Acting drunk."

"You mean her movements are uncoordinated?"

Tad nodded. The heifer was tied up so Dan undid the rope and tried to get her to walk for him back and forth, but she slipped wildly about, her legs out of her control, almost going down as he turned her back toward her stall.

Dan took her temperature and, while he waited, asked, "Scouring at all?"

Tad shook his head.

"Eating?"

Another shake.

"No temperature. Could be one of several things. Obviously some problem with its brain. Tapeworm cyst, tumor, lead poisoning . . ." Dan looked round the stable for anything at all which the heifers might have got at, but saw no tractor oil or windows where they could have reached the putty, nor old flaking paint. "Seems unlikely in here. Whatever it is, it's well advanced. I'll take blood samples. The other showing any signs?"

Yet another shake of that head.

He took the blood samples, packed his bag and said, "I'll be back tomorrow. I don't like the look of her at all." Dan stood looking at the two cows, his mind ranging around several possibilities, unable to put his finger exactly on the problem. "She hasn't been out in the field these last few weeks?"

Tad shook his head.

"I see. Keep an eye on her. Ring if she gets worse later today

and I'll come out. It's puzzling, very puzzling. In any case, I'll
see you tomorrow, Tad. Good morning to you." Dan touched
his cap, gave a final look round the stable and left. It was the
first time in his working life that he'd managed to conduct a
visit with so few words being exchanged. What a strange man.
What a farm. A funny mixture of farm and scrapyard, with the
remains of cars and lorries and vans strewn in corners of the
yard and in the adjacent fields. Not modern vehicles, but old
nineteen thirties and forties ones, beaten into submission by
the weather and total neglect.

After a morning filled with calls, Dan went back to the
practice with a shop-bought lunch, intending to sit on the outside bench to eat it and think. Think about Rose, mainly, and
however he was going to overcome his loss. Beautiful, beautiful
Rose. Why had she chosen him, with nothing to recommend
him compared with the men she could have had? Was he a
whim? Someone to satisfy an idle summer? An amusing incident? No, that was unworthy of him. The passion she gave him
was real love, that could never be in doubt. He certainly loved
her, or he would not have asked her to marry him. Involuntarily
he reached out to take hold of her. He gazed down at his empty
hand and longed for her, not only for her bodily presence
beside him but for her companionship, her friendship and her
humor. Dan remembered how often they'd laughed together,
how . . . His thoughts were interrupted by Perkins bounding
out of the door on his way out for his afternoon walk.

Miriam shut the door behind her, pulled her coat collar
closer and then realized someone was on the seat. "Dan! What
on earth are you doing sitting out here on a day like this? Why
don't you go inside?"

He smiled up at her, saying, "Needed to think."

Miriam perched on the end of the bench while Perkins did
his big greeting scene, small teeth exposed in a grin, tail wagging

madly, ears pricked, front feet on the bench, taking the admiration like a regular pro.

Dan rubbed his hand on Perkins's head. "Now, Perkins, what are you doing interrupting a fella's quiet lunch? Eh?"

Perkins heaved himself up and settled upright beside Dan, shuffling along the bench until he was resting his shoulder against his. Dan removed the remains of his sandwich away from Perkins's temptation. "They can be a great comfort, can't they, dogs?"

"They can. In times of need."

"Very understanding."

Perkins felt tempted to lick Dan's face in appreciation of his approval, but just in time remembered the good manners he'd been taught and snuffled in his ear instead.

"Exactly." Miriam didn't look at Dan's face, that private look he had warranted her discretion. "Good friends, especially Airedales."

"Indeed."

"I'll leave you to finish your lunch. Come, Perkins." She stood up, facing the icy wind swirling down from the slopes. "We'll be off." Without looking at him she squeezed Dan's shoulder, gave it a pat and set off, with Perkins leaping around her legs in excitement. Her back to Dan, she raised both arms in the air and waved goodbye.

He called out to her. "Thanks for taking on the ordering."

"My pleasure!" came back to him on the wind.

What a joy, thought Dan, to come home after a hard day to someone like Miriam—warm and welcoming and sympathetic. Yet she wasn't sloppy and sentimental, honey-tongued or over-sweet, simply a loving, sensitive woman. It would be worth another try to gain that world for himself, for at the moment he was living only half a life.

The back door opened and it was Kate. "Oh, there you are, Dan. I've looked all over for you. Tad Porter's been on the phone. Can you go out to see his cow again? She's worse."

It was a moment before he answered her, taking a deep breath to ensure he gave nothing away with a shaky voice, to be apologized for, blaming it on a frog in his throat. Kate was no fool. "Thanks. It's a puzzle. I'll go there first before Beulah Bank. OK."

Tad was waiting for him in the yard, still as a statue, head hanging low like a sick animal. With a jerk of his head to Dan he turned to go into the stable. A sickening feeling of disappointment came over Dan as he followed him. The cow was convulsing. Tad spoke first. "Third time i' two hours. She's for t'knacker's yard. T'other's sick an' all." Tad leaned against the doorpost. "Yer ta late."

"I'm so sorry. This is lead poisoning or I'm a Dutchman. You said they hadn't been out for weeks."

"Aye. Well. They're Connie's heifers, and she's 'ad 'em out. 'For a change,' she said." He shook his head in despair at her fanciful ways. "Been out in t'field and wouldn't come when she called. Taken 'em in there a lot this winter when I'm up top with the sheep. Easier, being nearer than their own. 'Appen that's it."

"Old batteries?"

Tad looked away. "Perhaps."

"That's it, then. Lead poisoning. Youngsters are notoriously curious, you don't need me to tell you that. Well, either I leave her to die or we put her out of her agony."

"Give her a jab; let's have done with it. Missus'll be upset."

"Does she want to be here? Should she make the decision?"

"No."

"Are you sure?"

"I said no. Get it done."

So Dan despatched the cow out of her misery, and felt inadequate and angry with himself. "This live one . . ."

"Going same way. Tha might as well give her a jab too, and 'ave done."

"There's a chance here. She isn't convulsing yet. Once that starts it's all too late."

"It's the money." He pondered the situation for a while, during which Dan stood patiently waiting.

"It's worth a try? Isn't it?"

Tad appeared to make up his mind. "Grand lass is this one. Let's have a go."

Dan took blood samples, labeled them and injected the heifer with the appropriate drug for lead poisoning. "Are these the only two young ones you have?"

Tad nodded. "She has two house cows for her cheese making and cream for t'market and that, and these two she was hoping to bring on. We're sheep really, tha knows."

"Right. I'll be back first thing tomorrow. I should have the results when I come, so we'll know one way or the other." He left with a cheerful good afternoon and a touch to his cap. When he glanced back before revving up, Tad was still propping up the door frame studying his remaining heifer.

He'd damn well have to save it or the whole day would have been a disastrous write-off. What hadn't helped his day was encountering Letty in the mall when he'd shopped for his lunch. She'd emerged from the beauty salon right at his feet as he queued outside the sandwich bar. Even to his masculine eye there'd been a complete sea change in Letty's appearance, and he couldn't ignore it. Gone was the pale, fading-into-the-background Letty; her cheeks had a soft, warm bloom to them, and her slightly prominent eyes had been effectively made less so by skillful eye makeup. On her lips she had a rose-tinted lipstick, which softened them and filled them out. Her hair had been highlighted and cut into a smart bob, which flattered her face. He saw she had potential to look attractive. "Why, it's you, Letty! You look wonderful! What have you been doing to yourself?"

Momentarily Letty had bridled with pleasure, then recollected herself. "Don't I usually look wonderful?"

With anyone else but Letty that would have been a statement over which the two of them could have laughed, but not with her. "Well, I didn't mean . . . it's just that you look extra specially wonderful today. Been treating yourself?"

"No. It was a complimentary appointment, came through the mail."

"Well, they've certainly done a fantastic job on you. You seem to be getting some surprises of late, first the flowers from an unknown admirer and now this."

Letty, flustered by his teasing, had blurted out, "I've also won a weekend for two from our local travel agent."

"No-o-o-o! Some people have all the luck. Where to?"

"Our choice in Europe and we're going to Paris. We've never been, you see, Colin and me."

She was close enough to nudge and Dan had done just that and winked. "Romantic weekend in Paris! Eh?"

"Don't be ridiculous. Romantic! Huh!"

The queue had moved up and Dan had to go inside. Letty said, "I'll wait, I want a word."

Dan had bought his sandwich and a piece of carrot cake, and came out swinging a jaunty carrier bag to find her awaiting him, arms folded, ensconced on a seat. He had stood in front of her like a small schoolboy in the headmistress's study.

He remembered the expression on Letty's face when she looked up at him. "What on earth are you thinking of, encouraging this idea of selling things?"

"As you are so keen to maximize the earnings of the practice, I would have thought it would have had your approval."

"Well, it hasn't. It is diminishing. Selling *stuff*! As though we have to scratch about in corners looking for income. It is a professional business, not a pet shop!"

"I see your point, but we have to move with the times and, yes, it will bring in money, but also we shall be giving a service to our clients. What's more, we shan't be selling junk; Miriam will see to that."

"Miriam! Huh!"

Affronted by Letty's disdain for Miriam, Dan sprang to her defense. "I happen to have a high regard for Miriam."

"Do you indeed? Not surprising considering how much she likes you. You've got her round your little finger. If you say 'jump,' she'll say 'how high?'"

Dan had struggled to control the anger he felt rising in his heart. "I wouldn't dream of putting a lovely person like Miriam in such a position. I value her too much. However, when all is said and done, Mungo is keen; Colin approves; so does Zoe, though somewhat reluctantly; Miriam has volunteered to do all the ordering et cetera; and the girls can't wait to get started. So I'm afraid you've been outmaneuvered." He'd leaned over confidentially and, speaking softly into her ear, said, "By the way, the angry headmistress look you've put on doesn't suit the new Letty." Dan held up his lunch bag. "Must go. Busy day. You look great. Colin won't recognize you."

He'd charged off toward the car park and therefore didn't see Letty, a moment later, give herself a smile of approval at her reflection in the bookshop window.

But what had made his day even worse was having the misfortune to bump into Lord Askew coming out of the car park. Dan touched his cap and greeted him, intending to pass by without saying more than a pleasant "Good afternoon."

But Lord Askew would have none of it. "How you doing, Brown? Eh?"

"Fine, my lord. And you?"

Lord Askew had looked beyond Dan's shoulder and said, "All the better if I had you on board."

"Roan no better?"

"Trouble is my vet can't see what you can see. Are you certain?"

"Ninety-nine point five percent certain. Need to examine him, of course."

Impatiently Lord Askew had replied, "I know that. I know that. Would you come as a second opinion? For me."

Dan had considered his request and, although it didn't comply with what he had originally said, he decided someone had to give way if he was ever going to get the equine work. "I'll phone your vet and make arrangements."

"Standen-Briggs. Giles. As one gentleman to another, thank you. I make no promises mind."

"No promises."

There were people in Barleybridge that afternoon who witnessed the handshake between the two of them and paused to wonder why on earth the new vet and that old basket Lord Askew could be doing such a thing. But they were, because they'd seen them, and Lord Askew had looked well pleased.

Dan, reviewing his day, had not been quite as pleased, but felt he'd made a significant step forward. He was picking up his things prior to leaving for home and a night on call when he heard Kate saying she must get off or she'd miss the next bus. "I'll give you a lift if you like, Kate. Car off the road?"

"It is. I have a nasty feeling it might be terminal."

"Well, all cars do reach that stage eventually, not worth the repair."

"I would be grateful, but won't it be out of your way?"

"Frankly, yes, it will, but I've had such a dreadful day some pleasant company would be welcome."

"I'm feeling flush tonight. Shall we stop for a drink on the way? My treat." She looked at him and thought what a pity it was that he lived alone; as Mia would say, he'd make someone a good husband.

"That would be nice."

They chatted about this and that, finished their drinks and when Dan offered to buy them another, Kate accepted because she was enjoying herself so much, listening to tales of Dan's exploits in the Middle East. He dug in his wallet for a note, moaned that he'd forgotten to call at the ATM and might not actually have enough cash to pay for two drinks, and finally dragged out a crumpled note which looked as though it hadn't seen the light of day for some considerable time. Dan smoothed it out, saying "I hope you don't think that's a sign that I'm mean with my money. I don't normally have to *pry* notes out of my wallet."

He headed off to the bar and, as Kate watched him go, she saw he'd dropped a photograph on the floor. She picked it up and thought, "Wowww!"

It was of a girl, a natural beauty, who positively sizzled sex appeal. Her personality came right off the picture and zonked you in the eye. She turned it over and saw the words "Rose. At home." She had the kind of face Kate would have given the world for. The house behind her, well! If that was "at home," Kate could have done with being on her way there right now. It was just how she imagined the wealthy lived on the East Coast of the States. Such style. She guessed there'd be a pool the size of a lake, bathrooms galore, a kitchen to die for and . . . but Dan was coming back so she laid it on the table. He put down the drinks and saw the photo.

"You dropped it on the floor when you pulled out the ten-pound note. I couldn't help but look. I'm sorry."

Dan looked at it but didn't speak. He left it lying there and it made for awkwardness between them—Kate embarrassed; Dan lost in thought. He picked up his orange juice, and the ice beat a tattoo in the glass. Kate sipped her drink, outfaced by his heavy silence—so heavy it was almost palpable. She thought, *If this silence lasts another minute, I shall die. Who the blazes is she to upset him like this? Mind you . . .*

The minute passed, and suddenly Dan picked up the picture and stored it away in his wallet. "Someone I knew in the US of A. Ever been?"

"No. Is it nice?"

He downed his juice in one go and stood up. "Nice isn't a big enough word to describe it. Go there some time. It's amazing, larger than life. With your sense of humor you'd have a ball. I'm ready to go. Have you finished?"

Kate gulped down her drink and stood up, glad to be leaving.

He chatted about something and nothing all the way home, and she wished she could take on some of the burden of trying to keep normality between them but she couldn't. She bet that girl in the photograph would have coped wonderfully well. No crippling embarrassment for her, oh no! She'd simply have sparkled a little, and the difficult moment would have slipped away. When they reached her house, Kate made to get out, happy to be escaping, but Dan insisted he open her door for her and wouldn't leave until she was safely inside.

"Goodnight and thanks for the lift."

"My pleasure, Kate."

Kate went in to find Mia worried. "He said he'd be back about six and it's nearly eight. Do you think your dad's all right?"

Chapter

·9·

They waited until half past nine, growing more and more anxious as the minutes passed. Kate adopted the role of placid acceptance that Gerry could have met someone, or broken down, or gone for a drink, or got held up at the office, or was taking someone out for a meal to help push some deal through, but at bottom, as the seconds ticked away, she had begun to grow exceedingly anxious. "After all, Mia, he's been late before."

"But before, he's always rung and let me know. He knows how I worry."

"Well, don't. He'll be here." With relief Kate remembered his meetings. "I know. It'll be a model railway meeting, and he's forgotten to say."

Mia looked relieved. "Of course! They're always on a Thursday and it's Thursday. Honestly, I am stupid." She stood up and cheerfully began to fill the kettle. "He'll be ready for this. You know how he talks himself to a standstill when he goes." She glanced at the clock. "He'll be in any minute now, you'll see."

Kate occupied herself writing a letter to a school friend, but she'd written four sides and her father still hadn't come home. She felt as though a cannonball had replaced her heart. A terrible feeling of desolation came over her.

Mia asked her whom she was writing to, and she couldn't answer. Looking down at the letter, she hadn't the vaguest idea to whom it was addressed. Had she a screw loose? Was this how it affected you? Unable to answer the simplest question? Kate looked up at Mia and saw reflected in her eyes the fright she herself felt. "I . . ."

Mia took advantage of Kate's pause to say, "You feel like I do? There really is something wrong, isn't there?"

"Of course there isn't. Honestly, Mia, if you haven't got something to worry about, you find something. You know Dad; he'll be fine."

"You don't sound very convinced."

"Well, I am. Honestly. I am. He's probably going to come rolling home in a taxi."

"Kate! Gerry's never the worse for drink."

"Actually that's not quite true, is it? I can remember the time he went to that reunion . . ."

"That was different."

"And when he won Salesman of the Year. Remember that? How you laughed."

"Well, that was different too. He deserved to get drunk. He wouldn't drink and drive, though, would he? He's strict about that, Gerry is. Isn't he?"

"Very." Kate looked down at her letter and hadn't the heart to write anymore. She closed the writing pad and pushed it away. "Look, we're both of us being ridiculous. Make the tea. I bet he's here before you've poured it."

But he wasn't, and Kate had eaten two chocolate biscuits and drunk two cups of tea, and still he hadn't arrived. They heard a car and looked at each other, embarrassed at having been so concerned. But it wasn't Gerry; it was Lance from next door on late shift.

"If we ring the police, they'll think we're crackers. After all, it's only eleven. They'll laugh and be tempted to say he's having a night out on the town."

Mia was shocked. "Gerry! A night out on the tiles!"

"Yes, but they don't know Dad, do they, like we do? They don't know he doesn't. Plenty of men do, you see."

Determined to be reasonable, Mia said, "When it gets to midnight, I'm ringing the police. You go to bed."

"I shan't."

"Did you hear me? You go to bed."

"I shan't. It's my dad."

"It's my husband. Go to bed."

"You only want me to go so I won't see how worried you are. Well, we'll share it. I'm not a child."

"No."

That cannonball in her chest had grown larger. Mia was quite right; her dad would have let them know if he could. He knew how Mia worried. So why couldn't he let them know? "We are fools. I'll ring his mobile."

"Of course. We are idiots. He's never without it."

But the mobile rang and rang. So Dad had been separated from his phone. Why? She left a text message for him. "He'll have left it in his car, and he'll be in the meeting, or the pub. Let's stop worrying. Dad knows how to take care of himself. Always has."

Mia thought a moment and then replied, "Of course you're right. Well, I'm off to bed. We'll look silly if we both sit up and he rolls in, fit as a fiddle and wondering what the fuss is about. You use the bathroom first. I'll tidy up."

But Mia didn't go to bed. She sat downstairs, desperately

trying to read the novel that had been recommended by a neighbor. It was the story of a woman who'd had more crises in her life than seemed possible, but she was rising above it all and triumphing in the end. Losing three husbands in an assortment of incidents which stretched the imagination to its limits became more than Mia could believe, so she snapped the book shut thirty pages before the end and decided to read no more. By now it was half past one. She heard a step on the stairs. "Kate?"

"You said you were going to bed."

"Well, I got reading. It's a load of rubbish, though, so I'm off to bed now."

"Can't sleep for wondering."

"You'll be cold. Go and get your dressing gown, and we'll have a cup of Ovaltine or something."

"I'm all right. I'll make it."

They sat until two o'clock, avoiding conversation and especially avoiding looking each other in the eye.

Mia got up to wash the mugs. "I'll ring first thing in the morning."

"Who will you ring?"

"I don't know."

"Hospitals?"

Mia nodded.

"Police?"

She nodded again, not trusting herself to speak.

"Shall I?"

"No. I'm his wife." Mia took a deep breath and confessed to her fears: "It's a nightmare I'm not brave enough to face."

"We'll face it together. You and me."

Mia turned from the sink and gave her half a smile. "Let's be honest with each other: something must have happened to him."

"Of course it hasn't. What is it they say? 'No news is good news.'"

"That's right. He'll be parked up somewhere because he's realized he's too tired to drive. He's fallen asleep in his car by mistake, hasn't he?"

Kate had too much common sense to have any truck with ghosts or psychic something or others, but the moment Mia said that, it triggered the idea in her mind that somewhere he was doing just that, except he wasn't asleep. He was dead. She shuddered.

"I said you'd be cold. Go on, go back to bed. You've work tomorrow."

DAWN found the two of them sleeping with their heads resting on their arms on the kitchen table. Kate woke, panicking, puzzled why she was sitting in the kitchen and not in bed. Dad! She got up, stiff with cold. She stretched and felt her bones creak. Dad! How could she have *slept*? Guilt sidled through her veins. "Mia, are you awake? We've slept in."

"Ring up. Please."

"I'll have a drink of water first; I'm so dry." As she put down the empty glass on the draining board, the doorbell rang.

Mia, still fully dressed, stalked like an automaton down the narrow hall. Kate stood in the kitchen thinking, *It'll be the milk-man wanting his money. It must be. Please let it be the milkman wanting his money. Please. It's Friday, so it must be him.* She heard Mia invite whoever it was inside. So it wasn't the milk-man. She went to stand in the kitchen doorway and, looking down the hallway, saw two police officers; and just before she fainted, she heard one of them say, "Mrs. Howard? . . . found . . . on the hard shoulder . . . sitting in the car . . . Unfortunately, he'd passed away . . . Apparently natural causes. I'm so very sorry."

. . .

THE whole ghastly shrieking nightmare put the two of them into a permanent state of shock. Mia formally identified him, and once his body was released after the postmortem, they rigidly went through the process of organizing the funeral.

Every night when she went to bed, Kate felt as though she were lying at least a foot above the mattress. She couldn't sleep. She couldn't rest. Couldn't eat. Couldn't smile. Couldn't anything. Every part of her was paralyzed by the suddenness of his going. The whole of her life was on hold. Her car was still at the garage. She wasn't going in to the practice. Not to see him ever again. She couldn't accept it, couldn't, wouldn't believe it. She couldn't talk to anyone at all. Not even Mia. And what *she* was going through Kate could only guess, for she remained stoically getting on with life as though Gerry would walk in through the door each evening and hadn't died of a heart attack after he'd pulled onto the hard shoulder, apparently not feeling well.

Kate dragged herself through the funeral, and when it came to the time for his nearest and dearest to toss earth onto the coffin, that appalling, flesh-crawling act, Mia did her duty, but Kate shook her head, her mind shying away from the finality of doing that very dreadful thing.

After they'd all gone, Mia said, "I shall sell his car. I don't want that Beetle thing. And we shall move out of here. I can't stay here, not with him gone. It's always been his house, not mine. This nineteen thirties stuff he had such a passion for isn't my passion at all."

"I've always thought you loved it. But I want to stay here. We could always sell the furniture and buy some new. Redecorate."

"We shan't. And his train set—that'll have to go."

"Mia, let's move slowly. We'll feel better in a while; then we can decide. Christmas isn't the time for selling up anyway. Let's wait till spring."

"Don't think I'll change my mind because I shan't. I think

we'll go away for Christmas. Can't have it here, just the two of us. Disaster, that would be. We'll join a house party or something, where it's all organized. Together. No one need know we've just lost your dad. There's sure to be a cancellation somewhere, and I don't care where. Then we'll sell the house when we get back and make a new start. You and me. Just you and me. By ourselves."

They were sitting in the front room on the hard green sofa with its hard arms, drinking a bottle of wine from Mia's store in the cellar. This sofa had been part of Kate's life ever since she could remember. Could she manage without it? She doubted she could, but apparently Mia could.

Arranged on the mantelpiece were the sympathy cards. Not a single one from a blood relative. All of them were from the practice or Mia's art class or the Model Railway Society or Dad's office or the gallery where Mia occasionally had an exhibition. So now she, Kate Howard, had no living relative. Only Mia, and she looked as though she was going to make life a living hell with all her unexpected ideas. What worried Kate was that Mia had never cried, not once, whereas Kate herself had wept buckets.

"Another top-up?"

Kate shook her head. "No, thanks. I'm going to bed."

"If you want to sleep in our room for company, that's all right with me."

Kate shook her head. "No, thanks. Nice of you to offer, but . . . well, we've got to get used to it, haven't we?"

"I'm afraid so." She took a sip from her glass. "I thought we'd live into old age together, but we shan't, not now. He's been my anchor since the day I met him. I know we were not really alike, in temperament and interests, but we complemented each other, as you might say. I shall miss him."

"Of course you will."

"So will you."

"Even if he was an old curmudgeon sometimes. But now you remember only the best bits, don't you?"

Mia didn't look at her. "Oh yes. That's human nature." She twirled her wineglass by the stem. "You've to get on with things, you know. If he is looking down at us, think of the pleasure he'll have when you get into college. He'll be marching all over heaven telling even the Angel Gabriel what you've achieved."

"Now he's gone, there's no one living with the same blood in their veins as I have. No one at all. Except my mother, and she doesn't count. But I've got you, haven't I?"

"We'll manage, you and me, very well. A flat, a modern flat is what I want. Minimalism. That's what I shall go for."

"Mia!"

"He wouldn't mind, wouldn't your dad."

Kate wasn't too sure about that. She was certain he'd like the idea of their living on in his nineteen-thirties world, but if it pleased Mia, then . . . She wandered upstairs to bed, settling herself for sleep, feeling akin to an empty shell, utterly without life inside her, but at the last moment before she slept, she remembered Dan's words as he stood beside her at the grave-side, gripping her arm to comfort her. "Take heart, Kate. Stick by Mia and fulfill your dad's ambitions for you. That's the best gift you can give him now."

Two days after the funeral, Kate had her first day at work. She arrived home at half past four, exhausted by keeping up the pretense of being able to cope, no problem. Mia had made a cup of tea, and they sat together in the kitchen making desultory conversation. Mia had obviously made an attempt to begin painting again, but had not got far. She noticed Kate looking at her materials laid out at the end of the table with the brushes clean of paint and the paint rag still pristine. "I'll clear it away. I haven't the heart . . . to paint right now."

"Never mind, it'll happen when you're ready."

"I'm not going to answer the sympathy cards. What can you say but 'thanks'? There isn't another thing to say."

"No, there isn't, is there?"

"I've booked us away for Christmas. Two cancellations. North Devon, Ilfracombe, not too far to go. Father Christmas and all that jazz. But it'll be easier than staying here."

"I'm not going to the staff do."

"Why not? Your dad wouldn't mind, I'm sure. He wasn't much of a one for parties, but he'd have liked you to go." She reached across and took hold of Kate's hand. "Go on."

"No. I'd only be a wet blanket. They wouldn't know what to say, a week since Dad . . . you know . . . and a week to Christmas. It'll be kinder to keep right out of it."

"It was nice of Dan to come to the funeral."

"Yes."

"He's a nice chap, a very nice chap. Knows just what to say, as if he's been through it."

"That's it, Mia! You're not just a pretty face. She's died, that's it."

"Who's died?"

Kate stood up. "The girl in his photograph. He was so funny about it, withdrawn, you know. How terribly sad."

"Explain."

So Kate described the incident in the pub when he dropped the photograph, and Mia said, "Well, it makes sense, I suppose."

The doorbell rang and neither of them wanted to answer it, not anymore, but it rang again with such insistence that Kate, as she was on her feet, volunteered to go.

Standing on the doorstep was a very well-dressed woman, elegant almost, about her own height with hair which could only be described as coiffured. Immaculate makeup, narrow face and unfathomable eyes. A tad too thin. Conscious she wasn't looking her best, Kate said, "Yes?"

"I've come to see Katrina Howard, and I'm sure you must be she."

"That's me."

"I read about your father in the paper. I'm so sorry. Good thing he was chairman of the Model Railway Society, otherwise I don't suppose he would have hit the headlines and I would never have known. I would have been here earlier, but I've been so busy. Work, you know. How are you?"

"I'm all right."

"There's a Mrs. Howard, isn't there?"

Kate sensed a crisis looming. "You're asking some funny questions. Who are you exactly?"

"I'm Tessa Fenton."

"Tessa Fenton?"

"Yes, you don't know the name, do you?"

"It seems familiar but I can't . . ."

"I would have thought your father would have told you. I'm your mother, Katrina." She smiled, exposing unbelievably even teeth.

Kate thought she might be going to faint for the second time in her life. Her mother! Her mother? Her world went black, then red, then she refocused her eyes and saw *her mother standing there in front of her*. She grasped the door frame with both hands to steady herself.

Her mother filled Kate's silence with, "Aren't you going to ask me in? We can hardly talk on the doorstep."

"Yes. Yes. Come in." Then she thought about Mia. "Wait there. I'll tell Mia. She may not . . . Sit on the chair."

Kate went into the kitchen and closed the door behind her. Mia was standing by the sink putting on her rubber gloves.

"Mia! Oh, Mia!"

Mia spun round at the sound of panic in Kate's voice. "What's happened?"

"Are you ready for a shock?"

Mia blanched and sat down rather rapidly. "What?"

"Well, I don't know how to tell you this, but there's a woman come to see me." She took a deep, shuddering breath as though suffocating. "She says she's my mother. Tessa Fenton."

"Dear God!"

"She's in the hall. May I ask her in?"

Mia stood up, looking incredibly flustered. "Take her into the sitting room and talk, while I rush upstairs and tidy myself. She musn't see me like this. I'm a mess." Mia ripped off the rubber gloves and flung them in the sink.

"Right. I don't know what to say."

"Let her do the talking then, and you listen . . . I don't know why she's decided to turn up right now." *And how I wish she hadn't*, thought Mia as she raced up the stairs. This was the one thing she had dreaded for years. Gerry had always said she'd never come, but now she had and . . . Mia judged her impact in the bathroom mirror. Whisked her hair into order. Flicked powder on her face. Rushed lipstick round her mouth. Too red. Mouth like a tart's. Lavatory paper. Rubbed it off. Tried a pink one. Liked it better. Despised her dress. Decided to change. Messed her hair. Combed it again. Breathed deeply. Took herself in hand. Walked down the stairs, heart hammering, mouth dry, to meet a woman she could cheerfully have murdered on sight. When she took in the expensive detail of her aubergine business suit, the confidence, the worldly look of her, Mia's fingers itched to grip a carving knife to stab her right below that big silver brooch on her lapel, where she judged her heart would be if she'd had one. But there was no doubting she was genuine, for when she looked at her, Mia realized where Kate got her good looks from; except Kate's expression was sweet, whereas hers was . . .

Graciously the woman extended her hand toward Mia. "How do you do? You must be Gerry's wife. Katrina and I need to thank you for all the care you've given her over the years."

Mia's dry mouth made it difficult to answer. She ran her tongue round her front teeth, but it made little difference. "No thanks needed. It's been a privilege to care for Kate. An absolute privilege." She shook hands and found Tessa's slight, excessively manicured hand with its aubergine painted nails bony and dry, but the grip firm. "Won't you sit down? A drink. Tea, coffee or something stronger?"

"Whiskey and water?"

"Fine."

Made stiff with anxiety, Mia marched into the kitchen to comply with Tessa's request. Huh! Whiskey! The shock of Gerry's death had affected her badly, too badly for tears, but this . . . If she lost Kate, that would be the end of life. Resistance, disapproval, silence would only drive her further away. She must appear welcoming.

The glass needed a polish, the top of the whiskey bottle was too tight, where was the little jug she usually chose for cream? Eventually everything was organized, and she strutted, rigid with pain, back into the sitting room, balancing her best melamine sandwich tray in her hand, a smile stitched on her face.

Tessa was inviting Kate to tea.

Tea! After all the years of neglect. Tea?

Mia fielded a desperate glance from Kate and smiled stiffly. "Tea. What a lovely idea!" she said brightly.

"Look, here's my telephone number." Tessa pulled a business card from her wallet. "Ring me. I know I live a good distance away, but it's straight down the motorway, no problem, an hour is all it's taken me tonight, though I do drive fast, I have to confess. I'm not in court, with it being Christmas, so you can ring me and we'll make a date. After Christmas I'm incredibly busy, and it won't be so easy. You can see my house, where I live, see what you think, but I'm sure you'll love it. You can't stay here, in this . . . place." She looked around the sitting room disdainfully. "Not here."

"We're not. Kate and I are moving, after Christmas."

Nonplussed by Kate's silence, Tessa clutched eagerly at the idea. "Christmas! What are you doing at Christmas? You could come to me, first Christmas without your father. Do say you'll come. We can really talk, get to know each other, then you can make up your mind. You'll love my home." She said this looking only at Kate and not including Mia.

Mia had been perching on the edge of the sofa, too taut to sit properly, a great lump in her throat; she stood up and excused herself. "Things to do . . . in the kitchen. Nice to have met you, I'm sure." Arriving at the kitchen sink she put on her rubber gloves again and started to clear up. Money. It all came down to money in the end. How it oiled the wheels, greased the cogs, smoothed the path! What a temptation for a girl who'd longed for years to meet her mother.

She heard Kate showing her mother out and couldn't resist listening at the door. The voices were muffled, but she caught Tessa's commanding tones saying, "May I kiss you au revoir? . . . You have *me* now . . . I want to know all about you . . ."

Then Kate said something and Tessa's voice came again: "You're lovely. I'm so proud to have a daughter like you. We'll make up for lost time, you'll see."

Mia's hands trembled as she swished the dish mop around a cup. She braced herself for Kate's return to the kitchen, but heard her footsteps on the stairs. She spent the next half hour cleaning and recleaning the kitchen worktops and anything and everything which might be in the slightest need of a wipe, then went up to find her. Kate was sitting on her bed, turning the little identification band from the hospital round and round in her fingers, head bent, deep in thought.

"Kate?"

"I can't believe I've met her at last, after all these years. Fancy her seeking me out. Doesn't she look gorgeous? So utterly splendid? *So well off!*" She looked up at Mia, who saw she'd been crying. "Fact remains, though, she did dump me."

Mia put her arms round her and held her tightly while Kate wept again and Mia longed for the eloquence which would enable her to find the right words to comfort Kate; the emotions were there, but not the words to express them. So Mia cuddled Kate just like when she was tiny, uttering the baby words of comfort as she did so, and it helped as it had always done.

When the crying stopped, Mia leaned away from her, stroked her hair back into place, wiped her cheeks for her and said, "There, now. Feel better?"

Kate nodded. "Shall I go for tea?"

Mia could have said no emphatically because at bottom she was panicking about Tessa, thinking of the bait her wealth would offer Kate, but instead she said generously, "You're nineteen, old enough to decide for yourself."

"What would you do?"

"Oh, I'd go for tea. I couldn't do any other. Just to see, you know. Curious, that's me."

"I will, then. But not for Christmas. That's ours."

"Thank you, I love you for that." Mia walked onto the landing, calling out, "I can see where you get your looks from, you're just like . . . her." She'd got out of Kate's sight only just in time, for, like the opening of a dam, tears began to flood down her thin cheeks, and she fled to lock herself in the lavatory. Tears for Gerry but, more so, tears at the thought of losing Kate poured silently down, soaking her handkerchief, leaving her hollow and spent.

THE following morning, as soon as the post office opened, Kate was dispatched to buy postage stamps for a mailing to all their clients, which Dan had initiated mainly to announce the opening of their "shop." His steady flow of ideas gave extra work for everyone, and they all, except Kate, grumbled at him.

"I can't see why you grumble; everything he does is to improve our service to the clients and bring in more money." She struggled into her coat and put on her gloves. "While it's quiet, we can stuff the envelopes and stick on the stamps; and as soon as Christmas is over, we can stagger to the post with them all done and dusted."

Stephie answered her tartly by reminding her that they all knew she thought the sun shone out of Dan.

"I don't. I just think he has some good ideas, that's all. I'm off. Do you want anything?"

"No, thanks."

Joy gave her the cash for the stamps, and with it carefully hidden in the deepest pocket of her winter coat, Kate set off. It was quicker to walk than bother taking the car and having a problem finding a parking space, it being Christmas. She strode off down the hill into the mall, thinking all the time about her mother's visit, hugging the event to herself, not daring to confide in anyone at work about their meeting the previous evening. She was still debating about whether or not to ring her to make an arrangement for tea. Kate felt chary of encouraging too close a contact so quickly. How could her mother be so thoughtless as to imagine that she would be welcomed with open arms, or that she should be. For years Kate had fantasized about her, imagining how she looked, how she dressed, what it would feel like to say "Mum"; yet presented with the opportunity, she drew back. It seemed like taking a step forward from which there would be no retreat, and Kate wasn't sure that was what she wanted. Hanging about in the back of her mind was a question: Why did her mother suddenly want her after years of total silence?

She'd ring her after Christmas; that would be soon enough, but she'd have to tell her not to call her Katrina—she couldn't stand that name—and she wouldn't allow herself to be bought. She wished her dad had been there to advise her, but she knew already what he would have said: *Don't hurt Mia; we owe her a lot.* So she'd make sure she didn't. She'd wait till after Christmas just to show her mother that she, Kate, her long-lost daughter, wasn't all that keen.

Kate turned into the mall and headed for the post office. The queue, of course, was long and winding, and ended right at the entrance. Settling herself for a considerable wait, she let her mind wander, thinking mainly about what it would be like spending Christmas away from home and without Dad. She'd have to be lively for Mia's sake, for Mia hadn't rallied since her mother's visit and it worried her . . .

A man's voice she thought she recognized cut through her thoughts. Whose was it? She glanced discreetly down the long, winding tail of the queue, thinking she might see a client she recognized, but saw no one she knew—but there was the voice again. This time she clearly heard it ask, "By air?" And she spotted him. It was the clerk sitting at the number six window.

But who was he? She couldn't quite see because of the reflection of the lights on the glass screen in front of him, but as the queue moved, she saw the face of number six quite plainly. Who on earth was he? Then she realized. It was the man who'd brought Copperfield in to the clinic. There were now only seven customers ahead of her, and it would be just her luck to have number six available when it was her turn. That strange, disembodied voice called out, "Cashier number three!" They all moved up a couple of steps, and now Kate knew definitely that she was right. There he was, sitting as calm as you please, being polite and helpful, smiling and kind, when all the time he was a cruel torturer... And his car wasn't even licensed, when he worked where he could get one without any effort at all!

Now there were only four customers ahead of her, and number six was free. He musn't see her because he might recognize her. Still, if it was true that he really had found the cat by the parking garage, then she had nothing to fear, but somehow his subsequent behavior belied his innocence. Kate sighed with relief when her turn came while number six was deeply occupied arguing rather nastily with his customer, and she was called for cashier number one. She bought the stamps and raced back as fast as she could.

Breathlessly she burst into Joy's office. "Joy, I've seen the man who brought Copperfield in. He's a clerk in the post office. Can Stephie go down and make sure I'm right?"

Joy shot up from her chair and said, "Really? A clerk in the post office? I don't believe it."

"It's him. I'm certain."

"I'll have his guts for garters, I will. I've a good mind to go down there myself right now and give him a piece of my mind. Better still, I'll tie him to my bumper and drag him along behind like he did Copperfield; then he'll see what it's like for himself."

Kate advised caution. "Wouldn't it be better to tell Sergeant Bird?"

"You're right. My poor darling Copper. Let justice be done. Stephie! Off you go. Identify the brute."

"He's sitting at number six. Hurry up. He might go for lunch or something."

Stephie, eager for blood, flung on her coat and rushed off.

Thirty minutes later she came charging back into reception, breathless and close to collapse. When she could speak, she said, "It's him. Definitely. I'm one hundred percent sure. Ring old Dickie."

THE wheels of the law grind slowly, and it was two days before Sergeant Bird came back to relate the news about Copperfield's torturer. He leaned his forearms on the top of the desk and prepared himself for a long confidential discussion.

Joy joined Stephie and Kate, and they listened open-mouthed to his story.

"Well, him in the post office isn't the guilty party."

"Aw! We were sure it was him."

"But . . ."

"Yes?"

"But we have got the culprit."

"Oh!"

"It was his son."

"No-o-o-o."

Self-importantly, Sergeant Bird took off his cap and placed it on the desk. "Took the father to the station, showed him the photos. He said he knew nothing about it at all. Didn't know what we were talking about, but eventually . . ."

"Yes?"

"I got him to tell me the truth. I told him, "You've been identified by two people from the practice; we know it's you.

We've got the security video to prove it, so come on, tell me what really happened." Sergeant Bird took out his handkerchief and wiped his forehead.

"And . . . ?"

"Turned out he was covering for his fifteen-year-old son."

"Fifteen!"

"He should have known better," said Joy.

"He should, I suppose, but his mother's left home and he's gone to pieces, got in with a rough lot. Still doesn't excuse what he did to that poor cat. His dad is heartbroken about it."

"Was it just the boy himself or the crowd he's got in with?"

Sergeant Bird nodded. "The crowd he's got in with. But he won't split. Just clams up."

"Huh! Send him round here. I'll have it out of him in a second," Joy barked out.

Sergeant Bird took offense at Joy's lack of confidence in his ability as an officer. He removed his forearms from the desk top, drew himself up to his full height, put his cap back on and said, "Barleybridge police are quite capable of extracting all necessary information. We may not be the Metropolitan police, but we're equally well trained."

Joy touched his arm. "I'm sorry. It's just that we're so angry about this. So upset about what the poor thing has had to go through. It isn't as if you can *explain* to him. He's turning into a lovely cat, though. There was trouble to begin with because our Tiger took exception to him coming, but now she's his slave; there's no other word to describe her behavior. Follows him around with adoring eyes. Wherever he goes, she goes and, if she can, she creeps into his basket with him for the night. Duncan is charmed with the pair of them. More power to your elbow, Sergeant, we'll be glad to hear the next installment. Thanks for all you've done." Joy left the desk expecting he'd be leaving, but he didn't. He shuffled from one foot to the other, blew his nose, cleared his throat, mentioned the crisp, bright weather and were they all set for Christmas?

Kate took pity on him and, leaning across the desk, whispered confidentially, "She's gone for lunch. The new sandwich bar. But you'll have to be quick. Mr. Price starts operating at half past one and she'll be needed."

Sergeant Bird fled reception as though the hounds of hell were after him.

"He won't have any luck. Bunty's not daft."

"She might be desperate, though." Kate grinned.

Stephie was scandalized. "I know she's getting on a bit, but Dickie Bird! Come on!"

"He's a good man. He'd make someone a good husband, as Mia would say."

"A dull and boring good husband. Speaking of Mia, how is she coping since . . . your . . . dad? Come to that, how are you?"

Kate paused while she assessed how she felt and decided she was just about coping. "Not bad, thanks. It's Mia I'm worried about. She's very depressed and I'm dreading Christmas."

"I was sorry you didn't come to the staff Christmas do."

"Couldn't face it, and I didn't want to spoil it for everyone else."

"I can see what you mean. I'm dreading Christmas too. Family all turning up, you know. At least I can escape here on Boxing Day for a couple of hours for the emergency clinic."

The main door opened, and they both looked up to find Bunty, loaded with shopping, wiping her feet on the doormat.

Stephie asked her if she'd seen Dickie Bird because he'd gone to find her at the new sandwich bar.

"No. I changed my mind and went last-minute shopping instead."

"He'll be disappointed. He shot out of here like greased lightning."

Bunty shrugged her shoulders and walked through to the back.

Stephie nudged Kate, saying "I've just had a thought. She can't marry him."

"Why can't she? She'd be the right size because she's so small."

"Because she'd be called Bunty Bird. I mean, there are limits!"

They both collapsed in giggles and had great difficulty controlling themselves when Mungo came in to begin his afternoon operating list.

"What's the joke?"

"Just laughing because Dickie Bird fancies Bunty."

"She could do worse." He picked up the file of case notes Stephie had ready for him and, turning his back to them both, viewed the shelves which had been put up to accommodate the "knickknacks," as Dan called them. "You know, I think we . . ." He paused while he watched the person who had just opened the glass door walk across to reception.

"Katrina! Just passing. Thought I'd call to tell you all the plans I've made for the two of us for Christmas."

Chapter

·10·

Dan made sure he was dressed in his best on the day he
was to give a second opinion on Lord Askew's daughter's roan. He wore his corduroy jacket just back from
the cleaner's, with the matching cap, a light-brown shirt and
the trousers which toned with it, a stunning countrified tie and
his best brogues. He inspected his teeth and face in the mirror
in the staff cloakroom, retightened the knot of his tie, gave
himself a wink and strode out, confident that he couldn't have
looked smarter.

He'd also remembered to wash down the Land Rover, so
when he drove into the stable yard right on the dot of ten, he
gave a first-rate impression. Unfortunately, there was no one
there to appreciate him—not a living being in sight. Through
the archway into the farm part of the estate he could see activity,
so he went to ask for help. "Hello, Chris. Dan Brown. Remember me?"

"You're hard to forget."

"Come to see that roan."

"We've heard nothing else all week. Hope for your sake
you're right."

"I am."

Chris put his head on one side while he contemplated Dan's confidence in his own judgment. "There'll be the devil to pay, I can tell you, if you're wrong. His lordship's been in a foul mood all week."

Impatient, Dan asked, "So where are they?"

"Lady Mary likes to make an entrance. She wouldn't dream of being early."

"Where are the others? They definitely said ten o'clock."

"Got held up, I expect. Must press on." Chris saluted with a single finger, casually raised, and spun away, leaving Dan alone. He wandered back into the stable yard and found Lord Askew had arrived.

"Morning, Brown." Lord Askew shook hands and then bellowed, "Gavin!"

Gavin appeared from the tack room. "My lord!"

"Lady Mary's here, is she?"

"Not to my knowledge."

"Bring Galaxy out."

Gavin glanced at Dan and, judging by the black look he received, Dan guessed he wasn't flavor of the month in the stable yard. Simultaneously the roan was brought out, the equine vet Giles Standen-Briggs arrived and Lady Mary made her entrance.

Lord Askew introduced Dan to Lady Mary. She gave him her hand to shake, and he found his gripped mercilessly. "Good morning. So, you're the chap who knows better than the rest of us?"

Dan couldn't resist laughing and saying with a smile, "My reputation goes before me." He released his hand and wondered how such a beautiful, fragile-looking woman could have such a deep voice and powerful grip. She reminded him of Rose: that same very slender beauty without being emaciated, the blond hair, the athleticism, the magnetism too. One look into Lady Mary's steely blue eyes, though, and he knew exactly where she stood: four-square for her own way and her own opinions. She'd be hard to convince.

Giles Standen-Briggs he dismissed: the right manners, the right postures, the right clothes but no substance. "Good morning, Giles. Pleasure to meet you. Let's get down to business, shall we? I'm pressed for time. Right, Gavin. Walk him back and forth, right to the end of the yard and back twice, if you please. Keep your eyes on his front feet this time. See how he's on his toes more than he should be."

He heard Giles snort his amusement, but he ignored it. Lady Mary stood silent, watching. Lord Askew said, "I'm damned if I can see . . ."

"Now, Gavin, at a fast trot, twice. Watch his stride . . . watch the length of his stride." They all four watched Gavin huffing his way across the yard in front of them with Galaxy stepping out with eye-catching grace and poise. "See there, look, as I said, just that slightly shortened stride. It's always there every time. Look. See?"

Gavin brought Galaxy to a halt in front of them. Giles Standen-Briggs, rubbing his chin, shook his head. "You're wrong. I can't see it. Smooth, perfect action. No hint of hesitation at all. No limp."

"If he goes on working at the pace he does, at the competitive level he does, he'll be unable to work before long. Great pity, since he's a grand horse and with his spirit he'll keep going for as long as Lady Mary demands it of him." He turned to her and said, "You don't want him lame and unable to compete, do you? Not with his potential."

She was looking thoughtful. "Take him again, trotting . . . fast." Gavin looked askance at her, but minded not to refuse. He set off once more, back and forth in front of them.

Lord Askew watched, Giles Standen-Briggs watched and so did Lady Mary. As Galaxy came to a halt, she said, "How come, Giles, you've never noticed what Dan Brown sees? You see Galaxy regularly. What's the point of my father paying you thousands to look after our horses if you can't identify the simplest problem? This man only saw him once, by chance, and picked it up."

"I don't agree there might be a problem."

Lady Mary's eyebrows shot up her forehead. "If you don't, then you are a fool." She turned to Dan. "What do you say it is?"

Dan studied his hands for a moment to give himself time to phrase his opinions without breaking ranks with Giles Standen-Briggs. "It's my opinion he has navicular disease. I'd have to consult with my colleague on the right course of action."

"My God! What's that? It sounds terminal."

"It will be if something isn't done. But I shall have to discuss the matter with Giles, as I said."

"Closing ranks, are we? I want a decision, please. Today. Galaxy is the best horse I've ever had. He's young but he's *right*, and if he can be made to reach his potential, I shall be forever in your debt. He's everything any rider could ask for: spirited, tenacious, willing to learn, full of courage. Are we talking surgery?"

"That has the best chance of success, yes."

"Have your talk, then. I shall be in the tack room when you've come to your decision."

Dan took some time to convince Giles that he was right. Finally he persuaded him at least to X-ray the feet, and that would prove the matter either way. If Dan was right, then an operation would be on the agenda. If not, Dan would retire gracefully to lick his wounds.

Lady Mary was examining a new saddle which had just

been delivered, but broke off immediately when the two of them came to the tack room doorway. "Well?"

Dan could see she was anxious but endeavoring to hide it as best she could. "We've decided on an X-ray, sometime today. When the plates have been processed, I'll view them back at Giles's practice and we'll decide the best thing to do."

"Can we manage without surgery?"

"There are ways, like fixing him with circular shoes instead of the traditional shape, that would alleviate but not cure the problem. Or sometimes trimming the hoof differently to counteract his tendency to walk tiptoed, but with such a young horse, frankly, if I am proved right, surgery is the better solution. The operation is called a navicular suspensory ligament desmotomy."

"My God, it sounds terrible! If you consider it necessary then . . . hang the expense. Surely an operation on a horse as valuable as Galaxy should be done by experts in the field like the Royal Veterinary College?"

Dan had to smile. "That's for you to decide. He'll have padded bandages for about four weeks, with gentle walking for a while and then slow progression, until after about three months he'll be fit for training again. Everything done in slow progression. Asking too much too soon would undo all our work. However, what must be clearly understood is the fact that we can give no one hundred percent guarantee that the operation will work and none that if it does work, he will be absolutely A1 for the rest of his life. It's damned bad luck this happening to a horse with his promise. Without taking the chance, though, he has no hope at all. It will quite simply get worse."

"I see. You do appear to know what you're talking about. We'll go ahead with the X-ray, then. Can it be done here, Giles?"

Giles nodded. "I have the equipment and I can be here this afternoon to do it."

"Thank you. We'll make our decision when you've seen the results." She turned to Dan, holding out her hand. "I'll say good morning to you; Dan, is it? You're going to feel all kinds of a fool if the results prove you wrong." She gave him a wry smile, and he had to smile back at her.

"I will indeed."

Lord Askew, who'd left all the discussion to her, took Dan to one side before he left. He was worried and showed it. "Damn bad news, this. I don't want her let down. There'll be the devil to pay with her if this doesn't succeed. She's spent hours training Galaxy, and he *is* as good as she says. Could take her to the top of the tree, don't you know."

"I realize that and I can assure you . . ."

Lord Askew waved a dismissive hand. "Only the best, if it comes to an operation. The best in the field. You understand me. I won't have her disappointed." He looked across at Lady Mary, and Dan saw the passionate love he held for her right there in his eyes.

By five o'clock that afternoon Dan had been proved right. He and Giles Standen-Briggs had a discussion and agreed surgery was the answer.

Giles looked shaken but didn't admit to it. He took a moment to reassemble his ego, then said calmly, "I'll contact the college; see if they're willing. OK?"

"Of course. That's fine by me. Lord Askew says the best in the field, so that's what we'll do." He drove back to the practice, vindicated and full of satisfaction.

He sought out Mungo immediately and found him putting the finishing touches to an operation on a cat with two broken legs. "There we are, Bunty; you know the routine. Ring the client, tell them the good news, be your sweetest, there's a love, they'll be well-nigh hysterical by now." He peeled off his operating gown and saw Dan. "Ah! It's you. What news on Galaxy?"

"Thankfully, I've been proved right."

Mungo gave a great "Ah!" of approval.

"It's the Royal Veterinary College for Galaxy, nothing less will do."

"Of course. Beware Lady Mary: sweet as pie if things go her way, but she'll have you scrambled for breakfast if anything goes wrong. I'd like to go over the operation with you if you'd be so kind. Pure interest, you know, though I am staking a lot on the success of it; you must see that."

Dan laughed. "Of course. I can just disappear off into the sunset while you'll be left to carry the can. We've discussed it thoroughly with Lady Mary and Lord Askew, and they wholeheartedly agree with the decision."

"And Giles Standen-Briggs?"

Dan paused a moment before replying, "The X-ray has proved him wrong, and he hasn't taken kindly to that, but he's bearing up."

"Treat him with care. We don't need any antagonism between the two practices."

Bunty left the operating room carrying the patient, and as he closed the door after her, Dan asked, "Supposing it works out. Shall we take on the equine side if it's offered?"

"Let's leave it till after, shall we? The whole picture might change."

"Fair enough. You haven't got someone else, then, to replace me?"

Mungo, scrubbing his hands at the sink, said above the noise of the running tap, "No. I'd have told you if I had. I have advertised again, though. I'm of two minds. Miriam wants you to stay and almost everyone else is halfhearted or downright against you. That first chap kept us hanging on far too long. I reckon he only applied for our job as a lever to get more money out of the practice where he is now. But I don't have to take anyone on if I decide for you to stay." As he dried his hands, he looked Dan in the eye and went on, "Are you still of the same mind?"

"I'd like to stay, yes. Buy a house. Settle down."

"A lot hangs on this operation."

"I know."

"I'm not sure about taking on equine. Getting his farm work back, yes, but horses . . ." Mungo shook his head. "Whole new ball game. Equipment, new setup. No, I'm not sure."

"If you invite me to stay, I have capital, and I wouldn't mind . . ."

"Right, right. I hear what you say. I'll think about it." Mungo put on a clean operating gown. "Must press on."

Bunty and Sarah Two came in carrying a comatose black spaniel. "You have the notes, Mungo, he's all ready for the anesthetic."

Dan took his leave. Mungo rechecked the case file and bent to his task.

"MIRIAM! I'm starving." She was in the kitchen testing a chicken casserole for flavor.

"This is the very last remains of the Christmas food. I swear, honest to God, I shan't buy as much food next Christmas as I did this. We seem to have been eating up for *years*." She grinned at him, put her hands round the back of his neck and drew him to her for a kiss.

After he'd savored her kiss for a few moments he asked, "You've heard?"

"No, what? I've been out all afternoon."

"Where've you been?"

"Walking with Perkins. That's why he's not come to greet you. He's flaked out in his basket."

"The lazy devil. You'll be pleased to hear that Dan has come out smelling of roses."

"No! With Galaxy, I assume?"

Mungo nodded. "He's almost too good to be true. Not only that, Tad Porter is over the moon because Dan's saved Connie Porter's young house cow from lead poisoning; and I met Phil Parsons in the town this morning, and he feels Dan's the best vet we've had in years. Reckons he saved his bull, Sunny Boy, from choking to death."

Triumphantly, Miriam said, "What did I tell you? Didn't I say?"

"I've placed the advert for Dan's job, so it's too late to withdraw, but I really do think we should keep him."

Miriam thumped her fist on his arm. "I knew I was right; and surely to goodness old Askew will want us back, and very possibly we'll get the equine work too. Dan must have an instinctive eye for horses."

"He's volunteered money if and when . . ."

"Really?"

"That would mean a partnership, though."

"Well, why not? With Lord Askew, to say nothing of Lady Mary, on our side we would do well. Oh, Mungo! Aren't you excited? A whole new chapter for us."

"I know. Do we want it? Apart from you, all the wives in the practice have their knife into Dan. Well, women. Zoe, Letty, Joy, Stephie, the two Sarahs and, on occasion, Bunty. Perhaps it wouldn't be worth it."

"One word from you and the whole picture would change. That smile of yours could melt an iceberg."

"Rubbish."

"It's true. Honestly. The casserole's ready. Go and sit down."

"Still, we'll wait and see if the tide turns in our favor. Old Askew might have more allegiance to Standen-Briggs than we've bargained for."

"Not if Lady Mary takes a shine to Dan. I wonder, could we persuade him to pay her some attention while she waits to see if the operation is a success?"

"Miriam! *If?* Do you doubt Dan's prognosis?" Mungo raised his eyebrows at her, and she had to laugh.

"Of course not. I have every faith in him. What he needs is a good wife, though, and why not Lady Mary? She doesn't inherit, because there's a string of sons, so no one could question his pedigree, could they?"

"I've only met her once and, though I admit she has breeding and is very beautiful, having her as a wife would be hell. I don't think Dan would sit very comfortably with a wife who wants it all her own way."

"I didn't say he *had* to *marry* her in order to get Lord Askew's account. Just flirt a little, keep her on our side."

"Are there no depths to which you will not sink?"

Miriam had to laugh. "None."

"Colin manages with a wife who gets all her own way. Though 'manages' just about sums it up."

"So you haven't noticed the change, then?"

"Change?"

Miriam nodded her head. "Oh yes! For my sins I had coffee with Letty in the mall this morning. Her suggestion. She'd been to the beauty shop before I met her, and I must say the result was excellent. Also, instead of those clothes which make her fade into the background, that dreadful cream suit, for instance, she was wearing a little raspberry-colored number Colin had chosen for her in Paris. That weekend seems to have, well, I don't know what, but mellowed things a little. From something she said, I have an idea Colin's been putting his foot down."

"Colin? That'll be a first."

"What she needed, though. Finished, darling?"

"Yes, thanks. Only don't find any other leftovers. Just give them to Perkins, and let's have done with them. I don't want to see any more of this trifle."

"I feel the same. Poor Perkins . . . New Year's. What shall we do?"

"Don't know; haven't got that far yet. Let's clear up and sit down in front of the TV. I'm on call. Pray it's a quiet night."

Miriam got up from her chair and, ignoring Perkins clamoring for their leftovers, went to put her arms round Mungo. "Poor you. You know the knickknacks? It's a pity Dan had the idea so close to Christmas. We'd have made a killing if we'd had more time. Most of the stock is promised for delivery by the New Year, and I can't wait to get cracking. He does have good ideas, you know, does Dan. It would be rather fun if he did get himself some female company. It would fill his life up tremendously, wouldn't it? Just round things off for him, sort of? Go and sit down. I'll clear up."

THREE weekends after his opinion had been sought about Galaxy, Dan was on duty when he received a call from Lady Mary. "Dan Brown? Mary Askew here." He picked up on the pent-up excitement in her voice and wondered what she wanted him for.

"Yes, it's me, Lady Mary."

"Dan, Galaxy's back from the Vet College. I thought you'd like to know that the operation has gone well. We've just unloaded him, and he's in his stable, tucked up and looking fine."

"I'm very pleased to hear that. Very pleased indeed. What a relief."

"Amazing place."

"You went with him?"

"Oh yes, couldn't let him go all that way on his own. Amazing facilities there and so charming, all of them. Did you train there?"

"I did."

"Then you'll know what I'm talking about. Would you call Monday to change his bandages? Just this once. Show me and Gavin what to do?"

"Of course, I'd be delighted, but what about Standen-Briggs? Surely . . ."

He heard a sharp, impatient breath. "I asked *you*." Dan thought she would say something more, but for a moment she didn't. Then, "Well? Will you come?"

"I thought Giles would be . . ."

"I asked *you*. Hang Giles. He couldn't even recognize what you could see immediately."

"Very well, but I feel uncomfortable about it."

"Bother that. Come. Lunchtime Monday and we'll have lunch and talk. About progress. OK? See you. The name's Mary."

Her receiver snapped down before he could reply. He didn't really want lunch and still less did he want to upset Giles Standen-Briggs by attending Galaxy when he wasn't officially his vet. *The name's Mary.* God! He didn't want to get involved there. Those steely blue eyes didn't appeal one little bit. Lunch!

But in the event, it all turned out better than he had anticipated. Galaxy cooperated wonderfully well when the bandages were changed, and Lady Mary and Gavin were excellent pupils. When it came to lunch, it was laid in Lady Mary's small sitting room in the big house. The butler opened the wine and left them to it.

The day was chill even for January, and Dan appreciated the huge open fire. The lunch table had been drawn close to it, and what with the food and the warmth he soon relaxed. Lady Mary was an entertaining hostess and spoke knowledgeably about horseflesh and competing. The whole subject fired her up, and while she was completely absorbed in talking about it, her face was alight and her eyes less steely.

Then she got down to the real purpose of his visit. "Daddy will do what I want, whatever. Being the only girl and the youngest in a family of five boys, I only have to dab my eyes and he crumbles. Mummy's not quite so amenable. Being a woman, she sees straight through my subterfuges, but Daddy! If I insist that we change vets, would you . . ."

"Would I what?"

"Don't be so damn dumb. You know what I mean. If I persuaded Daddy to drop Standen-Briggs, would you be our vet?"

Dan shook his head slowly. "Look here. You're rather jumping the gun. We don't know how successful we've been, do we? Also, your father asked me in for a second opinion, and that is the basis I came on. Fortunately, I was proved right, but that doesn't mean Giles is a fool. Nor does it mean I want to be your equine vet on a permanent basis. I may not even be here permanently anyway."

"You mean that gorgeous Mungo Price doesn't want to keep you? We'll see about that." She layered a pile of brie onto a biscuit and snapped it in half with her beautiful snow-white teeth. When she'd eaten it, she went on, "What I want I get, and I want you. You've instinct as well as knowledge, and I don't know which is the more important. So, would you?"

"I'm not sure. I'm not playing hard to get . . ."

"I know you're not that kind of person, Dan. You and I are alike. We speak our minds, straight from the shoulder."

"Then I'll speak mine."

She waved the other half of her biscuit at him and popped it in her mouth. While chewing it, she said, "Speak up. I'm waiting."

"I have experience and I have instinct. I've worked in racing stables in the Middle East, and I know what I'm talking about when it comes to horses, but . . . I do not want to be exclusively equine. I like variety. I actually like cows and sheep, and lambing time is upon us at the moment and I enjoy it, believe it or not. What's more, I would not want to be running back and forth at your every whim like some kind of tame errand boy. I'm not by nature a lackey; I'm not Gavin. Also, I have Giles to consider and Mungo's wishes to think of, so there's no way I am giving you an answer right away."

"More wine?"

"A little, please. But I am honored that you would consider me."

"And so you should be. I'm very picky about who gets close to my horses. We've twelve all together with my brothers' and Daddy's, and Mummy breeds donkeys, so it would be a lucrative account. Leave Giles to me. He'll do exactly as I say. You can deal with Mungo." Leaning back in her chair, she said, "You are arrogant at bottom, aren't you? Most men would jump at the chance to run back and forth when it was me they were running back and forth for."

"Would they indeed?" Dan smiled sweetly as he added, "I'm not much impressed by titles."

Lady Mary was startled by his frankness. "Mm. Well, that's certainly refreshing. So, shall you finish the wine?"

"I'm driving and I have calls to make."

"Of course. I'll put the idea to Daddy and let you know."

"I make no promises. Just glad Galaxy is doing well, but it's early days. Don't rush him, will you? He needs time. He's a wonderful animal. It must be a privilege to work with him."

"It is. Oh yes. He responds so well and he looks so good, doesn't he?"

"He does. There's a kind of elegance about him, powerful as he is. Wonderful find."

"Daddy came back with him one day, and I knew as soon as I saw him that he'd chosen well."

"Lucky girl."

"I've worked hard with him."

"Still a lucky girl. Doesn't matter how hard you work; if the horse hasn't got that something extra, you're wasting your time."

Lady Mary shrugged her shoulders.

"Thank you for the lunch. I have thoroughly enjoyed it. Your butler took my coat?"

Lady Mary reached across to the bell pull by the fireside and tugged it. The butler shot in through the door saying, "My lady?"

"Mr. Brown's coat, Lister, please."

She went out into the stable yard to see him leave. He wound down the window of the Land Rover and thanked her again for lunch.

"My pleasure, Dan. My pleasure. I'll give you a buzz shortly. I mean it, I'm having you, so you'd better accept the fact."

Dan waved goodbye, thinking *heaven preserve me from ruthless women*. Out of sight of her he punched the air in triumph.

Chapter

·11·

Mia and Kate had tried so very hard to join in with the Christmas activities at the hotel, hoping that the other guests wouldn't guess how very low they were feeling. The first Christmas Day without Gerry was almost too much for Mia and keeping back the tears an impossibility; twice Kate was up in the night trying to comfort her. At least sharing a room on the basis of cost meant she was there for Mia when she needed her. But Kate felt extremes of pain herself, and try as she might to be bright and festive, she failed dismally. Deceit added to her burden, for she hadn't told Mia that her mother had been to the practice the morning after arriving at their door so unexpectedly, full of plans for Christmas.

Completely ignoring the presence of Mungo and Stephie, she had addressed herself to Kate. "I was booked in a hotel for lunch on Christmas Day and they've squeezed you in too, and I thought we'd have a cozy girls' evening together, catching up on our lives, and then for Boxing Day I've arranged . . ."

Kate had interrupted her more forcibly than she'd really intended, but somehow she'd had to put a stop to her plans. "I never said I would come for Christmas. We said we were going away, and I'm not letting Mia down."

Her mother's face had collapsed with hurt. "But now we've met we can be together at long last, surely. Our first Christmas. I've such plans for the two of us." Her enthusiasm gathered pace again. "I'm going to the States in May, and I'd love it if you would come, and . . ."

"I have my exams this summer. There's no way I can go to the States, not even for a weekend." Kate felt as though she were being mown down by a juggernaut, and hysteria began to rise in her throat.

"I just don't understand you. Don't you realize I'm your own mother?"

"Of course I do. But you can't expect to come into my life at this late stage and have me fall in with your plans at the snap of your fingers. It's not reasonable."

Out had come the lace-edged handkerchief, and the eyes were carefully dabbed without smearing the mascara. "But I thought . . . I'm so disappointed."

"That isn't my fault. I never promised anything at all."

"When shall I see you?"

"After Christmas I'll give you a ring, I promise. I have your card, and we'll meet up and have tea or something and talk. There's a lot for us to talk about."

"This is not at all what I expected."

"Please. I am trying. I've sent you a Christmas card. I can't do any more at the moment. At this minute I'm working and I'm needed. I'll ring as soon as I get back. Thank you for coming."

Mungo watched Kate and realized what a tight hold she was keeping on her feelings.

Her mother tried being hurt all over again. "I'm so disappointed."

"Well, I'm glad we've met at last. I've always wondered what you were like, but Dad dying like he did . . . it's all too . . . much."

The whole emotionally charged scene was abruptly shattered by a further crisis as a client rushed in carrying in his arms a big mongrel dog with blood running from its two front paws. "He's been wading in a pond and he's cut his feet; it's terrible. They're in ribbons. There must have been broken glass. Do something. Quick!"

Spurred into action, Mungo dashed to open a consulting room door while Kate grabbed a wad of tissues to catch at least some of the blood and fled with the client into the consulting room. By the time the crisis was over and the dog safe in Graham's hands, and she'd wiped up the trail of blood on the floor of reception, Kate's mother had gone. "I'm going for my break. Is that all right?"

Stephie, who'd witnessed Kate's distress, nodded. "Of course, take as long as you like. I didn't know . . ."

"Neither did I till last night."

Kate had made herself a cup of tea and gone to take refuge in the accounts office to drink it. Rage had boiled up inside her. Now she knew that the loving, smiley person she'd always imagined her mother to be simply didn't exist. But when she reasoned it out, if her mother had been kind and motherly, she would never have dumped her. In truth, she was as hard as nails; that was why she'd done what she'd done. With her clenched fist Kate wiped away the tear escaping down her cheek. It felt cold, so she put her hands on the radiator to warm herself, but that did nothing to stop her trembling.

Insensitive was another word which sprang to mind. How could she imagine for one moment that she, Kate, would let Mia spend Christmas on her own? Did her mother have no understanding of feelings? Did she, in fact, have any genuine feelings? That was the question, because the dabbing of the hand-kerchief to her eyes was a total sham. It was simply her method of trying to get her own way. Well, if that was how the cookie crumbled, then Kate Howard wasn't fool enough to fall for it.

The trembling had almost stopped, so Kate picked up her cup and drank her tea. The hotness of it spread through her, and gradually she began to get herself together. OK, she wanted to get to know her, see her sometimes, but *live with her*? No chance.

What really hurt was the heart-searing realization that the mother standing at the desk this morning no way matched up to the mother of her imagination. Kate remembered how as a child she'd spent hours dreaming about her own mother, imag-ining eating hot buttered toast by the fire on winter evenings, seeing her proud, smiling face in the audience at school con-certs, being met by her at the school gate—all those simple things which illuminated a small child's life. Instead it was Mia who'd done all those things for her. As her dad had said, it was Mia who cherished her. How right he was.

There was a knock at the door and Miriam had come in. She'd paused in the doorway for a moment and then she'd put her arms around Kate. "Mungo said, so I've come, if it helps. What a quandary, my dear."

"Do you know the worst thing? What must hurt Mia so much is that she's been my mother all these years, and I've never, ever, called her Mum. Not once. How could I have been so thoughtless? I'm so ashamed."

Miriam, with no answer to that, had squeezed her shoulders and remained silent.

KATE had rung her mother as soon as she'd got back from hol-iday with Mia, but there'd been no reply to the messages she'd left on her answer machine. Now, Kate felt dumped all over again. Why had she sought her out if she was to forget her immediately?

Then, out of the blue, the phone rang at home one evening and it was Tessa, begging forgiveness. "I was so upset, Kate, about not seeing you at Christmas, and I just couldn't . . ." There was a break in her voice, and then she continued more decisively, "I felt so low. I'm sorry, Kate, I really am. When I heard your voice on the answer machine, I could have cried. But I've got over it now, and I'm asking you to come to see me. Will you, please?"

Kate didn't answer immediately.

"Please, Kate."

"Of course, I'll come to your house and see it as you suggested. When shall I come?"

"Saturday? I'll be free that day."

"Right. About three?"

"Lovely. I'll pop a map in the post."

The rest of the week Kate spent in a whirl of anticipation. She tried her best to hide her excitement from Mia. But Mia saw through her. "I don't mind you being excited, you know. You don't need to be secretive about your mother. I'd like to know."

"Dad said I wasn't to hurt you and I don't want to, but I can't help but be excited."

"It's only natural. I shan't be able to wait until you get back to hear all about it. The house and that, you know."

"Thanks, she's been so upset about me not going for Christmas. That's why she hasn't rung me back."

"Understandable. Yes, understandable."

Kate recognized from the tone of her voice that Mia was striving hard to be reasonable and finding it very difficult, so she changed the subject. "You know the man who's bought Dad's train set? When is he coming to collect it? Because we need to clear up some of the rubbish he's got up there and make sure Mr. Whatever-he's-called gets what he's bought and nothing personal of Dad's."

"You're right. I'd better get on with it."

"If you like, I'll do it," Kate said gently.

Relieved, Mia replied, "Do you mind? I can't face it."

"I'll start right now. I've done all my work for Miss Beaumont for tomorrow night, so why not?"

Gratefully, Mia answered, "Wonderful. If there's anything we should keep, put it in a box all together and when I feel better . . ." She made a vague gesture with her hand. "I'll . . . you know."

"Right. Here goes."

Kate switched on the light at the top of the attic stairs and for a mad, mad moment thought her dad was sitting in his chair waiting for her. It must have been the way the shadows fell as her eyes adjusted to the bright light. Her heart missed a beat and her throat tightened. It was time this train set went, because it was so strongly associated in her mind with her father that she could feel him here as though he'd left his soul behind in the attic when his heart stopped beating.

It felt intrusive handling all his boxes of train paraphernalia. Shoeboxes filled with signals, and rails, and tiny sandwich boards with old slogans half rubbed away, damaged bushes, sheets of imitation brick for the outsides of station buildings, bogies with wheels missing, rusting wheels, the odd window taken from a discarded signal box. Oh, look! She remembered him replacing his old signal box. Of course! Here it was, useless, but loved too much to be thrown away. An invoice for old carriages he'd pounced on in triumph at a sale. She'd been with him that day;

clear as crystal came the memory of his excitement at finding them and of her hand in his, and being half afraid of the crowds looming above her four-year-old head.

Shoeboxes had been his favorites for storing precious things: one full of notices and handbills about exhibitions. Oh! Here was the one for the time he went to London and had upset Mia by buying an early engine which had cost the earth, when in truth they'd needed a new boiler more.

Another held a motley collection of tiny people and animals for use on platforms and the like. Some badly made, others, as he got more skillful, she supposed, admirable in their minuteness, and wasn't that tiny skirt on that tiny girl a bit cut from that favorite old summer dress of hers? And that red coat the woman was wearing? Surely she'd worn that coat to infant school? Searching the box was like seeing her life revealed year by year. How odd that she'd never noticed before.

Kate blew the dust off another box, sealed with sticky tape. She peeled away the dusty stickiness, took off the lid and there, staring at her, was a photograph of herself in the garden by the trellis in a dress she didn't recognize. Oh, God! It wasn't her, it was her mother! Startled, she swiftly put the lid back on again. When her heart had slowed its pounding, she cautiously opened the box again and reverently began looking at a past she shared with her dad. But it wasn't just the past, it was her mother's too. He'd saved birthday cards and Christmas cards she'd sent him. Notes she'd left for him when she'd had to go out before he got home, even a note she'd left for the milkman one day long ago. Curiously Kate studied her mother's handwriting and saw it was very like her own.

Separately, all together in an envelope, she found photographs obviously taken by her dad because he was renowned for his lopsided photos. Some were blurred as though his hands were trembling as he held the camera, but there was no doubt of their subject matter: they were of her mother first and last. Her mother, slim and dark; her mother dressed up for something special; in a swimsuit by the sea; several of her mother obviously pregnant; her mother at the door of what appeared to be a hospital holding . . . yes, holding a baby. So, that must be me. Her and me. Me with her. My mother. Kate drank in this picture in all its aspects, unable to stop looking at it, thrilled to the core. Eventually she put them all back into the envelope, her feelings totally confused. There were letters too, in another envelope in the box, mostly ones from Dad to Mum. He'd had a way with words in those days, had Dad. They were love letters she wouldn't have minded receiving. She wondered what her mother had thought of them.

Kate put the box on one side to take downstairs and hide in her wardrobe. That box most certainly mustn't go with the rest.

Then, most painful of all, she found hidden under a shelf behind a vast pile of old model railway magazines another thick envelope of letters he'd written but never sent. All with "Tessa" written on the envelopes and stored in date order. They were dated regularly throughout the first year of Kate's life and then they trailed off and, around her first birthday, they stopped altogether. That was when Mia had replaced her. One by one Kate opened them and read all about her dad's tender love for her mum in every line: a pining and a longing which revealed so poignantly a depth of feeling she never knew he was capable of. Poor Dad! Loving her like that. How did he survive her going?

"Kate! Are you all right up there? That serial we're watching—it's just about to start. Are you coming?"

Guiltily she shoved the letters into the shoebox along with the photos and squeezed the lid on. "I'm on my way." In haste, so as to prevent Mia from coming up, she got together all the boxes which could be taken with the train layout and, taking

the one into which she'd crammed all her dad's own memora-
bilia under her arm, she switched off the attic light, went down
to her bedroom, pushed aside a pile of shoes she should have
thrown away months ago, put the box in the bottom of her
wardrobe and heaped the shoes back inside to hide it, so Mia
wouldn't find it.

Somehow she found it difficult to meet Mia's eyes when she
got downstairs and sat staring at the TV, scarcely able to follow
the plot because her mind was so full of what she'd just read.
Her dad had suddenly, in one evening, become quite a different
person from the one she thought she knew. For her father's
sake Kate realized she'd have to give her mother time if nothing else. Simply because he had loved her so.

Mia patted her hand. "Finished it all?"

Kate nodded.

"Nothing to keep?"

"No. It's all in piles. Waiting."

"He'll be here to take it away on Saturday. The check's gone
through the bank now, so the money's secure. There wasn't anything for me to see, then?"

"No."

"I see."

Kate leaped up. "I'll make us a drink." Before Mia could
agree with her, she'd disappeared into the kitchen. Now it was
Mia's turn to be unable to follow the TV. Because she knew
Kate so well, she guessed she was hiding something. What, she
didn't know, but there was something Kate didn't want her to
know. If there was something up there about how much Gerry
had loved that Tessa, there was no need to hide it; she'd always
known. A stranger pair there couldn't have been. Tessa had
been a fool, because she, Mia, had reaped all the benefits of loving Gerry and having Kate. Nothing, *nothing* Tessa could do
could take the last eighteen years from her, so she'd hug that to

her heart no matter what happened. Saturday would be here before she knew it, and what had been Gerry's passion would go out of the house for good with that model railway man; and perhaps, worse, she'd lose Kate that day too.

KATE, eager to see her mother, was at the house promptly at three o'clock. She parked at one side of the U-shaped drive because the road was too busy for her to park at the curb, but there was no one there. She stood back from the front door and looked up at the house. It was very new, beautifully painted, with lavish bay windows and expensive net curtains at each of them—being so close to the road, they were necessary. Two smartly clipped bay trees grew in square cast-iron tubs at either side of the door, and the beginnings of a wisteria, a favorite of Mia's, grew on the far side of the right-hand window.

She tried the doorbell again and smiled at the tune it played. Mia would have laughed at it had she been with her. So . . . the big meeting of mother with daughter had finished before it started. Kate went to sit in her car to wait. Just in case. She might turn up. Just might. *I'll wait until half past three; she could have been held up in traffic.* Kate wondered what car she drove and played a game of guessing while she waited. Every part of the house and front garden was as neat as a pin and shouted money. Well, stuff it. Tears welled in her eyes. Her mother seemed to be making a career out of dumping her. Then, as she prepared to pull out to drive away, she saw in her rear mirror a BMW turn into the drive and park. So instead she reversed, parked and got out.

Her mother leaped out. "Kate! I'm so sorry! I went shopping and didn't realize the time. Can you forgive me?" From the backseat she hauled several expensive-looking carrier bags. "This is all for you."

Kate's heart sank and resistance to enticement grew inside her, but when she saw what her mother had bought for her she caved in and accepted. "How did you know my size?"

"I didn't. I guessed."

"I don't know how to thank you; it's all so lovely. This top and these trousers! I've been longing for a pair like these for weeks." But she didn't give her a kiss of thanks as she would have given Mia.

"Tea! I'm parched. Have a look around while I get it ready. The bedroom at the back will be yours if you like it." She wagged a teasing finger at her and disappeared into the back.

Kate wandered about the house, admiring her taste in furniture and the good eye she had for interior decoration. She loved the collection of silver snuff boxes she had, and the modern art on the walls, and the huge, inviting, cuddly goatskin rug before the ornate electric fire. When Kate saw the bedroom her mother had said would be hers if she so chose, she gasped with delight. Such an elegant quilted throw on the big single bed, the huge matching curtains looped back by tasseled cords, a long-pile carpet invited her to try the texture of it with appreciative fingers. It was a bedroom she could only dream about, and with its own bathroom too. Surely it wasn't real marble on the floor? It was. My God! A pink marble bathroom. What a joy!

When she got back to the drawing room, the tea was laid out on a trolley, all lace doilies and delicate china, with a Georgian silver teapot—the whole works.

"Tell me, Kate, what do you think?"

"You have a lovely home."

"I've got an eye for choosing furnishings, haven't I?"

The question popped out of her mouth before Kate could stop it. "You've never married, then?"

"No, never. Not to say I haven't had the opportunity but . . . sugar?"

"No, thanks. Why?"

"Didn't see any reason why I should. I have a good job and simply didn't have any interest in any encumbrances. Do you think I should have?"

Kate shook her head. "Nothing to do with me; I just wondered." She munched on a tiny sandwich, so unlike one made by Mia, which would have had the filling pouring out over the edges and be lavishly buttered and chunky. Mia always joked that it was her generous nature which made her sandwiches turn out like they did. "You've never had any more children? I mean, I haven't got a brother or a sister somewhere?"

Her mother shook her head emphatically. "No, you have not. Once was enough." She looked as though, given the chance, she would have snatched back that last sentence. "Childbirth isn't all it's cracked up to be."

"Being a mother isn't all it's cracked up to be either, apparently. Well, not as far as you're concerned."

Her mother looked hurt. "Kate! How unkind."

Kate waited for the lace handkerchief to come out, but it didn't. "You did leave me. At two weeks old. That takes some effort to understand. In fact, I can't understand and probably never will." Kate couldn't work out why she was coming out with such unkind things; some devil seemed to be goading her. "Didn't you give me a thought? Didn't you care about who would look after me when you were gone?"

"Of course I did. You had Gerry. I'm not entirely heartless."

"No?"

"No. I lost my identity when you were born. I wasn't me. I was Katrina's mother and not Tessa Fenton, solicitor. And you woke in the night to be fed. Night and day demanding food. It was exhausting. I wasn't cut out for it. Believe me, I was tormented by what I did."

Kate helped herself to another sandwich and said with a

sarcastic edge to her voice, "Well, you needn't have worried; Mia's done an excellent job."

"She may have, but she can't give you what I can give you." She waved her hand in the air, encompassing the elegance of her drawing room. "A house like this to live in, a room like yours upstairs, clothes like these, and if you get to college, which I've no doubt you will, being your mother's daughter, you'll have no worries about money. I'll see to that."

Kate gasped for the second time that afternoon. "You really mean that, don't you?"

"Of course. I wouldn't have said it if I didn't. You come to live with me, and you'll want for nothing. Trips abroad, clothes, money to spend. I'll buy a flat for you near college. I'm not having you in student accommodation."

"Oh!"

Her mother leaned across and put a gentle hand on her knee. "You see, you've turned out just as I would have wished. You need to lose a bit of weight, say, perhaps a stone, well, half a stone maybe, and then . . ." She bunched her fingers and kissed them. "With the kind of clothes I can afford for you, you'll be stunning. More tea, Katrina?"

"Yes, please." She held out her cup. Noticed the expensive bracelet and ring her mother wore, the long, beautifully lacquered nails, the impeccable cuff of her white shirt and thought about Mia's neatly filed short nails, and the sweetness of *her* hands and the healing they seemed to bring when they touched her. "When I've drunk this I must be going."

"But we haven't talked."

"What is there to say?"

"You could tell me what Gerry was like as a father. What Mia's like. How you enjoyed Christmas."

Kate, shocked by her use of the word "enjoyed" in connection with her first Christmas after her dad's death, snarled,

"*Enjoyed* Christmas? How could we *enjoy* it? We'd just lost Dad. It was vile. Absolutely vile. Both of us hated it, but it was better than staying at home, just the two of us without him. Don't you understand anything at all?" She sprang to her feet, angry with her mother and with herself, and bitterly disappointed. "I'm sorry for shouting, but this, all this that you're offering me. I can't help but ask why? After all these years. Why? Why bother?"

Her mother got to her feet to emphasize her point. "Because I thought I should when you'd lost your father. It made you an orphan and it didn't seem right. Not when I knew about you, saw in the paper you were still living in the same house. I had to do something. I didn't know how you would be placed, and when I did, I knew something had to be done about it. You can't live in that dreadful house. You needed rescuing."

"Rescuing? From what? A stepmother who loves me? A home that's mine? Where I'm comfortable and happy? Is that what I need rescuing from? Believe me, I don't." Kate gathered her bag and coat, looked at the carrier bags holding the clothes she was expected to take with her and decided not to take them. "I'll be in touch."

"No, Katrina, no. Don't go like this. It's not fair."

"Not fair?"

"To me. I've done my best." This time the lace handkerchief did come out.

"And another thing: I'm called Kate, not Katrina; I hate it. Thank you for the tea. Do you want me to have the clothes after the way I've behaved? I expect you'll be able to take them back to the shop if you don't."

Her mother sat down on the sofa, and looked small and beaten. In a defeated kind of voice she said, "Take them; you may as well as they were bought for you."

Kate hesitated and decided it would be just too churlish to

refuse, and they were all that she longed for but couldn't afford. At least her mother got that right. "Thank you, then. Thank you very much. I will. Sorry for losing my temper, but I couldn't help it."

Her mother looked up, eyes glowing, not a tear in sight, but a smile of satisfaction on her face. "Thank you, Katrin—Kate. Thank you. I don't mean to be thoughtless. It's just that I never have anyone else's feelings to consider, so it's hard for me. But I'm a quick learner. Forgiven?"

"Forgiven."

She went with Kate to the car and helped her put the bags on the backseat. "I'm sorry to have upset you, Kate. I didn't mean to. Will you come again?"

"Of course. Perhaps we could go out for a meal, my treat?"

"That would be lovely. Next weekend?"

"I'm working next weekend, so we'll make it a fortnight."

"I'll pop my diet sheet in the post in the meantime. All right?" Her mother moved as though to kiss her goodbye, but Kate aborted that idea by getting into the car.

"I'll ring and we'll make arrangements. Thank you for tea and the clothes, and I'm sorry if I've been rude."

Before her mother could reply Kate pulled away and drove home, churning with conflicting emotions which crisscrossed her mind so rapidly that each was only half formed before another took its place.

KATE threw herself into her work to avoid having to sort out her feelings about her mother. The new clothes she'd flung on hangers and left in the wardrobe, not able to bear to wear them.

It was Dan who saved her sanity one night when he got a call to a difficult lambing at Tad Porter's just as he was about to leave for home. "How about coming with me, Kate? Fancy it? Seen a lambing before?"

"No, I haven't. Are you sure? I'd love to."

"Of course."

He courteously opened the passenger door for her, stored her boots along with his in his giant plastic washing-up bowl and drove off at his usual hell-for-leather pace. They'd driven right out of the town before he spoke. "Take your mind off things."

Kate continued looking glumly out of the window.

"Is she that bad, this mother of yours? Or isn't that the problem?"

"Between you and me?"

Dan nodded. They'd turned off the Magnum Percy road onto the lane which ended at Tad Porter's. He pulled in to allow a car to pass him on the steep narrow road and then replied, "You don't like her, do you?"

"I didn't say I didn't like her; we're just not the same kind of people, and she is trying to buy me. It's as if I'm being auctioned. Except she's the only one bidding. I'll do the gate."

Dan negotiated the turn into Tad Porter's, and after Kate had closed the gate behind him, she got back in, saying "Tries to buy me, you know, with clothes and money and things."

"Ah!"

"But I know why she left me and ran away."

"You do?"

"She has no feelings whatsoever. Except for herself and what she wants."

"Ah!" Dan braked.

"I'll get my boots."

Despite the cold, Dan stripped down to a short-sleeved shirt and boxer shorts, then he put on his parturition gown, which finished just above his waist, then his waterproof trousers, tied the gown firmly to his lower ribs with a piece of twine kept specially for the purpose and tucked the legs of the trousers into his steel-capped boots.

As Kate put on her boots, Connie Porter came out of the house, wrapped in an enormous tartan blanket carrying a bucket of water and a bar of soap. "Good evening, Dan."

"Good evening, Mrs. Porter. You know Kate, don't you?"

"No, but how do you do? I'm Connie to everyone but you."

"Connie it is, then."

"Tad won't be his usual chatty self. He's been up three nights in succession. The lambs are coming thick and fast. Best year we've had since I don't know when; that many twins you wouldn't believe. You can wash up in the outside lavvy when you've done. I've put new soap and clean towels in there, and come in afterward and I'll find something for you to eat. Tad's in the lambing shed, in the corner of the first field through the gate. Right problem he's got."

Dan led the way across the field, guided by the lights of the lambing shed, with Kate close behind carrying the bucket, accustoming her eyes to the intense dark of the night. The air seemed filled with the sound of calling lambs and their mothers' answering bleats. Far away down the slope were the scattered twinkling lights of Magnum Percy, where people were cozy by their fires, but Kate wouldn't have swapped places for anything, even though her cheeks were already numb with cold.

Tad Porter greeted them at the opening of his lambing shed. In the scant light afforded by the lamps hanging at strategic points, Kate saw that the shed was packed full of sheep and bleating lambs: some penned off, others free to wander about knee deep in straw. Closest to her were twin lambs feeding from their patient mother, long tails waggling briskly as the warm milk gushed down their throats. Here and there lambs were curled asleep, keeping close to their mothers' warm, comforting bodies. She couldn't help but let out a long "Aw."

Dan grinned. "Great, eh? Evening, Tad. Which one's the problem?"

"This ewe here." He went to stand by a pen which contained only one ewe with no lamb with her. "I've tried to sort her out, but them's that entangled. Has twins ev'ry year, she does. They're allus right little goers."

Dan washed his hands and arms in the bucket of icy water Kate had carried for him, then he pushed aside Tad's makeshift bed piled high with blankets, climbed over the partition and invited Kate with a jerk of his head to do the same. Despite the shelter of the huge expanse of corrugated-iron roofing and sides protecting the ewes and lambs from the chill, Kate found the icy cold almost intolerable. When she remembered how little money farmers were getting now for lambs at market, she wondered at their tenacity in tolerating such inhuman working conditions.

Dan was on his knees beside the ewe, feeling inside her. "Hold her head for me, Kate." He concentrated on the job, muttering from time to time. "There's another head."

"That's two heads."

"Another pair of back legs. Like you said, Tad, what a tangle."

Kate felt compelled to address the ewe. "There, there, you let Dan give you a hand. Don't worry, he'll soon get you sorted." Then she felt embarrassed and ridiculous.

Dan gave her a smile. "Thanks for the vote of confidence. Tad! There's two in here for sure, like you said, all entangled. I think the first to come out has something wrong with it; it won't come out at all. I'm going to turn it round and bring it out back end first."

"Do yer best. That's what yer here for." He leaned his lean length against a supporting post, pulled a thick sack more closely round his shoulders and lit up his pipe, preparing for a long wait. "I've had fifteen born today so far. One's in t'oven cos it's a poor doer, but Connie'll bring it round."

Dan, kneeling in the straw struggling to make sense of the lambs, with two thirds of his powerful forearm inside the ewe, suddenly said, "Ah! Here we go. Number one." Out slid a tiny lamb, wet and messy and lifeless, with both its front legs seriously crippled. He broke its cord with a quick nip of his thumb and forefinger and, laying it to one side, went back to dealing with the second lamb. Kate kept her eyes from the dead lamb. She couldn't bear to look at it. What should have been a beautiful moment had turned very sour.

The second lamb came the correct way round, its little nose and forefeet arriving first, and with relief Kate saw this one was perfect, but it didn't breathe immediately.

"Clear its mouth and nose and then rub it, Kate, rub it with that old cloth. Go on. Vigorously. Go on. Do it! Hard! Harder!"

Kate was stunned to find herself with the lamb's life in her hands. In a daze she heard Dan say, "Hard, harder than that; it won't break." So she did as he said and rubbed its chest so vigorously that the lamb was actually moving up and down in the straw with every rub. Just as she was about to admit defeat it took a breath, gave a half-strangled bleat and began breathing regularly. Kate could have cried with relief.

"Good girl! Well done . . ."

Kate kept rubbing the lamb in case it decided to stop its fight for life. She was in such a panic that any thought of market prices and whether it was worth it had flown from her mind and been replaced by a desperate desire for the tiny thing to live. It just had to! Her first lamb. Her very, very first. This was brilliant.

She wished she could pick it up and hug it, mess and all. It was just so . . . so . . . wonderful. That was the word. Wonderful. Kate burst into tears.

Dan gave his attention to the health of the ewe. Feeling round inside her he said, "That's it, everything all right in there. One good one at least. No point in trying to revive the other, Tad."

"Ah, well, it 'appens. Yer learn to be philosophical in this game. Ewe's all right, is she?"

"All clear. I'll give her an injection to boost her a bit. She's had a hard time of it."

Tad observed, "She's been struggling to deliver for some time, and I tried to help but it was no good."

"Kate, my bag, please." Dan spoke sharply because he wanted her to stop crying. When she didn't react, he added loudly, "Now."

Kate gulped down her tears and went to get the bag for Dan, wiping her cheeks with the heel of her hand. "Here you are." To comfort herself, she knelt down in the straw to stroke the little lamb and to her surprise found that beneath the soft wool its head was hard and almost rocklike, when she'd always imagined lambs' heads would be soft and woolly.

The ewe, having got rid of her burden, began to take an interest in her lamb and before they left the shed it was trying to get up on its wobbly legs. Kate looked back at the lamb she'd helped to revive before she left the shed and loved it. The sight of its utter sweetness, the absolute beauty of it, was just mind-blowing.

She and Dan struggled across the dark field by the light of Dan's torch and eventually found the outside lavvy. "You wash up first, Kate." The water was ice-cold, but the coal tar soap smelled good, and rubbing herself with the hard, rough towel line-dried in the fresh air put life back into her.

As she watched Dan wash his arms and hands, Kate said, "I'm so sorry, Dan. I didn't know I'd cry."

"That's life, as they say. We can't win every time, Kate. Only most of the time, and it's something you never quite get used to, losing an animal. I'll get my clothes on and wash this lot off, then we'll go in."

When he was dressed, Dan called, "Come on, then, let's see what Connie has for us."

"They all look so sweet. The two of them. I did it, though, for the second one, didn't I? I made it breathe."

Dan took her arm, delighted by her pleasure in her triumph. "You did indeed, but like Tad said, we've to be philosophical about the failures. Go in. Boots off first. Connie! There were twins, but the first one was a no go, I'm afraid."

"That's life. Sit yourselves down. Lamb casserole. OK?"

Kate's stomach heaved. The very thought: lamb casserole. How could they? Lamb casserole! Those dear little lambs, the one she'd helped to revive! How could they?

Dan saw her horror and for her sake tried to cover the moment by saying, "Smells good, Connie. Is Tad coming in for some?"

"He'll be in."

"You're more than generous. Hadn't expected a meal, had we, Kate?" Dan nudged her sharply.

"No, we hadn't. It's very kind, very kind." Somewhat painfully she added, "I'm really hungry."

The casserole was brought out of the oven as soon as they'd seated themselves at Connie's big pine table. With a clean sack for an oven cloth she carefully placed it on a big hand-woven mat in the middle of the table. On the top of the casserole was a thick layer of thinly sliced wonderfully crisped potatoes, browned and delicious-looking to anyone with even half an appetite, but to someone out in the fields all day and night earning their livelihood it would look like something from paradise. As Connie dug her huge serving spoon into the dish, the rich smell of the thick, shining, brown, herby gravy as it dripped

down reached Kate's nostrils, and hunger overcame her squea-
mishness. By the time her plate was in front of her, full to the
very edge with meat and gravy and glorious vegetables, Kate
couldn't wait to pick up her knife and fork. There was a large
glass of foaming homemade beer to accompany it, and the two
complemented each other superbly.

"A feast fit for a king," Dan mumbled through his first
mouthful of food.

Connie smiled, well satisfied. "Well, when my Tad's been
out there all day he needs some packing, believe me."

After the meal, Connie took the lamb from the warming
oven and asked Kate if she'd like to feed it, if they had time.
Dan agreed they had; the warmth of the fire and the satisfaction of the huge meal he'd consumed made him reluctant to
leave, and he was glad of an excuse to enjoy the warmth a while
longer.

Kate knelt on the hearthrug and took the bottle from Connie. The frail lamb took a deal of encouragement to persuade it
to begin feeding. When it did, it worked hard, but quickly
became exhausted and could only finish half the bottle.

"Never mind, that's better than he's been doing. You're a
good lass. You've a way with animals."

"How often will you have to feed him?"

"Every two hours night and day till he shapes up." Connie
hitched up the tartan blanket round her shoulders.

Dan stood up. "We'll be off, then. Thanks for the meal,
Connie, much appreciated. Ready, Kate?"

"Every two hours! How do you manage without sleep?"

"Catch up when the lambing season's done. Same every year.
Goodnight and thanks."

Dan snatched up his bag and headed for the door. He glanced
round at the spartan room—the cold stone floor, the ancient
oak settle by the fire, the huge old cooking range, the morbidly

challenging religious picture over the mantelpiece, the old, old comfortable chairs—and brooded gratefully on the warm hospitality they'd received. "Thanks again, Connie. You're a remarkable cook. Might be seeing you again soon."

"More than likely." Connie followed them out and went into the outside lavvy. They heard the catch snap shut.

Kate whispered, "Have they no inside toilet, then?"

"I don't expect so."

"They are so poor and yet so generous."

"Upland farming is always difficult even in the best of times. OK?"

He put the Land Rover in gear, released the brake and set off to return to Barleybridge. "Care for a drink, Kate?"

"Might as well, if you've time. I'd like that."

They settled themselves in a quiet corner of the Askew Arms. The main bar and the restaurant where Dan had had that awkward lunch with Lord Askew were busy, but they chose to sit in the smaller, relatively quiet bar.

"I think I'll go to the ladies' room and tidy up. Coming straight from a lambing, I must look a mess."

"You don't, but OK. I'll order. What would you like?"

"A sweet cider, please."

When she came back, the drinks had been served and Dan was patiently waiting. He grinned at her as she approached. "What did you think, then?"

"When she said lamb casserole, I thought I would die. I suppose I've learned a lesson tonight. Quite what it is I don't know. The other lesson I've learned is that nature can be cruel. That lamb . . ."

"I know, but at least we got one good one, thanks to you."

"And thanks to you. I wouldn't have known where to start sorting that jumble out."

"Practice, that's what it is. Nothing but experience. I love it.

I'll take you with me another time when it's convenient and you can do an examination. Would you like that?"

Kate nodded her agreement. "Very much."

"So satisfying and new lambs are so . . .'"

"Jolly, and sweet, and lovable?"

Dan smiled.

"But was I put face to face with the reality when Connie said what she'd cooked. I thought I would be sick." Kate shuddered at the memory.

"It's the harsh reality of farming. It's their living, and sentiment mustn't come into it. Well, occasionally it does and they keep a pet one."

"Cheers!" Kate raised her glass and toasted Dan. "Heard any more about Lord Askew and his horses?"

"Making progress. I had dinner with Lady Mary last night."

"No! You didn't!"

"Yes, jolly pleasant too. She can be very amusing."

"She has a dangerous reputation. I hear she devours nice men."

"This man's not for devouring."

"Oh, no? Wait till she's worked her charm on you."

"Not my type."

"What is your type, then?" Kate looked at him over the rim of her glass, curious to know his answer.

She'd taken a long drink and put down her glass before he answered her. "Immaterial. I'm not in the market."

Unsure of her ground and of his reasons for saying what he did, she blurted out, "You've forsworn women, have you?"

"No. I'm simply not free."

"I see." Kate could have cut out her tongue for saying what she had and quite simply didn't know how to rescue the situation. She flushed bright red and hadn't a clue what to say anymore. What on earth did he mean he "wasn't free"?

Cutting through her embarrassment, Dan asked, "Another drink, Kate?"

"No thanks, I'd better be going. Sorry to have said what I did. I didn't mean to pry. I'll walk to the practice to get my car. Thanks for the drink and for inviting me to the lambing."

Dan stood up. "My pleasure." He endeavored to be pleasant, but his effort didn't quite succeed because his eyes remained blank. "I'll drive you; it's a long walk in the cold." He picked up his keys from the table and, taking hold of her elbow, led her outside.

They drove the short distance to the practice in silence. Eventually, just as he pulled up in the car park, leaving the engine running so there was no question of him wanting to stay talking, he said, "One day perhaps I'll explain, but not right now. It's all very personal. Thanks for your company, you make a good assistant."

"Except for crying like an idiot."

"No, it shows you have a heart and a deep concern for animals. So long as you've done everything in your power to make things come right, that's the secret. Have no regrets." Dan waited until she'd started up her car and then with a wave drove away. Kate wasn't quite sure if his advice referred to veterinary work or his private life. Whichever, the advice made good sense. Even so, she was no nearer to finding out what made Dan so uptight about women. He must have very deep feelings for that girl in the photo for him to be so seriously affected by her. If she was dead, then why wasn't he free? If she wasn't, where was she?

Chapter

·12·

Kate was on duty at the desk by herself the following day when Sergeant Bird arrived full of excitement. "Just going off duty. You won't believe it, but we've caught the beggars who tortured poor Copperfield." He clenched both fists and banged them on the desk. "All five of 'em. Not only that, I've got them for all the car thieving in the parking garage. They'll be drawing their pensions by the time they get out."

"Really? Good work!"

"Oh yes, brilliant!" He thumped the desk again.

"How did you do it?"

"Well, we were looking at the security film from the parking garage, and this time they were on the film. We'd caught them red-handed doing the stealing, and like a flash it came to me that I knew one of the lads. Took a day or two for it to click, but then it dawned." Sergeant Bird took time off to contemplate his delight at his inspirational moment, while Kate hung in suspense, waiting. "One of them was the lad I'd interviewed about poor Copperfield."

Kate stood transfixed, fingers poised over the keyboard. She couldn't help it, he was so passionate, so . . . " 'That's him!' I shouted. 'I know him. It's that little sod Bobby Turner.' "

"So?"

"So this time we got him to the station, showed him the video and bob's yer uncle he came clean. The game's up, I told him. Might as well do yourself a favor. So of course he agreed to cooperate, and we've got the lot in the nick at the moment. They were all in it together, tying that poor cat to the back of a bike and racing him down the slopes at the car park. Terrible. Terrible. Every last one of 'em we've got. What a coup."

"How many did you say were involved?"

"Five. Thought doing that to him was a joke, the nasty little beggars. It's only thanks to Bunty and Mungo that Copperfield's still alive. But . . ."

"Yes?"

"But . . ." He paused for dramatic effect. "They're only the tip of the iceberg; they were stealing the cars to order for an international gang."

"In Barleybridge?"

Sergeant Bird nodded. "In Barleybridge. It's not only London where they have the big gangs. Oh, no. So it could lead to a big arrest." He winked significantly at Kate.

"Well, all thanks to you. I'm so pleased. Wait till I tell the others. If you go on like this, there'll be nobody left in Barleybridge. We'll all be in the nick. I have to confess I went through a red light the other day and . . ."

Abruptly he lost interest. "Bunty in?"

"Yes, but she's . . ."

But Sergeant Bird had gone in the back to find her. He returned in a moment, white as a sheet. In fact, almost as green as a pea. Kate had to inquire about his health. He replied in an awestruck voice, "My God!"

"What is it?"

He looked down at his hands in horror. "Her hands were covered in blood and you could see . . ." He fled reception with the speed of light. Kate put down her pen and rushed outside after him. Poor Sergeant Bird was being disgustingly sick in Miriam's ornamental bushes right outside the front door.

"You'd better come in and sit down a minute. I'll get you a glass of water."

She helped him in and sat him on the nearest chair. He sat shaking, his handkerchief held to his mouth. After he'd sipped the water, he wiped away the beads of sweat on his forehead and said more calmly, "You could have warned me they were operating. It was ghastly. I'd no idea."

"Some of Mungo's operations are a bit intrusive."

"Intrusive! It looked like a slaughterhouse in there. Mungo shouted at me to get out. He's never spoken to me like that before."

"He doesn't mean it. He gets tense when he's operating; his ops are very tricky, you see, very intricate. Not like a common garden neutering. Don't take it to heart. We've all had to learn to ignore his outbursts when he's doing a difficult op. Must get on. Sit there till you feel better."

As she finished speaking, the alarm sounded from Mungo's operating room and Kate heard the *thud thud* of Sarah One's clumpy shoes as she rushed in to assist. Kate maintained a calm exterior, remembering what Joy said about not alarming the clients, but inside she was turbulent with anxiety. Obviously something was going badly wrong with the operation. Then she heard the hurried tattoo of Joy's shoes as she too hastened to help. There were raised voices, controlled but anxious: the tension in the air moved in palpable waves down the corridor. Tied as she was to the reception desk, Kate could only worry.

Then Joy's unhurried footsteps came back down the corridor. Sarah's clumpy shoes returned to the other operating room, where she was working with Rhodri, and Kate had to know. She left the desk and put her head round Joy's office door saying quietly, "Joy, everything all right?"

She whispered, "Fingers crossed. Heart stopped. Got it going, though. Seems fine now. Mungo's just closing up."

"Who was it?"

"Cadbury, that chocolate Labrador bitch. The client had been warned it was risky, but they decided to go through with it. I tell you, we thought she was a goner. It was one heck of a dodgy moment back there. Tea all round, I think."

"A cup for Sergeant Bird too."

Joy raised an eyebrow at the prospect of making tea for him as well. When Kate had explained, she smiled rather grimly and went to put the kettle on. To Kate's surprise, Bunty emerged into the reception area carrying a mug of tea, which she gave to the Sergeant and then sat down beside him, saying "I've put sugar in for you."

There was something about their body language that alerted Kate, and while she attended to the clients she kept a wary eye on the pair of them. She heard Bunty say, "But of course there was blood on my hands, well, on my gloves; we were *operating*, for heaven's sake."

"I know, I know, but it was just such a shock. I've never seen . . . you . . ."

"Then you've seen the real me. All right? Got to go, another op."

"Please apologize for me to Mungo."

"Of course. Drink your tea."

Sergeant Bird nodded. "You won't have heard. I've got the scum who tortured poor Copperfield."

"Good. Throw the book at them. See you, Aubrey."

Kate covertly watched Sergeant Bird's face as Bunty left him. It was a strange mixture of admiration and, well, let's face it . . . love. And she had called him Aubrey, which no one else ever did, and Bunty had avoided catching her eye as she passed her. Well, surprise, surprise!

KATE had a further surprise that evening when she was scheduled to take her mother out for a meal. They'd agreed to meet by the fountain in the mall, and when Kate spotted her mother walking toward her, she almost died. Her outfit was more suited to a reception at 10 Downing Street than a meal at a modest Italian restaurant. Kate was thankful that Mia had turned down her invitation to join the two of them. Her mother's appearance would only have put her back up. "It's very considerate of you," Mia had said, "but, no, I won't, thank you. It's something between you and her, and I shall be in the way."

"Of course you won't. Please come. I want you to come."

"Well, if you don't mind, I won't, Kate. I feel you and she have to get to know each other, and I shall just be a nuisance. Now go along and have a good time. Remember, there's all the rest of your lifetime, so don't go rushing anything, will you?"

Kate gave herself a last look in the mirror. "There's no need to worry. I shan't be going to live with her or anything. It's tempting, but no thanks."

"I see."

"Look, Mia, I mean it. I'm not going to live with her. I want to stay with you." Out of the blue came the terrible idea that maybe Mia was being reasonable because she actually wanted her to go. Kate's heart shot into her throat; she spun round and looked her straight in the face, but she couldn't tell from Mia's blank expression what she was thinking. "Do you *want* me to go; is that it?"

Mia's face crumpled and she held out her arms. "Go? Of course not. Of course not." They hugged each other tightly.

"I'm trying not to stand in your way, if that's what you want. I'm just trying to be sensible, not to put pressure on you, you know. Oh, Kate! If only Gerry . . ." Mia drew back, wiped her eyes and, putting a smile on her face, added, "I know there'll be a time when you'll launch out on your own; that's inevitable, but right now isn't the time and I want you to stay. Till you're qualified, you know."

"You've got such faith in me. I just hope I won't let you down."

Mia sniffed. "You won't. Now get off or you'll be late. Have a good time."

So now what should she do? Change her plans to accommodate her mother's outfit? There was no way that she, Kate, could afford anywhere more expensive than the Casa Rosa, and that was that.

"Kate, dear!" Her mother bent forward to kiss her cheek and gave Kate a noseful of expensive perfume. "I'm not late, am I?"

"No, you're not."

"Where are we going to eat? The Askew Arms?"

"No, at the Casa Rosa, just down here, round the corner."

"The Casa Rosa? I've never heard of it. Is it Italian?"

Kate nodded. "It is very nice, though."

"I'm sure." Her mother looked disconcerted. "Look. I know money must be tight. Mia won't have much, I expect, and you certainly won't, working as an accounts clerk at that practice. So why not let it be my treat? Eh? How about it? We'll go to the Askew Arms."

Getting no reply, her mother took hold of her arm and shook it affectionately. "What do you say?"

"I don't know."

"Go on. I can afford it, you can't. Let me treat you and we'll have a lovely talk. The food is astonishingly superior, considering the size of Barleybridge."

Kate studied the smart navy suit her mother wore, the lustrous pearls at the neck, the immaculate makeup, the large pearl earrings, the gold lapel brooch studded with pearls.

"I'm dressed up to make a good impression. I'm nervous you see."

Stubbornly Kate replied, "It is my invitation. I've booked the table. I'm paying."

Her mother sighed. "Very well, so be it."

Just as they reached the restaurant door her mother asked, "I hope the kitchens are all right. I've asked to inspect kitchens before now."

"Not tonight, you won't."

The evening went downhill from there. They found no common ground. In fact, it was hard to believe that their relationship was that of mother and daughter. Her mother did her best to retrieve the situation, but even her skills couldn't surmount the awkwardness between them. Finally, as Kate paid the bill, her mother whispered, "You should have let me take you to the Askew Arms. It would have been much better."

With her change pushed into her purse, and a zipper which wouldn't close and a handbag which for no reason had become too small to hold it, Kate slammed out with a curt goodnight to the waiter and marched her way down the mall toward the car park, her mother trotting along behind her on her high heels.

"Wait! Let me catch up."

But Kate didn't wait. She stormed along on the verge of tears, angry and disappointed.

"Kate!" Her mother labored up the stairs to the second floor, trying to catch her up. "I'm parked on the first floor, Kate!"

Kate stopped and turned round. "I think we'd better not see each other again. I'll return the clothes. I haven't worn them. It's for the best." She looked anywhere but at her mother, breathing hard and thoroughly distressed.

"What have I done wrong? I've tried my best."

Kate took a deep breath and let her temper rip. "You are rude and arrogant with no thought for anyone's feelings but your own. Selfish, that's what you are. How could I possibly have afforded the Askew Arms? It's way out of my bracket at the moment, and you should have realized that. If I'd suggested a fish and chip shop, you should have gone without a murmur. I'm so disappointed." Her temper spent, Kate added sadly, "But it's no good, is it? We're not made for each other. Thanks for trying anyway."

"I have tried. I really have. I want it to work. I want you to come and live with me and let me support you. You can't cope with five years at college without some help. That's big money. I'm certain Gerry won't have left you big money, and Mia hasn't any, has she? It'll cost me nothing really to help. Let me?"

"I don't know."

"I'll phone in another week, and you'll come round for tea. Don't bring the clothes back, though, those are yours whatever. Smile for me? Mm? We'll try again."

"All right, then. We'll try. Goodnight." As Kate turned away to walk to her car, her mobile rang. She fumbled about in her bag and eventually found it and conducted her conversation with Dan with her mother listening.

"Kate? Dan here. Where are you? I'm off to a lambing at Porter's Fold. Coming?"

"Oh, Dan, yes! I'm in the mall parking garage. Where are you?"

"About a hundred yards away, I was going to pick you up from home on my way through. Good thing I rang first. Let's think. I know, I'll pull in at the fountain end."

"Right. Three minutes." To her mother she said, "A lambing. Got to go. Give me a ring like you said." On winged feet she fled down the stairs, heart zinging with delight. This was a world in which she knew where she was, not that slipping, sliding world her mother lived in, where you never knew what was truth and what wasn't.

Dan was just pulling up as she arrived, and she leaped in with relief. "What's the problem?"

"Don't know, but Connie's worried and they need support. He must be nearly dead on his feet. Belt up." Dan surged off into the first gap he could find and headed for Magnum Percy.

This time it was Connie who was in the lambing shed, wrapped in her tartan blanket. "Tad's asleep like a man felled, so I've come out. We've lost two lambs today. These are the ones causing a problem at the moment."

In the same pen where the ewe had given birth to the twins only the night before stood two ewes in dire straits. Their bulging stomachs told their own story. "Looks like twins again, Connie. Right, let's get to work. May I ask if Kate could examine one? Just for experience. Would you mind?"

"Not at all. I'll leave you to it and go and see how Tad is." She heaved the tartan blanket more closely about her neck before she left the shelter of the shed and disappeared into the night.

In an old set of parturition clothes belonging to Dan, Kate knelt down in the straw. Dan squeezed some lubrication cream into the ewe and left Kate to get on with her examination. She hadn't the first idea of what sensations she would experience but she was eager to have a try. It was tight getting her hand in through the ridge of the pelvic bone, but once through that there was more room and inside felt warm and wettish. Kate felt a head, and a jumble of legs, bony and angular, but as for making sense of what she felt, that was beyond her.

She withdrew her hand and turned to see what progress Dan had made. He had one lamb out on the straw and was struggling with the second one. It popped out with ease. "How do you do it? I can't make any sense of what I could feel. There could be three or four in there for all I know."

"Let me look. Check these two for me."

Dan had the two lambs out on the straw almost quicker than it takes to say "The first one needed turning round; he was coming back end first."

When they left the barn and set off to wash up in the out-side lavvy, as Connie called it, there were four spanking lambs and two proud mothers in the pen. Connie gave them both a hot toddy before they left. "Thanks for all you've done. Just couldn't manage it myself. You're blinking good at your job, Dan, there's no doubt about that. I hear his lordship will be taking you back on."

"Really? I hadn't heard."

"So they were all saying in the market on Wednesday. Horses and farm they were saying. I'm surprised you don't know. They all knew in the market; that's the place to be if you want to hear the latest. Here, I've just had a thought. Come in the dairy and choose some cheese for yourselves. I've had some good reports about this batch."

Kate and Dan put down their empty glasses and followed her out. The tartan blanket hitched up round her shoulders against the biting wind, Connie led them into the dairy, which was better equipped than the house, as though all Connie's creativity were centered in there rather than her home. Well-scrubbed stone shelves, immaculate, gleaming, stainless-steel pans and bowls, huge shining spoons and ladles, and best of all, shelves holding a small selection of cheeses waiting to mature.

"These are ready, these at this end, up to there. Choose one. Go on."

"It's very kind of you," said Dan, "but please let me pay you for it. I can't expect you just to give me it."

Connie stood tall and answered sharply, "I shall be offended if you offer me money."

Kate, anxious not to give any more offense, said, "Dan lives on his own and there's only two of us at home; how about if we share a cheese? Otherwise it'll take us months to eat it up." She smiled her sweetest smile at Connie, who gave in with only a slight demur.

"I see your point. I'll cut the one you choose into two halves and wrap them for you." She busied about getting paper and a huge shining knife down from her knife rack and stood waiting.

Dan nudged Kate. "Go on, you choose."

They all appeared the same to Kate, but she took her time choosing, knowing it would please Connie.

As they left Porter's Fold, Kate said, "I feel very embarrassed about this cheese. She can't really afford to give it away, can she?"

"No, but like she said, she'd be offended if we'd insisted. Very proud the two of them."

"I see that. A lot of veterinary work is with the people, isn't it, as much the animals. I wish I were good at that."

"I've always thought you were."

"No, Dan, I'm not, not where it counts. I've made such a hash of taking my mother out this evening, you wouldn't believe." She explained how angry she'd been and how disappointed. "You see, Mia would have fallen in with my plans without a murmur because she *understands*. But my mother? Oh no! An Italian restaurant in the mall wasn't good enough. Even the clothes she wore were all wrong for Barleybridge. She was all set for the Askew Arms no less, you see. I can't afford to afford that, if you see what I mean. I need to keep a hold on any money I have because of college." Kate gave a great sigh and continued looking out of the side window, deep in thought.

Dan patted her knee. "Come on, Kate, it'll take time, you know."

"Still, we made a good job of those lambs, and that's more important. Well, to me it is." She beamed a great smile at him, and he smiled back at her, glad to see her spirits had lifted.

"So, seeing as I keep using you as my life counselor, what do you advise me to do? Keep on seeing her?"

"Of course. You must. Forget the dreams of childhood and your disappointment at her not matching up to them, and meet her as an adult on an equal footing."

"Mm."

"She can't replace Mia, can she?" He got no reply. "Can she?" Kate snapped out. "Of course not."

"There you are, then. Tessa happens to have given birth to you, but Mia is your mother. You might find Tessa's very lonely, and your father dying has given her a window, as you might say. Here we are, then."

"Yes." Kate stared out at the fountain thrusting water fifteen or more feet into the air as though she hadn't seen it before. "Oh! Yes, here we are. Right, I'll be off. Thanks Dan, for thinking of me; it's been a wonderful experience and gives me a real impetus to succeed. Thanks for the lift." She hunted in her bag for her car keys.

"Don't forget your cheese."

"Oh, right. You know they've caught the people who tortured poor Copperfield? Dickie Bird came in this morning to tell us; not only that, but they are also the same ones who are stealing the cars from the parking garage, so he's killed two birds with one stone, as you might say. He's got some daft idea about their being part of an international gang stealing cars to order. I ask you, honestly, in sleepy old Barleybridge! He's been watching too many American gangster films."

"There are people with pots of money around here. He could be right."

"I suppose. Good night. Thanks again. See you tomorrow."

Chapter

·13·

The letter asking Mungo if the practice would take on Lord Askew's equine work and also take back the farm animal work was on Mungo's desk the following morning. Joy opened it and sprang to her feet, shouting, "Eureka!" before she'd finished reading the first paragraph.

> *... in consequence of this a meeting next week to discuss the ... suggest Thursday at twelve noon at the practice or at Askew Hall whichever you prefer ...*

Joy raced up the stairs to the flat and burst in to find Miriam and Mungo still eating breakfast. "He's done it!"

"Who's done what, Joy?" Miriam asked.

"Sorry! It's this." She thrust the letter under Mungo's nose. "See?"

Mungo, sensing the importance of the moment, slowly picked up his reading glasses, placed them on his nose, and solemnly read the letter all the way through before he spoke, his face showing no reaction whatever. Then he leaped to his feet, put his hands round Joy's waist, kissed her heartily twice and swung her round.

Miriam picked up the letter from where Mungo had dropped it on the table and read the magical words. "What did I tell you. All due to Dan."

"Exactly!"

With a wry grin on her face, Miriam asked Mungo, "He can stay, then?"

"Of course. What else? I never thought the beggar would do it, but he has. So we're equine too now. Champagne all round tonight before they leave?" Mungo raised a questioning eyebrow at Miriam.

"Shall we keep mum until it's all agreed? Knowing Dan, he could drive a hard bargain, or perhaps more likely, knowing Lord Askew, *he* could drive a hard bargain and *us* not agree."

"Perhaps you're right, yes, of course. But what a climbdown on his part."

Miriam corrected him. "No, Mungo, what a wise man he is. He knows how clever Dan is and wants him for himself."

Joy declared she rather thought it might be Lady Mary who'd swung things in their direction. "I know for a fact that Dan has had dinner with her twice in the last few weeks."

Miriam looked up from reading the letter again and asked, "Has he? I didn't know. You don't think . . ."

"I've work to do even if you two haven't, so stop your matchmaking the pair of you and start the day." Mungo went off to the bathroom to clean his teeth and left Joy and Miriam speculating.

Joy said, "He'd lead a hell of a life if anything ever came of it."

"Lord Askew as a father-in-law! God help him."

"Apparently Dan thinks he has a soft side to him."

"He must be the only person ever to think that. No one has a good word for his lordship." Miriam put the letter back in its envelope and placed it by Mungo's glasses. "And you, Joy, what about you? What if Dan wanted to be a partner. Would you agree?"

Rather primly and with tight lips, Joy answered, "As Zoe so rightly told me not long ago, I'm not a partner so I have no say in the matter."

"For heaven's sake, of course you have. You've the rest of the staff to carry with you about this. Well?" Miriam folded her arms and looked as though she had all morning to wait for Joy's reply.

"Well, at one time I would have opposed it, but I've got used to him now and there's no doubt about it, he brings nothing but credit to the practice and that can't be bad. Now he's apparently won back Lord Askew . . . So, yes. It's fine by me."

Miriam kissed her cheek. "Excellent! You see I was right. I've always said he would be good for us. I may not work in the practice, but I do have a nose for knowing what's going on."

Joy looked away, wondering just how much Miriam had guessed about her own love for Mungo. God, she hoped Miriam never found out. She couldn't bear it if she did. Fast on the heels of that thought she was hit as though by a sledgehammer with the realization that her reaction to Mungo swinging her round by her waist and kissing her had not brought the adrenaline rush it would have done at one time. As she pondered this astounding thought, he came back to pick up his glasses and the letter from the kitchen table, and she found that her heart scarcely stirred at the smile he gave her, and there was only the slightest tingling of jealousy at the sight of him kissing Miriam au revoir. So what had happened to her? Nonplussed by the void which had apparently opened up in her life, Joy thought she'd better go before her face gave anything away. "I'll come down with you."

She followed Mungo down the stairs, noticing that his hair grew as vigorously as ever. For twenty years she'd fiercely resisted the temptation to lay a loving hand on his neck where his hairline began, or more tempting still, caress his temples where his dark hair sprang so strongly. Somehow the urge to do so had almost bled away. But he was still a very desirable man. As Mungo walked down the stairs, he glanced back to look at her and winked. "We're forging ahead again, aren't we, Joy? Aren't you thrilled?"

"Oh, yes! We're moving on." But Joy wasn't sure whether she referred to the practice or to her passion for him.

When Mungo handed Dan the letter to read later that day, Dan was beside himself with delight. "This is marvelous! Just what we wanted, isn't it?" He looked up at Mungo and asked, "Isn't it?"

"Of course. We're all thrilled. It's a whole new world opening up for us, a new chapter. We'll get him here on home ground, you and me, and have it all out in the open. Get things clear right from the start."

"Absolutely. While I wouldn't mind building up the equine side, I don't want to be exclusively equine, remember. In any case, there wouldn't be enough work to begin with until we got more clients." Dan handed back the letter to Mungo and added, "That business of capital and wanting to be a partner, I'd like that."

"Let's get the meeting over with first. I'm in favor, but there's the others to consider before we can make concrete plans. Talking of plans, what's this about Lady Mary?"

"What about her?"

"Having dinner, I understand. The two of you."

"That's all. Nothing more."

Mungo held up his hands in surrender. "Right. Sorry. None of my business."

"No. Would you want me at this meeting?"

"Of course. You and I, but before the meeting I'll consult Colin and Zoe."

"Certainly. Must be off. I take it I'm staying, then?" Dan smiled. "I'd like it more than anything. But I'd buy a house and then the flat could be available for another vet should you decide to employ an additional one."

"Right. Thanks." Mungo held out his hand. "Let's shake hands on it."

WHAT really amazed Mungo that night was Letty's surprising response to his news. They'd agreed for Zoe and him to meet at Colin's house, and when they were seated, all with drinks in their hands, Mungo outlined what his proposals were. "I know there was a lot of opposition to Dan when he first came, but I'm rather hoping that you've all had a change of heart. There's no doubt about it that he's made changes which we didn't care for, but which have proved excellent once they were up and running. His knickknack idea has proved a winner from day one, and the changes he suggested to the small animal clinic hours are making that side of the practice pick up rapidly. Now we're faced with another big change. A fourth partner joining us, with capital, and transforming us into an equine practice. We musn't stand still . . . we've got to keep on going upward."

Zoe held out her glass for a refill and while Colin obliged, she commented, "We don't want change just for the sake of it, though."

"Absolutely not. But our premises cost thousands to maintain, and we're not out of the woods yet financially with the capital cost of the building. Dan's money would be a real boost. Plus the added income from Lord Askew, plus any more equine we might pick up . . ."

Colin interrupted with, "Don't be asking me to step in if he's away. I haven't done horses since I qualified. I wouldn't know where to begin."

Letty patted his knee. "Colin, don't underrate yourself."

Zoe was struck dumb with astonishment, and Mungo thought he hadn't heard correctly and had to ask her what she'd said.

"I said he musn't underrate himself."

"Oh no, certainly not, quite right, though I do see his point. I'd be alarmed myself, I have to confess." Then Mungo noticed what Miriam had told him, that Letty did look different: younger, less acidic, more friendly somehow. And it wasn't just her clothes and her makeup, though they were a vast improvement. It was something about her, a kind of melting, a sort of surrender. He shook off his analytical mode, thinking he was getting as bad as Miriam, and found that Zoe was being difficult.

"He's arrogant, that's his trouble; that's what gets my back up. He's always so *right*."

"But he is." This from Letty, which almost made the others' jaws drop in amazement.

"He is?" Mungo asked.

"Oh yes. Diagnostically he can't be bettered; let's face it."

Colin smiled a secret smile. "She's right."

"She is?" Mungo felt there was something going on he didn't understand.

"Oh, I am. I know I didn't like him to begin with, and he was very rude doing that Nazi salute when he saw me, but I deserved it. I was rude and very aggravating too."

Mungo now felt he was swimming in thick soup. "You were?"

"Oh yes. When really he's a very hardworking man putting in all the hours while we've been shorthanded. And to get Lord Askew back . . . and his horses to boot, is nothing short of miraculous." She downed the remains of her whiskey and held out her glass to Colin for a refill.

Colin continued to smile his secret smile, and Zoe and Mungo were still nonplussed while Letty, completely unaware of the surprise the others were experiencing, sat dreamily gazing into the gas fire. Out of nowhere she said, "We're thinking of having this fire taken out and fitting a wood-burning stove instead. Much more homely and welcoming, don't you think."

"Good idea," said Zoe. "But it's not for me. I don't like the work."

"But think of the pleasure."

Mungo decided he'd better get the discussion back online before he finally lost the plot. "So if I go ahead with this meeting, you'd be in agreement to have Dan as a partner I take it?"

Letty nodded vigorously. "Absolutely. Well, it's for Colin to say really, of course, he's the partner. But he does agree, don't you, Colin?"

"I most certainly do."

"Zoe, what about you?"

"Well, all things considered, I suppose I shall say yes. Let's hope he's sound financially, otherwise . . ." She gave a thumbsdown to indicate it was impossible without his money to back him up. "I've got a bit remote from practice politics since I've been at home with Oscar, but I'm back next week and I expect I'll be glad to have his support."

Mungo agreed with her by nodding his head. "He'll be buying a house, so the assistant's flat will be free. Shall we sell it, or keep it for an additional member of staff."

"With the poor state of farming at the moment, to be quite blunt, I can't honestly see us wanting to take on another vet for large animals. But I think hanging on to the flat would be prudent. Perhaps a member of the lay staff could use it for a while till we see some improvement." This from Colin, who for once

in his life had made a decision without first getting it approved
by Letty.

"So if Lord Askew and Dan and I make music at this meeting, I shall formally ask Dan to be a partner."

THE prospective partner in question was sitting in the flat on
the sofa which had once been Miriam's and Mungo's, brooding.
Partly wishing he were a fly on the wall in Colin's house and
thereby knew what was going on, and partly cogitating about
his life outside the practice.

To be frank, he hadn't got one. It was this blessed yearning
for Rose which was hampering everything he did. He wouldn't
for the world not have known her, but the fallout from their relationship was coloring his life to such a degree that it was hardly
worth living. Then he remembered how happy she always was,
how totally wholesome and scrumptious she was in bed, giving
every inch of herself to loving him, with nothing held back, and
how she'd taught him to do the very same. Dan thought about
how unspoiled she had remained, despite the wealth and political
power of her stepfather. He'd given her everything money could
offer, and yet she'd remained so very sweet.

Unconsciously his hand reached out to touch her as though
she were there with him on the sofa. He could almost smell her
perfume, feel the swirl of her hair as she turned toward him:
that long, ash-blond hair he so loved. She wore it plaited and
pleated and under control when she went out, but when they
were alone she'd have it hanging loose, scented and squeaky
clean.

She'd inherited her coloring from her mother. The domi-
neering old bitch had protected her only chick with a vicious-
ness which had to be witnessed to be believed. How Rose had
ever managed to survive her dominance and become such a

sweet, loving person he would never know. By all the rules Rose should have been mean-minded, devious, greedy and shallow, but she was none of those things, and he'd loved her with a passion that he knew would last to the end of his days. He couldn't cast her off.

He pulled her photograph out of his wallet, remembering the day he took it, the shimmering heat outside, the chill of the air-conditioned house, the almost frozen precision of the furnishings and decoration: the untouchable, sterile chairs, the stark barrenness of the dining hall, which killed one's appetite stone dead. All of it mirrored the destructive, strangling characteristics of her mother.

Whom could he find to replace his beloved Rose? He knew the answer before he formed the question: no one.

His phone rang and he snatched it up from under the cushion beside him like a drowning man grasping a lifeline. It was Phil Parsons babbling incomprehensibly something about Sunny Boy and Hamish, and could he come?

Glad of a diversion, Dan leaped to his feet and roared off in the Land Rover to Applegate Farm. Phil was standing, hopping anxiously from one foot to the other, in the farm gateway. "He's gone mad. Completely mad! He needs a jab."

Despite Phil's anxiety, Dan took time to put on his boots and some protective clothing. "Come on, hurry up!" As they strode together across the pitch-black yard an ambulance chugged heavily up the lane and parked behind Dan's vehicle.

"God, Phil! What's happened? An ambulance?"

Phil shouted to the ambulance men, "This way. This way." He waved his arm in a wide, sweeping gesture. "This way!" Dan switched on his torch to light the way through the gloom for the crew.

"Hurry up!" shouted Phil. "He's in a terrible mess." He led the way into the cow barn. Being winter, the so-called dairy cows were housed inside, and they were panicking. Lying to one side in the deep straw was Hamish, with Blossom kneeling beside him holding a bloodied towel to his chest. "Here he is. Please, save him! He's only a boy."

"Can we have more light?"

Phil hurtled about, lighting a couple of Calor gas lamps and hanging them from convenient nails in the beams. "Hurry up! The lad's dying."

As Dan's eyes became accustomed to the light he saw that several of the cows were gashed here and there as though they had been attacked. Streaks of blood had run down their flesh and were beginning to dry. In the ghastly silence which followed, the crew started work on Hamish. Then Dan could hear savage crashing and banging coming from Sunny Boy's stall.

Before he could question Phil about it, Blossom flung herself onto Dan, weeping and wailing. He put a protective arm round her shoulders and muttered comfort to her, though he'd no idea if his words were of any use because the ambulance crew were working with a kind of desperate energy which boded ill. His veterinary training made him able to turn his attention to the cows and he was pleased to find that none of them was in urgent need. A stitch here and there would suffice. It was the sound of Sunny Boy's frantic distress which really panicked him.

"Right. Let's get him to hospital. We've done what we can here."

Blossom screamed, "Hamish! My baby!" She left Dan and hurled herself toward Hamish, reeling back in shock when she saw the oxygen mask and the unconscious Hamish with his deathly white face and the ambulance man padding his chest in an attempt to stem the flow of blood. As they carried him out, she staggered after him into the cold night, wearing only a tiny cropped short-sleeved sweater and a skirt which just covered her bottom. "I'm coming! I'm coming, Hamish!" Her long, black-stockinged legs seemed to vanish from beneath her as she wobbled across the dark yard, so only the Day-Glo skirt and sweater appeared to be stumbling along behind the stretcher.

Phil stood in the barn, rigid with distress. Dan couldn't think of a word to utter. What was there to say? "They'll pull him round." "He's in the best place." "If anyone can save him, they will." Or the classic, useless, "Try not to worry." All this against a background of the noise coming from Sunny Boy's stall.

Dan cleared his throat. "We'll leave the cows here to settle a bit and then I'll inspect them and stitch any that need it. First, it's Sunny Boy. What the hell happened, Phil?"

It was only when he faced him that Dan realized Phil's balaclava below his eyes was soaked with tears. Silent, painful tears he couldn't control. As usual, only one eye matched up with the slits in the balaclava and Phil, with his one-eyed stare, said, "He went berserk."

"I see. What set him off?"

"Don't know. It just happened. Been all right with Hamish ever since the day he came. He went to give him his tidbits before he shut him up for the night while I checked the cows, and wham! Sunny Boy went for him. He'd got careless, had Hamish, bit too casual yer know, not brought up with animals he wasn't . . . isn't . . . and he'd gone in his stall and left the gate open. First I knew, Hamish was running in here with that damn great beggar after 'im, wild with temper, and before I knew it, he'd got Hamish cornered, got 'im down and stamped on 'im. The cows all took fright and he went for them, but they're more hurt by crashing into the walls and that than 'im."

Phil paused for breath. He gave a great shuddering sob and stood head bowed. The cows had stopped milling about, and all they could hear was Sunny Boy trashing his barn. "If Hamish . . . dies . . . Blossom 'ull never forgive me. God 'elp me." Phil took out his handkerchief and wiped his eyes. "She loves him like a son. And so do I." His shoulders heaved in sorrow.

"About Sunny Boy . . ."

Phil warned him. "Don't say it . . ."

In a low voice so as not to provoke him more than he could avoid, Dan said, "I have to say it. I'd be irresponsible if I didn't."

"*Don't say it.*"

"*I shall.* There must be something terribly wrong with him for this to happen. Like a brain tumor or BSE, whatever, he can't be trusted ever again."

Phil's chin was almost touching his chest.

"In fact, hard though it is for me to say this, I don't know if I want to be responsible for his health when he's so unpredictable."

Phil shook his head despairingly.

"That boy's life is hanging by a thread because of Sunny Boy's unpredictability."

Truculently Phil growled, "He should have shut the gate."

"If he had shut the gate, then Hamish would more than likely have been dead. Mangled dead. I'm serious, Phil. You've a big decision to make here."

"You wouldn't be saying that if it was someone you loved like I love Sunny Boy. You're a hard man. You don't understand pain, you don't." He thumped his chest with his clenched fist. "It's right here."

"I understand the pain all right, believe me." Privately Dan was thinking *I've got to persuade him to have Sunny Boy put down, but who the hell but me is there to do it?* They both listened and each thought the crashing about seemed to be getting worse. Dan said, "Well?"

"You asking me for a decision right now?"

Dan nodded. "How did you get him back in his stall?"

"I didn't, he went himself. He did a couple of turns round

the yard, then went in his stall; and I rushed and banged the gate shut, like as if he knew where he would feel safe."

"You were very brave. He could have turned on you."

"On me? Naw. Not me."

"I won't challenge you to prove that, just in case, but it seems to me he's gone totally irrational. Somehow I'm pretty sure it isn't BSE; the behaviour pattern isn't right. These cows are calming down now. Before I stitch them up, I'm going to climb up on something and have a look through that nicely cleaned window in Sunny Boy's barn and see what he's up to."

By the light of his torch, Dan found an old chair out in the yard and used it to climb on to look in. The stone walls of which his stall was made had withstood Sunny Boy's panic, as was only to be expected, but the gate had two bars snapped, and he was making inroads on the remaining ones. He was thrashing about uncontrollably, ramming his massive shoulders into the walls, thudding his head against his manger, rubbing it frantically against any available hard surface as though . . . that was it! It was as though he had an almighty pressure in his head and he couldn't bear it.

The answer was to wait until he was exhausted and then go in and give him the lethal shot. He could hear the house phone ringing. "Phil, your phone's ringing."

He heard Phil clump round to the house. Dan got down off the chair and waited. Phil came out. "Blossom. He's going into surgery as soon as."

"That sounds as if there's hope."

"It does. Blossom's beside herself. Well, now he's not dead there's no need to . . ."

Dan overrode this bright idea saying, "I can't go in as he is. Let's barricade the outside door in case he gets out of the stall . . ."

"Let me look." Phil borrowed Dan's torch and climbed up

to peer through the window. "Bloody hell." He stood on tiptoe. "Bloody hell! He's torn himself and no mistake. There's blood."

"I know."

"You can't leave him like that."

"I can."

"He'll need stitches."

"Tomorrow. I'll see to the cows and then I'm going home and coming back first thing in the morning to see to Sunny Boy."

"To stitch him, you mean?"

"No, I don't mean that."

Between them they got Phil's tractor and drove it up against the cow barn door so he couldn't possibly escape. Dan went back to the cowshed and began examining the cows, completely ignoring Phil. It took him an hour to attend to them and then he packed his bag and got ready to leave.

Phil had gone into the house in an attempt to shut the noise of Sunny Boy's frenzy out of his head. Dan opened the door and shouted, "Phil, I'm going. I'll be back first thing."

"You're not putting him down. I tell yer, yer not."

"Goodnight," Dan answered firmly.

COLIN went with him the following morning, and they were at the farm by a quarter to eight. They parked their vehicles on the cart track, put on their protective clothing and, with a sharp warning from Dan about the slurry pit, they trudged across the yard to the house. To Dan's relief there was an uncanny silence about the farm. The tractor was still parked at the cow barn door, and there was no sign of life.

"What the blazes! It doesn't change, does it." Colin gazed round first at the house and then the farm buildings and the filthy yard. "Years since I've been here. I'd forgotten."

Dan rattled the door knocker again. He thought he heard

voices inside the house, but no one came. "I'm going to have a look."

Colin followed him and watched while he climbed on the old chair. Dan peered in and saw Sunny Boy standing up, leaning heavily against a wall of his stall as though he wouldn't be able to stand if he didn't have its support.

"Take a look."

Colin climbed on the chair and looked in. "Gone quiet at least. But he looks odd. Almost comatose. Not asleep. More like he doesn't know what he's doing. Dazed, kind of. Doesn't seem like BSE to me, which it could have been, I suppose. No, the symptoms are not right."

"Just what I thought. Perhaps my theory about it being a brain tumor is right."

"God, he's a magnificent beast, isn't he? Such a shame to see him like this, Dan."

"Somehow we've got to persuade Phil to have him put down. He's too dangerous."

"I agree. He should never have kept him. What's wrong with artificial insemination?"

"He's proud of him."

"That's a load of sentimental tosh and you know it. The man's a farmer not an emotional do-gooder."

"I know that, but he loves him and you can see why."

They heard the house door slam shut and footsteps coming across the yard. Colin got down from the chair. It was Phil, his eyes looking as though they hadn't closed for a week.

"Morning, Phil. You remember Colin? Any news of Hamish?"

"Hanging by a thread. Blossom got home an hour ago. Crushed ribs, you see, and they've penetrated . . ." He wiped his eyes with an old rag.

"Well, at least he's holding on, that's something. I'm so

sorry about him. Well, Phil, I've brought Colin to give a second opinion. We both agree Sunny Boy is very, very ill, otherwise he would never have acted like he did. We both think his unpredictable behavior is due possibly to a brain tumor. There's absolutely nothing we can do about that. At the moment he looks as though he doesn't even know what he's doing."

Colin added, "The decision is yours."

"But we both feel . . ."

Colin interrupted with, "How about it, Phil? Hamish is more important than any animal to you, isn't he? Eh? Much more important, especially to Blossom, who's such a loving woman, as you well know. Even if Hamish recovers, you can't expect her to want to live here and see that magnificent animal still about."

Phil shook his head.

Colin continued, "He looks to be in such pain that it's almost cruel to leave him alive."

Dan said, "No vet likes putting an animal down, but we do know when it needs to be done for the animal's sake, and this is one of those moments, Phil."

"I hear what you say. I'll just have two minutes with him, and then . . ."

Dan couldn't believe he was hearing right. "Is that wise? He may not recognize you."

"Wise or not, he's not going without his closest friend saying goodbye."

He climbed in the tractor and backed it away from the door.

Colin and Dan stood in the doorway on red alert—quite still, watching. The gate hadn't been totally destroyed, and Phil climbed over the two still intact bottom bars and approached the bull quietly. Sunny Boy, occasionally shaking his head from side to side, was still leaning against the wall, dazed, his eyes clouded and lifeless. Phil spoke gently, holding out his hand with a few tidbits in it, but Sunny Boy never even recognized that his dearest friend was standing by him.

"Watch him, Phil. Watch him," Dan warned quietly.

By now Dan was almost in tears. It seemed so incredibly sad that at the last, Phil couldn't have the gratification of saying a proper goodbye to the pride of his life. Dan recalled his last goodbye to Rose, how he'd wondered that his brain could still send signals to his body when his heart had burst with such deep sorrow.

Ignoring the danger, Phil reached out to stroke Sunny Boy's dark-red flank, then he grew brave and stroked his huge forehead. Only the sound of Phil's quiet murmurs and the blowing of the breath of half a ton of bull broke the silence.

Phil backed away from him, stepped over the broken gate, and as he passed Colin and Dan said painfully, "I 'ave to say he's been getting unreliable for a while. Like that time he trampled on Scott. We thought it was the pain of his leg, but I think perhaps it was more than that. I've warned Hamish once or twice to be careful. It's come to something when I have to back away from 'im. Never had cause to do that in all his life. Get it done. It isn't 'im, not anymore." He stalked into the house and left Dan and Colin to do their job.

When Dan got back to the practice, Miriam asked him up to the flat for breakfast. "I know you've a list of calls, but come; I've put the kettle on. It's the least I can do."

She settled him at the kitchen table with a pot of coffee, cereals and croissants, a block of golden butter, and a dish of homemade marmalade and another of raspberry jam.

As he sat at the table, Dan rubbed his hands. "This looks wonderful. Thank you."

His thanks were so gloriously genuine that Miram placed a heartfelt kiss on his cheek. "You deserve it. It must have been harrowing at Phil Parsons's. How is he?"

"He went straight off to the hospital with Blossom. He's shattered. The hunt agreed to come for poor old Sunny Boy, and I didn't want him to see that. Neither did Blossom, so she persuaded him she was too tired to drive safely. They're an odd couple, on the surface so totally unsuited, yet . . ."

"Look at Bunty and Sergeant Bird . . ."

"What do you mean?"

"Oh, I shouldn't have said that. Don't tell anyone, but they're getting married on Saturday. She doesn't want anyone to know."

Dan's eyebrows shot up with surprise. "Now there is a very odd couple. I'd no idea."

"Poor Sergeant Bird. His mother died three or four years ago, and he's been desolate ever since. Needed a good woman, you know. Well, now he's got one."

Dan put aside his empty cereal bowl and began on the croissants.

Miriam clasped her hands round the mug of coffee she'd poured herself from Dan's pot, noticed how gratefully he was devouring his breakfast and said daringly, "You need someone to look after you too."

This was greeted by total silence. Dan put down his knife and picked up his cup, but didn't drink from it. "Do you have a twin?"

"No."

"Then I am destined to walk the path of life alone." He had somber vibrations in his voice when he said this, and Miriam had to laugh.

"Honestly, Dan, you are a flirt."

"I'm nothing of the kind. I'm speaking the truth. Mungo is a very lucky man."

"I'm lucky too."

"Yes. I can see that. There's much to be admired in Mungo."

"I'm so glad you're joining us. Oh! Perhaps I've jumped the gun there too. Sorry. My big mouth."

"If I didn't know you better, I'd think your gaffes today were deliberate."

"I'm so sorry. I seem to be off my guard this morning." Miriam felt extremely uncomfortable. She didn't really know what was the matter with her; she was usually the soul of discretion, and here she was with all her barriers down.

Dan finished his second croissant, drained his cup but didn't offer to leave.

"More coffee?"

"No, thanks. What was worse for Phil was Sunny Boy not recognizing him when he went in to say his goodbyes."

"I can imagine."

"That was the most awful bit." Dan stared at the plants on the windowsill. "Final goodbyes are never easy, are they."

"No."

"Damn stupid for a vet to be talking like this, but that great beast was like his own flesh and blood. I just hope to God Hamish survives."

"So do I." Tears brimmed in Miriam's eyes.

"I'm so sorry. I didn't think."

"That's all right. Just me being a bit soft in the head."

"Must go before I get maudlin."

They sat a while in companionable silence.

Head down so as not to catch his eye, Miriam dared to say, "One day, Dan, perhaps you'll be able to talk to me about her." When she finished speaking she looked him full in the face.

Dan's eyes registered shock momentarily, then he smiled. "Thanks for the breakfast. Much appreciated. Work to do." He paused for a moment with his hand on the kitchen doorknob, indecisive, lost in thought, then said, "Rose her name was . . . is."

Chapter

·14·

Of course Kate could have told her that, but the matter had never come up. Kate was far too absorbed anyway in her work and in sorting out the problem of her mother. She'd rung Kate exactly a week to the day from the appalling evening they'd had together in the Italian restaurant. Kate hadn't expected her to be so prompt, but she was, so maybe she did mean it when she said she wanted things to work out between them. They made arrangements for Kate to go for tea the following Saturday. Kate asked rather hesitantly if Mia could go with her if she wanted, and after a moment her mother had agreed.

But persuading Mia to go was altogether another matter.

"But I want you to go; I want you to see what it's like there. Please, for me."

"What good will it do? I don't want a relationship with her. You do. I don't. She's nothing to me. Because of her, your father could never love anyone again. She'd stolen him from me before your dad and I even met each other."

Kate was appalled about the thinking behind Mia's declaration, but she still wanted her there on Saturday. "But I want you to come."

"Why?"

Kate didn't really know why, but she said, "Because I want you to help me decide."

"Decide what?"

"I don't know."

"In that case, I won't go. Perhaps later when you know her better."

"I don't know if I want to know her better; that's the trouble."

"Only you can decide that."

"Please, Mia."

"No. I can't offer you what she can offer you. I can't provide you with pots of money, which she can, or the clothes and a better style of living and the holidays—none of that. All I've got to give is love and a roof over your head. Right? So off you go by yourself to make your own decisions. I won't stand in your way, and I don't want to hear any more about it." Mia got up and left the kitchen, came back in an instant, put her head round the door and added, "What's more, I don't fit in with her kind, not at all."

Kate had never known Mia to be so adamant, so irate; it made matters even worse and reaching a decision even more remote. Mia had changed toward her since her dad had died. But truth to tell, it wasn't so much since then; it was since her mother had turned up so unexpectedly.

Putting herself in Mia's position, it dawned on Kate that Mia felt threatened. Of course, that was it. Tessa had such tempting options to offer: money, a lovely home, position. And what had Mia to offer? Nothing except love, as she'd said, and a roof over her head. As if she, Kate, could leave Mia! She couldn't. That was what Mia needed to know.

Kate leaped to her feet and went to look for her. She found her in her bedroom, sitting on the bed. "Mia!"

Mia looked up at her, miserable and tearful. "I shouldn't have snapped, sorry."

"Yes, you should, because I've never made myself clear. You're my real mother, not Tessa. I'm not going to leave unless you prefer me to."

Mia shook her head disbelievingly.

Kate pressed on, "It's all terribly tempting—her money and such, the holidays, the support while I'm at college—but she doesn't love *me*; she loves the idea of a grown-up daughter who is old enough not to make babysitting a problem, someone she can mold into a likeness of herself. She wants me to be slim. I ask you, as if I shall ever be slim. Some chance! She fancies me well dressed. Smart. Up to the minute. A daughter to show off. Well, she's not getting that from me."

"Is that what you think? That she wants a model daughter?"

"Oh yes. The actual caring years are behind me, you see. I'm sure she'd much prefer me to be a doctor or a barrister or something. Being a vet is messy and cold and dirty and smelly, not nearly high profile enough. But being a vet is what I want to be. I've seen Scott . . ."

". . . of blessed memory . . ."

Kate had to smile. "Yes, of blessed memory, at work, and I've seen Dan—such completely different people but so dedicated. No matter how tired they are, how much they dislike the client, how unhappy they are about their own lives, the animals always come first. It's all so fascinating working out what's wrong. You can't ask a sheep or a cat where the pain is, or does it hurt when they cough; you have to work it out for yourself. That's the magic. That's what I *want to be*. A vet. When I see her next Saturday, you can bet she'll do her very best to persuade me otherwise. Well, she won't."

Mia took hold of Kate's hand and drew her down to sit beside her on the bed. "Your dad would have been so proud. So proud. I'm just sorry he didn't live to see you qualified."

"Talking about Dad, I didn't tell you everything about the attic."

"No, I know you didn't. I guessed there was something."

"There was a shoebox full of stuff about Tessa. Photographs and letters. I've half a mind to destroy it all, but for Dad's sake I feel I can't, not yet. If you want to see it, it's in the bottom of my wardrobe. But perhaps you don't, after what you've said."

Kate felt Mia's hand tremble slightly. "No, thank you. I don't want to know how much he loved her. He was fond of me in his own way, but not like he loved Tessa. I was useful and amenable and I loved you, and that had to suffice. For him and for me. But I do miss him. More than I ever thought. He was a good man, was your dad, and you were the light of his life. Do him proud, won't you?"

"I'll try. But I want you to know I'm not going to live with Tessa, because you're my mum and always will be."

Mia put her arms round Kate, and they hugged each other. Hard.

"Love you, Kate. I've seen a flat you might like. Will you come with me on Saturday to look round it, before you go to Tessa's. It's new and modern and bright, and there's a lovely window I could paint by, such wonderful light."

"Try and stop me." Kate stood up. "I'm not saying I shan't visit her or go shopping with her, or even on holiday with her, but . . . that's as far as it will go. Promise." She bent to kiss Mia and went downstairs.

A few minutes later she called up, "I've made a cup of tea."

"I'll be down." But Mia sat a while longer, feeling grateful for what Kate had said. Losing Gerry was bad enough, but to lose Kate . . . Perhaps she could housekeep for her when she qualified . . . or something. Mia thought of all the years she still had to live without the two of them. At forty-six, she possibly was only a bit more than halfway through her life. Well, she'd throw herself into living it to the full, and most important of all, she'd find a job, and at forty-six that was not impossible nowadays. A job where she met people and had a bit of excitement. Take hold of life and give it a good shake by the scruff, that's what she'd do. She straightened her shoulders, wiped away all trace of tears and went downstairs to drink tea with her Kate. Damn Tessa, she'd been stealing Gerry all these years, but it looked as if she wasn't going to steal Kate too. Kate, it would appear, was still *hers*.

In the event, Tessa phoned to say she had to be away for the weekend and could Kate come one evening during the week, say Thursday? So Kate did, but she found the long drive exhausting and arrived tired and certainly not in a diplomatic mood.

Thursday had been the day when Lord Askew came to agree to the practice taking over his equine work. Though it was Joy's day off, she came in and had been scurrying about right from the start, making sure everything was in apple pie order for the big moment. Hands on hips, she said, "Nothing, but nothing must go wrong today. Files at the ready, reception area spruce, chairs lined up, knickknacks in spanking order, and a goodly smell of disinfectant about the place, if you please."

Behind her back Stephie sniffed her disgust. "As if we don't do that every day. Anyone would think the queen was coming."

"Well, he is royalty around here, isn't he? And his account is important to us."

"I suppose. I'll get the spray ready to freshen things up."

The morning sped along at its usual pace, and before they

knew it, Dan was back from his calls, and Mungo and he were conferring on their strategy in Mungo's office. Kate was dispatched to carry down a tray Miriam had prepared with coffee pot and china cups so they could offer Lord Askew some refreshment in respectable cups instead of their collection of mugs given as gifts by the drug companies. It hardly appeared seemly to be offering him coffee in a mug advertising worming tablets. She'd intended going back to close the door at the bottom of the stairs to the flat, but a client had come in needing advice, and as Stephie was taking money and trying to answer the phone at the same time, Kate had to help; and all thoughts of the door slipped her mind.

At five minutes to twelve, just as Joy was beginning to come to the boil, there was the scuttle of dog claws on the reception floor, and Adolf the Rottweiler with Mr. Featherstonehough in tow appeared in reception. He omitted his usual pleasant greeting, and in a state of high tension he stuttered out, "He's got a lump come up on his groin. Can someone see him? It's inflamed, and he won't let me touch it." Adolf, too, was in a highly excitable state, on the verge of uncontrollable, and his front paws came up on the counter, and his great frothing mouth dripped pools of saliva on to the surface.

"Could you quiet him down, Mr. Featherstonehough, or it'll be impossible to examine him. Valentine's had a cancellation, so he'll be able to see you in about ten, fifteen minutes. Take a seat."

Mr. Featherstonehough dragged Adolf off the counter and went to find a seat. But just as Lord Askew opened the inner door, Adolf pulled free and went skidding across the polished floor toward the corridor leading to the back. Perkins appeared, and the wholesale fight to which they had all become accustomed began. Adolf coming in unexpectedly meant that they hadn't got the old fire bucket at the ready, and the fight progressed with almost terrifying ferocity. Total confusion reigned as clients lifted their feet, or grabbed their pets to avoid their flashing fangs. The air was filled with vicious snarling and growling.

Kate picked up a bucket filled with soapy water concealed in the accounts office, which had not been emptied from their cleaning frenzy earlier, and threw it, cloth and all, over the two dogs. Experience had improved her aim no end, and the two drew apart with the shock and shook themselves all over everyone. Perkins, his tail wagging furiously, eyes sparkling, grinned his delight at his own prowess, and Adolf, as he always did, went to lean his wet body against Mr. Featherstonehough, who'd also taken the brunt of the fallout from the bucket.

"Lively morning you're having." Lord Askew's great voice boomed through reception. "Feisty pair of dogs you've got. Like to see a bit of spirit, what the nation's short of. Now, young lady, kindly inform Mungo Price I'm here." Stephie disappeared to get Mungo.

The clients waiting their turns were glued to their chairs. More than one relied directly on him for their livelihood or their home and knew exactly how to mind their Ps and Qs. There came a chorus of "Good morning, my lord."

"Good morning to you all." He stood, this giant of a man, dominating them with his size and his bearing, a smile of approval on his lips. Kate began mopping up. Perkins went to have a word with Lord Askew. He showed his small front teeth in a grin and wagged his tail, looking up at him appealingly. For his pains he got his head, about the only dry part of him, well patted by Lord Askew's big beefy hand.

Mungo appeared, took the decision to ignore the whole fiasco and greeted his visitor with great style, leading him through the back to his office and asking Stephie to make the coffee as though nothing untoward had taken place. Kate had to admire him; she'd have been apologizing all over the place if she'd been Mungo. They could hear Lord Askew laughing loudly as they went out of sight.

The clients broke into quiet out-of-the-corner-of-their-mouths speech.

"Old bastard! Still, he took that well."

"Thieving old bastard yer mean."

"He's given 'em notice to quit next door to us."

"No!"

"Hard as nails he is." Several heads nodded at this.

The most vocal of the clients called out, "It's all over town he was coming back on your books, Stephie. Must be true, then."

Joy answered noncommittally on her behalf, and shot Kate and Stephie a warning glance. Kate, having mopped up the water, went to empty the bucket. Joy put their "slippery floor" warning sandwich board out on the wet patch, and peace was restored.

But the day had carried on in much the same chaotic fashion, so when Kate arrived at Tessa's, she was not her usual commonsense self. What she needed was Mia's kind of comfort. What she got was, "Are you keeping to that diet I gave you?"

"No, I'm not. I work hard, I'm studying and I've started playing badminton, but apart from that . . . no."

"I'm disappointed; just half a stone would make all the difference. Still, sit down. I thought you'd have been here earlier. I thought you finished at four."

"I should have done, but we were busy and I had the end-of-month accounts to finish."

"Go into the drawing room. I've got it all ready."

Kate plumped herself down on the sofa and tried to concentrate on what she had planned to say. But her mind drifted away to the day she'd just got through and to how thrilled she was that Dan had at last justified his existence and how she'd watched a jovial Lord Askew wend his way out, laughing and joking with Dan. What a coup for him! The rattle of the tea trolley brought her back to earth.

"Here we are. This must be just what you need." Tessa placed a delicate china plate in her hand and invited her to help herself.

"You know, I'm going to Norfolk for the weekend; why don't you come with me? Staying with friends who are clients of mine. They have a huge house, plenty of room and I'm sure they'd love to meet you."

"These sandwiches are lovely."

"Only the very best for my daughter. Which brings me to an idea I've had. I don't feel that being a vet is something I want my daughter to be. It's cold and dirty and . . . well, primeval almost, and you'll never be rich. But . . ." Tessa smoothed her skirt over her bony knees. "Why not try for the law? With me behind you . . ."

Head down so as to betray none of her feelings, Kate answered, "I hardly think so . . ."

"Why not?"

"Because"—Kate raised her head and looked full at her—"I don't want to."

"I see. That's not very helpful, is it?"

"No, it isn't, but it's the truth."

Tessa put down her plate rather sharply. "I'm doing my best here to make things come good between us. Why can't you be more cooperative?"

"Why should I? For the last nineteen years you have deliberately ignored my existence and now, because it suits you, you're all over me like a rash, even offering to change my career for me. I want to be a vet and a vet I shall be. I love it."

Tessa looked at Kate long and hard. "It's Mia, isn't it? She's poisoning your mind against me. Well, I can tell you she was welcome to Gerry, more than welcome. A more boring man, with his damned train sets and his biscuit factory, I couldn't hope to meet. It was no wonder I left."

"So why did you hop into bed with him? If he was so boring?"

Tessa shrugged her shoulders. "Bit of fun, really. Seeing how the other half lived, I expect."

Kate didn't reply for a moment, reminded how her dad had said he'd been a bit of rough for her. When she did, it stunned Tessa. "Never as long as I live will I either understand or forgive you for abandoning me. A more callous, mean, nasty, cruel thing to do to your own flesh and blood I cannot conceive. In fact, it makes me not even want to get to know you, because of the kind of person you must be to do such a thing."

"How dare you! You don't even begin to understand how I felt. I couldn't help myself." Out came the lace-edged handkerchief. "I really couldn't bear it."

"What's more, I will not hear one word against Mia. She is being so good to me about you, standing back and trying hard not to influence me. Nor do I want to hear one more bad word about Dad. I found all his letters to you. The photos he took, the letters he wrote to you after you left and never posted . . ."

"Letters to me, after I left that he never posted? What was the point of that, for God's sake?"

"To ease his broken heart, I expect. He adored you."

Tessa had the grace to look ashamed for a moment, but then that element of amazement at Gerry having been so devoted to her came back into her face. "Fancy, him with such passions. I'd no idea. Though I wouldn't have stayed even if I had realized. He was a bore. With his Beetle car and his obsession with keeping his house like some nineteen-thirties mausoleum. Hell!"

Kate felt as though her tea was choking her. She put her

cup on the trolley, her plate beside it and stood up. "If you imagine this is going to endear you to me, you are very wrong. The more I hear, the more I realize you and I have nothing in common. I've fantasized all my life about this wonderful mother I had, who one day would come and . . ." To her absolute fury, Kate burst into tears.

She blundered out of the room and headed down the hall, but the front door was locked and she hammered against it in despair with clenched fists.

She smelled Tessa's perfume close at hand, felt Tessa's arm round her shoulders and furiously shook it off. "Unlock this door. I want to go home. Please."

"My dear, I'm so sorry."

Kate snorted her disbelief. "For what?" She turned her tear-streaked, crumpled face toward Tessa and demanded, "Well? For what?"

"For letting you down so badly. For leaving you with Gerry. I know I shouldn't have done, but please forgive me. It's a long time ago now and . . . I realized before you were born that I'd made the most terrible mistake going to live with Gerry. He wanted me to marry him so you wouldn't be illegitimate. Well, he used the word bastard, which only served to emphasize the enormous gap there was between us. Frankly, I'd just lost my father, and I think I must have been looking for security, a base, someone to be a substitute for him, and at the time Gerry seemed to fit the bill. Then, when I found myself pregnant, I could have died. A baby from him! Oh, God! I didn't want one in the first place . . . but his! Heaven forbid. A girl like you, your mother's daughter, must have felt embarrassed sometimes at his coarseness, his lack of . . . well . . . refinement? I'm just so glad you've inherited my refinement. It makes me so proud. So do you understand my side of it a little better now?"

"Well, thanks for shedding so much light on the matter."

"I knew you'd understand." Tessa smiled and patted Kate's hand. "It's better to have cleared the air, isn't it?"

"You've certainly done that. You've made it all clear as crystal. You've made me feel a whole lot better, made me understand, you know."

"I have? Oh, that's good. I am glad."

"So much better, in fact, that I never want to see you again. I've tried to like you, but I just don't want to try anymore. It's finished. For good. Don't try to contact me ever. Never ever. I mean that. Goodbye." Kate found the latch for herself and left, closing her ears to the anguished howl her mother gave, possibly the only honest thing Tessa had done since that first fateful night they'd met.

Kate stormed down the steps onto the drive, couldn't unlock her car, managed it, got in, shut her coat in the door, released it, started the engine twice before it fired and drove out into the road in exactly the state of mind her father had always warned her against. Within two hundred yards she nudged the car in front as she stopped for the lights and was faced with a furious persnickety owner who physically threatened her, even though no damage had been done.

After they'd exchanged addresses, she pulled into a service road, switched off the engine and began to calm herself down. Five deep breaths later she knew she needed to get home. To Mia and the familiarity of that much-despised nineteen-thirties house her dad had so lovingly preserved. Stuff Tessa, just stuff her! Mother? Huh! Kate drove home, knowing that Tessa had killed dead the whole idea of being restored to that caring mother she'd so mistakenly conjured up all these years.

Chapter

·15·

Joy went up to see Miriam as soon as she got to work to make sure she was all prepared for the lunchtime celebrations. "I know I'm early, Miriam, but we're very busy today, and I thought I'd just confirm the arrangements."

"It's all in hand, don't worry. I've got everything out of the freezer, I've found a cloth to cover the desk, I've got the champagne in the fridge, and the paper plates and the glasses are all to hand. Don't fuss!"

"Sorry. But I want to make a good start for Dan. It's a big day and not just for him. I can't quite believe that Mungo has agreed; he's always been so set against equine."

"With the state of farming at the moment and no prospect of it improving, I rather think he's been forced into coming round to it. Have you time for breakfast?"

"I'll have a cup of tea. I don't need feeding. Duncan brought my breakfast to bed this morning."

"Did he? I didn't know he was that kind of person."

Joy smiled. "He isn't, but he's agreed to a new contract for a computer firm he's worked for before. Consequently, he'll be in another world for the next few months, so he's trying to appease me."

Hearing footsteps in the hall, Miriam said, "Here's Mungo. Sit down, Joy. Here's a cup." She handed Joy a cup and saucer, and Joy sat at the table. Mungo came into the kitchen and smiled at them both. "My two favorite women both breakfasting with me. What a pleasure." He gave Joy a kiss on her cheek, blew one to Miriam and sat down.

Joy kept her eyes on him, finding she could relish his freshly showered presence like a lovelorn teenager but without the old passionate longings. "You are a flirt, Mungo. A real flirt. No wonder we all adore you."

"You're being ridiculous."

Joy tapped his wrist with her forefinger. "No, I am not. All the girls think you're the absolute tops in men. Good-looking, handsome, athletic, charming. That smile of yours is worth millions."

"Nonsense."

"You'd have made a wonderful film star, romantic lead, you know; wouldn't he, Miriam?"

The phone rang and Mungo went to answer it.

Joy, enjoying being free from her anguish about Mungo, pressed her case with Miriam. "He would, you know. Don't you think so?"

"I'm biased." Miriam went to rescue a slice of toast which had sprung out of the toaster and landed in an African violet on the windowsill. "It doesn't hurt like it did, does it?" She gave Joy a smile as she spoke, but Joy didn't respond to it because she'd realized with a shock that it sounded as though Miriam must know her secret.

Miriam gave Joy the slice of toast, and absentmindedly Joy accepted it and reached for the butter. By mistake she spread raspberry jam on it too, which she didn't really care for at breakfast, but it served to cover her confusion. After all she'd said about never letting Miriam know, and here she was on the brink of it all being out in the open. What could she say to avoid a major revelation?

Before Joy had collected her thoughts, Miriam said in a small voice and almost reluctantly, "I've always known, you know."

Joy's head shot up in horror.

"Right from the first day I met you. It was the pain in your face when Mungo said I was his wife. It wasn't surprise I saw; it was terrible, terrible pain. I knew all right."

"Oh, God!" Joy was frozen with shock.

Miriam sat down and calmly began to eat her cereal. "Don't worry, Joy. But you did give yourself away, you know. It was the look in your eyes when I caught you watching him. The way you lit up when he spoke to you. Mungo doesn't realize, I'm sure, and I shan't say a word."

It was the sweetness of the way Miriam spoke, the gentleness, the obvious effort not to hurt which devastated Joy; there was no anger or jealousy, only sadness and understanding.

With her head in her hands, Joy tried to explain. "I've never wanted you to know . . . I'm more sorry than you'll ever know. I'd no idea you knew; you've always been so . . . Never let him know, please . . . I wouldn't want him to and I'm so sorry, Miriam; so sorry, but he's just so . . . "

"But what about Duncan? Does he know?"

Joy nodded.

"He must be so hurt. Why ever did you marry him feeling like you do? The poor, dear man."

Mungo came back. "My first client won't be in till later this morning. Car broken down on the way, so I can have a nice comfortable breakfast and read the paper before I go down." He looked closely at Miriam as she handed him his cup of tea. "All right, darling?"

"Fine."

Joy stood up, her toast left half eaten on her plate, her tea not touched. "I'll switch the phones through, then you can eat in peace. See you later, Miriam. We decided on twelve-thirty for Dan's celebration. He knows and he'll make sure to be back." She shot out of the kitchen with the speed of light.

"What's got into her?"

Smoothly Miriam said, "Getting worked up about the celebration. There's going to be quite a crowd. I've planned champagne and orange juice for those who don't drink. I'm not bothering with wine as there won't be enough time."

"Where? In here?"

"No. There's not enough time like I said. We're holding it in reception. If clients come they can join in. I've done plenty of food."

"You're a marvel, darling, you really are."

"I love doing it and after all, I've got my own way, haven't I?"

Mungo grinned at her. "You have, haven't you. We're all putty in your hands."

"Do I come across as manipulative? I do hope not."

"Of course you don't. Not at all. Just persuasive. Yes, that's right, persuasive."

Miriam had to laugh at his attempt at discretion. "All right. All right."

"I'll have more tea, please."

"Certainly. What does it feel like to be a film star?"

"She's talking rubbish and you know it. It's all nonsense. She's just pulling my leg. I'll get the paper."

Miriam smiled to herself as he left the kitchen, certain he hadn't realized about Joy's feelings for him. In her mind's eye she could see Joy's face the day Mungo had introduced her as his wife at the old surgery. The terrible shock she saw registered there and the pain. It had been disconcerting and because she was so nervous she hadn't been able to deal with it at the time. Afterward, from the security of her own deep love for Mungo, she'd taken it in her stride. Joy, she had realized, presented no threat to her and Mungo. The one most hurt must be Duncan.

When Mungo came back in, Miriam put an arm round his shoulders and hugged him. "Love you, darling."

"I love you. Seen this headline? What will they come up with next?"

MIRIAM organized the two Sarahs and Stephie to carry the food and drink down to reception. "This all looks gorgeous, Miriam, absolutely lovely. Better than a packed lunch any day. I don't suppose . . ." Sarah One raised her eyebrows, quizzing Miriam with a hopeful look.

"Get on with you. I've better things to be doing than making lunch for everyone every day. Take care down the stairs. I've laid out the cloth already."

By twelve-twenty-five they'd had a phone call from Dan to say he was running ten minutes late, but he'd be there.

"Typical!" said Stephie who'd taken his call. "Why can vets never be on time? Ten minutes. I guess that means twenty minutes really, but we can't start without him, can we?"

They'd all gathered: Bunty; the two Sarahs; Stephie; Annette; Kate; Letty; Colin; Zoe; Zoe's mother with little Oscar; Graham; Rhodri; Valentine and his wife, Nina; Mungo; Miriam; Duncan and Joy. All they needed was the man himself.

"Got a speech prepared, Mungo, have you?"

Mungo smiled at Letty. "Indeed I have. Not often we welcome a new partner, is it?"

"No. Sorry to be mentioning money, but it is all watertight, is it?"

"Of course. Naturally. All legal."

"Good. He'll be a great asset."

Hunger and pleasurable excitement were just beginning to get the better of them when the glass door opened and they all prepared to applaud, expecting it to be Dan at last. But it wasn't. On the mat stood a stunning young woman. From the top of her beautiful head all the way down to her feet, she shouted wealth and style.

"Hi, there!" She looked at them all staring at her and added, smiling, "Thanks for the welcoming committee."

Her slight American accent took them by surprise, and they fell silent.

She said, "I'm looking for Danny Brown?"

Miriam answered, "So are we. He'll be here any moment. And you are?"

"I'm his wife. Rose Franklin Brown."

If a bomb had dropped, they couldn't have been more stunned. En masse they stood open-mouthed with bewilderment. Kate recognized that this was the girl in the photograph, but she had become so convinced that she had died that the sight of her, apparently coming back from the dead, silenced her completely.

Rose surveyed them each in turn and eventually, getting no response from anyone, she asked, "I guess it must be a shock?"

"A surprise rather," said Miriam. "Yes. A real surprise. We're about to have a celebration lunch you see, because he's officially a partner from today. He's never said . . . though he did mention the name Rose to me once. You're from . . . ?"

"The States. Flown in, hired a car and driven here." She looked down at herself and said, "I must look a mess. I'd like to freshen up before I see him. Is that possible?"

Miriam stepped toward her. "Of course. Come upstairs to the flat and use our bathroom."

"Thank you. I appreciate that."

They all waited until they were sure Miriam had closed the door at the bottom of the stairs to the flat and then a hubbub broke out.

"Did you see those gorgeous clothes?"

"That fur coat will have to go."

"That fur coat must have cost a fortune."

"To say nothing of the handbag. Beautiful leather."

"And that wonderful blond hair. That's not come out of a bottle."

"I bet when she's done up, she'll look fabulous."

"I'd never dare to drive just like that." Stephie snapped her fingers. "Straight off the plane and here. What a woman!"

"But, Dan, *married*."

Letty commented, "Dan's a sly puss, isn't he? I wonder what the story is behind her sudden appearance, and pregnant too."

"Letty!"

"She is, I'm certain."

"There'll be hell to pay if it isn't his," Zoe said sotto voce, with an odd look in her eyes.

The comments stopped when they heard the door being opened and Miriam's footsteps.

They all looked expectantly at her as she came into reception.

"She's coming down when she's freshened up. She's lovely, isn't she? Such a sweetie! But she's totally exhausted. She needs to sleep and sleep and sleep."

Zoe commented, "Someone's going to get a surprise."

Letty proclaimed, "I think 'shock' would be more appropriate. I don't think he knows she's coming; otherwise you would think he would have said . . ." She broke off when they heard the back door open and Dan's quick step coming down the corridor.

Miriam swiftly stood in front of them all and put her finger to her lips. "Not a word."

The air of suppressed excitement bubbled about as Mungo said his speech of welcome to the practice, seconded by Colin, who, unusually for him, spoke with verve and enthusiasm, and was gazed upon approvingly by Letty. Graham, by practice tradition, opened the bottles of champagne, the two Sarahs poured out, and Valentine and Nina served it to everyone on two silver trays purloined from Miriam's kitchen.

Dan called for silence after the toast and made a speech. "First, I should like to say thank you to you all for making me so welcome to the practice. I know I made a bad start"—cries of agreement from everyone—"but I hope perhaps I may have made up for it by now. I have every intention of making a great success of the equine side of the practice, which, thanks to Mungo, I have been given the opportunity to do. I know some of my initiatives have not been welcome, but I think you have to admit that my knickknacks have proved a huge success and that the new staffing rosters are a boon." He raised his glass. "To everyone, your very good health and a very prosperous future for us all. I give you a toast: Barleybridge Veterinary Hospital and its great future!"

When they'd all drunk the toast, Miriam called out, "Food, glorious food! Please eat it all. I don't want any left for Mungo and me to finish up."

Zoe nudged Miriam and whispered, "She's a long time. Where's she got to?"

"I don't know."

"If she doesn't come down soon, you'll have to go and see. Do you think she really is pregnant, or is it Letty fantasizing? I can't think *she's* much of a judge, can you?"

"It was difficult to tell with her coat on. If she is, wow!"

Two clients appeared early for the afternoon clinic and found themselves being fêted with a champagne lunch.

Dan went round to each of the staff in turn to have a word

of thanks and say how much he was looking forward to working with them on a permanent basis. Eventually Miriam, after he'd completed his rounds, could wait no longer. She took him to one side and said, "Dan, there's someone up in our flat who's come to see you. Take a plate of food and a glass of champagne with you."

"Someone wanting to see me? Who is it?"

Miriam spread her hands and shrugged her shoulders. She selected food, arranged it on a plate, gave him a glass of champagne and pushed him gently toward the corridor. "Go on. Off you go."

"Why won't you tell me who it is?"

"Just go, Dan. Do as I say." She watched his progress toward the flat with tears in her eyes. Miriam had no idea what Rose's sudden arrival was all about, but she fervently hoped Dan was about to get everything he had ever wanted.

Dan put the glass of champagne down on the carpet while he opened the door to the flat. He picked it up and went into the hall. It was a moment before he smelled her perfume. In a daze he went to the kitchen but found it empty; he tried the dining room second, knowing full well he was putting off the dreadfully scary disappointment of finding it was someone else wearing the same scent as her, for he hardly dared to hope. It was such an impossibility. Finally he went where he should have gone in the first place: into the sitting room. Her fur coat lay on the arm of a chair. The smell of her perfume was stronger in here. Then he saw her, his beautiful Rose. Asleep, lying on the sofa. The powder compact he'd bought her in New York lay open, ready for use in her hand. Obviously, she'd been too exhausted to stay awake. She'd undone her hair, and it lay spread out over the arm of the sofa. Dan put down the food and the glass on a side table and went to kneel by her.

In total silence he studied every inch of her, savoring his

remembrances of her: her jokes, her laughter, her love of her work, her enthusiasm for life, her exuberance. His hand tentatively reached out to touch her as he'd done dozens of times since they'd parted, but this time was different, for she was here, breathing, sleeping. He put his ear close to her face and felt her breath on his cheek. Very gently he touched her hand, grasped her fingers, those delicate, expressive fingers he so loved. He knelt there, wallowing in his joy. Then he couldn't resist giving her cheek a light kiss.

Rose's eyes flicked open. "Danny, it's you! Forgive me! Forgive me for driving you away."

Dan was so choked by his emotions that his voice stopped in his throat.

"I've caused you such anguish. I had to come. I've come just as I am. I've left everything behind. Will you have me?"

Dan nodded, hardly daring to believe.

"I had to come, you see, to bring you him." She sat up so he could see for himself she was pregnant.

Dan simply couldn't take it in. One minute he was pining for her, the next she'd materialized in front of him, and pregnant too.

He laid a reverent hand on her stomach, and the barely distinguishable word "Rose" came from his mouth. She kissed his lips so sweetly, so gently, begging his forgiveness. "Am I forgiven, my darling? Am I? I'm here to stay if you'll have me."

Gruffly, Dan replied, "There's no need to ask. I let my temper get the better of me, but your mother had to be told. She'd driven me right to the edge. So, does she know you've left for good?"

Rose laughed. "She might by now. I walked out of the house, leaving her thinking I was having lunch for old times' sake with friends from the office, but instead went to the airport and boarded a flight. I couldn't deny you your son. We both need you. I'm so terribly tired, I just fell asleep. That drive. I'd forgotten English roads and roundabouts."

"And I'd forgotten how courageous you are. So you were pregnant then, as you half suspected?"

Rose nodded. "With a boy. My mother can't reconcile herself. She simply won't acknowledge I'm carrying a baby of yours. I'm glad to have made the decision to leave. If all this has proved nothing else, it has proved I cannot live without you."

"Nor me, you. I wrote but you didn't reply, so I sent e-mails. You read them?"

"I didn't get the letters; I guess my mother saw to that. But when your e-mails began coming, I lived for them. But I was so angry deep inside, I didn't reply. I'm a fool, an absolute fool." She took hold of his hand and, raising it to her lips, kissed it.

Dan shook his head. "Never that. Never a fool."

"And you're a partner, they tell me?"

Dan grinned. "I am indeed. I'm buying a house. When you've slept, I'll take you to see it. You'll love it. It will appeal to your Englishness. We can furnish it together. You and I."

Rose smoothed back his hair from his face, placed her hands either side of it and looked deeply into his eyes, studying every facet of the face of this man she adored more than life. How could she ever have allowed him to leave? How could she ever have listened to untruths and, worse, believed them? "Never again as long as I live shall I allow anyone to come between us. That's my solemn promise. Daniel Jonathan Franklin Brown shall be the first of many. Believe me. The first of June is B-day."

"It's going to take some getting used to, being a father."

"And being a mother."

"Will you need yours when it comes to the time?"

Rose shuddered. "God help me, but I never want to set eyes on her again."

"Will she guess where you've gone?"

"I hope not."

"Rose!"

"She'd only follow me. I'm exhausted, Danny. Can I go and sleep in your flat?"

"I'll take you home this minute. We'll leave introductions to another day. I know they'll all understand."

Rose stood up. "That sounds like the best offer I've had in months."

An excerpt from

COUNTRY LOVERS,

THE THIRD BOOK IN THE BARLEYBRIDGE SERIES,
COMING TO BOOKSTORES IN APRIL 2007

Chapter

· 1 ·

It was Joy, as practice manager, who struggled with the staff roster every month, and with Graham Murgatroyd off with flu, and Dan hovering distractedly waiting for the birth of his son and likely to be off for at least a week, and Rhodri behaving like the lovelorn chap he most decidedly was, it was providing more than usually difficult to plan June's staffing. She sat in her office in the last week in May, planning and replanning until her head spun. It was no good; she'd have to get Duncan to take a look. Joy rested her head against the back of her chair and closed her eyes. Briefly she dropped off, drained by a long, busy day. Moments later, someone clearing his throat disturbed her.

"Sorry, Joy, to disturb you but . . ."

"My fault. I've developed a splitting headache trying to plan the roster for June; it should have been done days ago." She rubbed her eyes to refresh them and saw Mungo looking down at her with sympathy. Her heart raced, though not quite as wildly as it had at times during the last twenty years. She sat upright. "What can I do for you?"

"Just to say I've finished operating for today, and I'm going up to the flat. I know you're shorthanded, so Miriam and I are not taking this weekend away we promised ourselves, just in case."

"That's wonderful. Thanks. If things get any worse, I shall be doing the operating myself!"

"You've had plenty of experience assisting me in the past. I've no doubt you'd do an excellent job."

Joy laughed. "I don't think so; things have moved on since I first helped you. New techniques, new equipment. No, no, our reputation would go straight down the pan! As they say, you're only as good as your last operation."

Mungo leaned across the desk and placed a kiss on her cheek. "Thanks for all you do and thanks for being such a good friend to Miriam. She does value your friendship."

Joy's eyes slid away from his face. "And I hers. Must press on. I'm taking this roster home to Duncan. He'll sort it for me. There's a solution somewhere, but I can't see it."

"Don't hesitate to ring if you need me. Anytime, and I mean it. It's just a difficult patch, and we have to gut it out."

"I'll ring; you can bet on that." Joy allowed herself to watch him leave, to smile at him when he turned to say, "Be seeing you," to enjoy his handsome bearing, his restless energy, those splendid eyes and the gentleness of his mouth. She swallowed hard. There I go again, she thought, just when I'd begun to think he didn't matter anymore. When he'd closed the door behind him, she clenched her fist and banged it on the desk in anger. Would she never learn he loved elsewhere? That his kiss was that of a comrade and not a lover and never would be.

Duncan. Duncan. She focused on Duncan's face as she'd seen it that morning when the alarm had gone, making no impression on him at all. He lay snugly tucked in right against her back, one arm laid carelessly across her waist. When she'd tried to get up, he'd held her down and grunted his contentment. But she'd managed to turn over so she could look at him. She was always surprised how young he looked first thing. Which he was, all of nine years younger.

Joy said, "Got to get up. Let me go."

"Five more minutes."

"No."

"Please." It was more of a command than a request. The arm across her waist had tightened and kept her there.

Joy tolerated the five minutes and then pushed off his arm and sat up on the edge of the bed. But he followed her and was kissing the back of her neck with his arm was round her waist again, gripping her.

"Duncan. Please. I'm going to be late."

Duncan turned away from her without a word.

She'd stood up and headed for the bathroom and a shower and for an assessment of her allure in the bathroom mirror. It hadn't made good viewing. That mood had stayed with her all day and was still with her as she parked her car and went into reception the following morning and found she was five minutes late.

Ordinarily she would have apologized for being slightly late, but this morning, instead, she could find fault with absolutely everything. In reception, Stephie and Annette came in for a few broadsides, Sarah Cockroft for leaving dirty, blood-streaked operating sheets out on the laundry worktop instead of putting them immediately in the washing machine, and finally Mungo for arriving late for his first appointment. "You should know better than to leave your first client waiting."

"Sorry."

Mungo saw the way the wind blew and escaped Joy's office as soon as he could, salving his conscience by being as charming as he possibly could to his client. "Please, forgive me. Do come this way."

"Don't worry yourself, Mr. Price, we know how busy you are."

Joy saw the owners of the dog shake his hand and smile, and she thought he could charm the devil himself, he could.

He ruffled the head of his patient and asked, "This is Teddy, is it? Hello, old chap." To the owners he said, "Now, tell me in your own words what the problem is."

Joy watched him lead them into his consulting room, and smiled grimly to herself. It really wasn't fair for one man to have so much charm and such good looks. She saw Annette putting her empty coffee mug down on the reception desk. "You know how much Mr. Price dislikes empty mugs standing about in public view. Take it away. Please."

Duncan had organized the roster to her satisfaction, and after she'd pinned it up on the staff notice board and made sure every one of the veterinary staff had a copy in their pigeon holes she put her own copy on the noticeboard in her room and sat down to think.

But not for long. Dan Brown came in to see her.

Dan had lost weight these last few weeks and was not looking quite as stocky or well built as he used to. But the craggy face and the penetrating brown eyes were still there and so, too, was his in-your-face-energy, which sometimes caught one on the raw, but not now, not since he'd won her over. She greeted him with warmth and affection. "Dan! You're soon back; is everything all right with Rose, you know?"

"She's fine; we got there early and they're delighted with her, and we've to go back next week same time if the baby hasn't happened in the meantime. She's furious that she can't drive herself anymore."

"Have they said she shouldn't?"

Dan gave the happiest laugh he'd given since she'd known him. "No. The truth is she can't get behind the wheel and reach the pedals."

"Oh, well! Go have a coffee or something and take a rest. You've no calls for the moment."

"None?"

"None whatsoever."

"Right. I will."

"You do that; it may be your last quiet day for some time!"

"We can't wait for the baby, you know. Just can't wait. Rose's stepdad has arrived and is out buying every item of baby equipment he can find. We wanted to wait . . . not tempt fate, you know."

As Dan went off to take his break, Joy said quietly to herself, "I can understand that." She had just finished speaking when she heard the most terrifying sounds coming from reception. The papers on her desk flew in all directions as she squeezed out of her chair and raced to see what was happening.

Joy was appalled at the scene that met her eyes. A very large, heavily built dog of uncertain ancestry had a cat in his mouth. The cat was hanging upside down, yowling and trying to swing itself round to scratch at the dog's face, its claws unsheathed, its mouth wide open, but the dog was hanging on tightly, his fangs exposed below his drawn-back dewlaps.

The waiting clients were panic-stricken, clutching their pets to them, lifting their feet to avoid the whirling dog. Mrs. Parr, the owner of the cat, was screaming with terror. "Get him off! Quick! Somebody! Get him off. Oh! Oh! Oh!"

But the dog was intent on his trophy and had no intention of giving it up.

The clients were behaving like a coop full of chickens with a fox at their throats, and Annette and Stephie were hysterical and no more use than a pair of mice.

Above the clamor Joy shouted, "Who owns this dog?"

A small, agitated man spoke up. "Bingo! Let go! Bingo! Let

go!" He was sweating so much his glasses were steaming up. "He hates cats."

Mrs. Parr shouted. "Get 'im off! Oh hell!" and promptly fainted. Another client began to beat at the dog with a magazine, which only served to infuriate Bingo even further. He altered his grip on the cat, was now holding it even more firmly, and the cat had stopped struggling. Joy grabbed his collar, and instantly, Dan, appearing apparently from nowhere, took over from her, stood astride of Bingo and deftly manhandled the dog's head to the ground, keeping a firm grip with both hands on its head and neck and his knee on its flanks. Taken by surprise the dog released its hold on the cat and it crawled away, trembling, its fur bristling and its mouth open wide, spitting hoarsely.

Joy took charge.

"Right. Stephie! Ring for an ambulance for Mrs. Parr. Annette! Capture the cat and put it in a cage in intensive care. Dan! Get that dog in the back and tie it up. Tight! I'll get a blanket for this lady."

She came back into reception with a blanket and a pillow. A client with her own cat safe from harm in its basket, got up to give her a hand.

Mungo came out with his clients to find uproar. If Joy hadn't been so preoccupied, she would have laughed at the astonished expression on his face. "What on earth . . . ?"

Dan finally managed to drag Bingo out. Annette caught the petrified cat and carried it away to make it safe, and Stephie called out, "The ambulance is on its way."

"Thanks, Stephie!"

Dan came back and faced Bingo's shivering owner. "He's yours?"

The man nodded.

"Why have you brought him in?"

"For his injections; it's time."

"Yes?"

Realizing that he was holding a very public discussion, Dan broke off and invited Bingo's owner into an empty consulting room.

The man shuffled after him, still sweating, still shivering.

"Sit down. Please." Dan pulled the desk chair forward and waited for the man to sit, then leaned against the examination table and asked, "Yes? Mr. . . . ?"

"Tucker. Alan Tucker." He pulled out a handkerchief and mopped his top lip. "She should have had the cat in a basket or something. It wasn't Bingo's fault. Not at all, no. The cat spat at him and tried to scratch him. What else is a self-respecting dog supposed to do? I ask you."

"Apparently you haven't got him under control, or you could have stopped him."

"Under control in circumstances like that? He's an angel at home. We've two children, little ones," he gauged their height with his hand, "this big, and he's like putty in their hands. They can ride on him, sit on him, cover him up with a blanket as if he's baby, anything they like and he never murmurs. It's only cats he can't stand."

Dan looked a little skeptical at this. "So you say."

Alan Tucker mopped his face with his handkerchief again. "She should never have brought her cat in without a cage . . . it was her fault."

"You have got a point there. But I can tell you this: Never once in all the years I've worked as a vet have I known of such an attack. All the animals are so overcome by the smells and the strangeness or have memories of having been here before for injections or treatment that they are usually very subdued. He was alarming."

"I still say it was the cat's fault . . ."

"Well, Mr. Tucker, quite what the owner of the cat will be thinking when she's come round, I don't know. It has all been very distressing. You are a client of ours, are you?"

"First time. We've only just moved here; changed my job, you know. Dog's all upset, you know, children too. New vet, new house, new garden, different walks—it's all been too much for Bingo, and then, on top of all that, that bloody cat."

"That's understandable. Now, I must see to the cat. But be aware, Mr. Tucker, that he's nervous. Keep an eye on him when he's with the children. He's big, and could do a lot of damage. I'm serious, a special eye till he's calmed down. OK?"

Mr. Tucker stood up. "Thanks for getting him under control. I was too shocked to do anything. Never seen him like that."

Dan opened the door. "Take care, Mr. Tucker. Bring him back when he's feeling happier. I'll get him for you, and then I'll see to the cat."

When Mr. Tucker came back into reception holding Bingo tightly, the ambulance had just arrived and Mrs. Parr was being taken out in a wheelchair. Mr. Tucker said to her, "I'm so sorry."

Ashen faced, she replied, "My cat. Where's my Muffin?"

Joy said, "We'll take care of her; she'll have the best of attention. The vet's examining her now. "

"Thanks. I really don't need to go to hospital. I only fainted. I think I'll just go home." She made to get out of the chair.

Joy gently pressed her back. "Believe me, it's best to have a checkup just in case. And it will make me feel easier in my mind that you've been looked at. I'll ring tomorrow and let you know about Muffin, or if you feel up to it, you ring later today. I'm so sorry this has happened."

After Mrs. Parr had gone, Stephie said, "Why were you so insistent that she go to the hospital? There was really nothing wrong with her."

"You're a doctor, are you?"

"You know I'm not."

"And neither am I. Best to make sure in case of legal proceedings."

"But she's nice; we've known her for years."

"She's never had her cat attacked before though, has she? She might feel she could be safe to bring her cat here, which is quite right, but today she wasn't . . . so . . . you never know." Joy wagged her finger at Stephie and disappeared into the back to find Dan.

He had carried the cat into a consulting room and was gently examining her. She wasn't in the best of moods for a close examination, and Dan was having to be very careful not to stress her more than necessary.

Dan glanced up at Joy as she watched his sensitive hands moving so sympathetically over the cat as he assessed her injuries. "She's been punctured here, look, one of his fangs. She's in deep shock. We'll have to set up a drip, can't do anything until she stabilizes. Nothing broken, I think."

"I'll set up the drip. The girls are all busy."

"Are you sure?"

"Absolutely. If Mrs. Parr had brought her in a cat carrier, none of this would have happened."

"Exactly. Mr. Tucker says the dog's as soft as butter usually. Just cats he can't stand."

With a wry smile Joy said, "That's plainly obvious."

"Even so, I've warned him to keep an eye on him. It really was a nasty attack."

Mungo took a couple of minutes between clients to find out what was happening. "No farm calls this morning?" he asked.

"None so far. Colin's out, but he only has three calls."

"So what about the cat? How is she?"

"Shocked. Joy's setting up a drip. I've found a hole where his fang caught her, but she's too shocked for me to do anything about it."

"New client, was he? Didn't recognize the owner."

"Yes. Claims the dog can't abide cats. Otherwise no problem."

Mungo shook his head. "Rose not pupped yet then?"

Dan laughed. "Not yet. You'd better not say that to her; she wouldn't find it funny at the moment."

"Exciting times we live in, eh?" Mungo clapped Dan on the shoulder, added, "Thanks for that just now. Got a client. Must go."

Muffin the cat was an exceptionally beautiful Siamese, and one after another the staff came to see her. "Isn't she gorgeous? Just gorgeous," Stephie said, and Annette thought she was utterly beautiful too and very take-homeable. "Hope she's going to be all right. The poor thing. I hate big dogs."

"Muffin. It's a poor choice of name for such an elegant cat. Sounds like a name for an ordinary cat, not an aristocrat."

Rhodri came in at this point.

Stephie turned to greet him. "Good morning, Rhodri, come to see our new patient?"

"Who organized this?"

"Dan did. You had a client, and we had to do something quicko."

"I see. Did no one think to consult me? I am the only small-animal vet on duty this morning."

This outburst silenced the two girls because they honestly didn't know how to answer him.

Rhodri turned on his heel and went back to his consulting room.

Stephie looked at Annette and they both pulled a face.

"Honestly! He gets worse. It's always poor Dan he has his knife into."

. . .

HALFWAY through the morning, Dan went home to Rose, promising Joy that if a farm call came in, he would go. Rose was seated in her favorite chair by the French windows, looking out to the garden. Beside her on a small table was the book she'd put down the moment she heard him coming. "Darling! What are you doing home at this time? How lovely."

"It's one of those strange mornings when there are no calls for me. It can't last, I'm quite sure. You all right?"

"I'm fine. Absolutely fine. So you've had an idle morning then?"

"No, not really, just a bit of an upset at the morning clinic."

"Dresden china I am not. Please tell me."

"Sorry. Huge great dog attacked a cat in the waiting room. Total uproar."

"Poor thing."

"I had to tackle it to the floor and then drag it out and tie it up."

"You didn't have to put it down?"

"It did occur to me that perhaps it would be for the best, but one can't just rush about putting dogs down; it's not done and it would give the practice a bad name."

Rose grinned up at him. "It most certainly would. I shall have a dog or a cat sometime. I always wanted a pet, but mother would never let me. Too messy, she said."

"Then you shall. You can choose, so long as it's not a huge one like a Saint Bernard. This cottage isn't big enough."

"Could you get me a glass of water, Danny, please? Save me having to heave myself out of this chair."

"Of course. Nothing stronger?"

"Like orange juice?" Rose smiled at him. It was a smile he had missed those months while they'd been apart. He should never have walked out on her. But the blazing row he'd had with her mother over an entirely mythical "woman" she swore he had hidden away had hurt him beyond belief. There had never been anyone but Rose. He found a glass, turned on the cold tap and let it run to make sure it was cold. As he watched the torrent of water gushing out, he remembered looking for Rose at that time and finding her climbing out of the pool after her daily dozen lengths. She had stood in front of him, water streaming from her, and said, "You're still here, then? Just go away. I can't bear it. Go away."

Dan hadn't been able to come to terms with the fact that she sided with her mother. "You know there isn't anyone else. No one. On his earth. No one but you," he'd told her.

He'd seen her hesitate, but a lifetime of agreeing with her mother had overcome her natural inclination to believe him. Fortunately, she'd soon discovered the truth.

He turned off the tap, took the glass to her, and as he handed it over, he bent to kiss the top of her head. "Love you."

Rose drank the glass right to the bottom before she said, "I don't deserve you, my darling. I simply don't."

"Clean slate, we said. You stay right there, and watch me mow the lawn. Got to do something. Can't sit about. I'll open the window. If you need anything, give me a shout."

He glanced at her once or twice and saw she'd picked up her book again. Then the next time he checked, the book had slipped off her knee and she was asleep. Do her good. She didn't get much sleep at night now. It was just what she needed. He paused for a moment to admire her. Everywhere she went people stared. And no wonder. She really was beautiful. Halfway through cutting the lawn his mobile rang. It was a call to Tattersall's Cop. One of Callum's goats was ill, and he was worried. He didn't want to bring it in because his wife, Nuala, who was very ill, couldn't be left. Dan left the mower where it was, wrote a note and put it on the table beside Rose and left.

To get to Tattersall's Cop, Dan had to cross the river in the center of Barleybridge by the Weymouth Bridge and then take the left fork, called Cop Lane, in Wootton. He was struck once again as he approached Callum's farm by how smart it looked. Dan sometimes thought that Callum spent too much time keeping the premises in order. While that was commendable and something other farmers could do well to think about, keeping the farm immaculate didn't fill the coffers.

"Good morning, Callum. What's the problem?"

"It's little Sybil."

Callum had bought the complete stock of a goat farmer who'd died, and among them were seven pygmy goats—perky, bright versions of full-sized goats, born with more than their fair share of curiosity. They'd been brought into a pen close to the house, and leaning on the gate alongside Callum, Dan paused to study them for a moment before going in. "They all look fit. Which is Sybil, then?"

"The all-black one." All seven of them were springing around the pen on a familiarization tour. They were a mixture of black, white and fawn, and looked as though they'd all been in the washing machine that morning, so fresh and smart did they look. What with their appealing looks and their cheeky antics, Dan couldn't help but smile at them.

"Settling down nicely, are they?"

"All of them are. Think they'd been getting a bit neglected toward the end. Nothing serious, mind, but neglected."

"What did you want them for, Callum?"

"Fancied a change and Nuala was keen."

"How is she?"

Callum didn't reply for a moment, and then he said, "You'll

see for yourself in a minute; she's coming out to see you. Wants to know about your wife."

"I see. So why am I here? There doesn't seem much wrong with Sybil."

"I reckon it's worms. Appetite like you wouldn't believe."

Dan climbed over the gate and was immediately mobbed by all seven of the goats. Dan crouched to examine Sybil and found himself with pygmy goats endeavoring to raid his pockets, steal his mobile, climb on his back, and generally get in on the act by making their own diagnosis.

"How long have you been farming, Callum?"

"Fifteen years or thereabouts. Why?"

"Don't you know what happens when you put a billy in with nanny goats?"

Callum's eyebrows shot up when he'd absorbed what Dan had said. "Oh, God! You don't mean . . ."

"I do. Sybil's in kid."

Callum rubbed his hands with glee. "No! Never thought it might be that. Nuala'll be delighted. Delighted. Well, I never. That's great. Sure it is." His tanned face almost split in two with delight.

"Not long to go, I shouldn't think." He stood up, trying to escape the goats' attentions without knocking any of them down. "In fact, this one looks as if . . ."

"That's Cassandra, she's Nuala's favorite."

". . . she might be too."

Callum's Nuala came out of the house and walked slowly toward them, every delicate step an effort. Dan hoped his face didn't register the shock he felt when he saw her. She was emaciated beyond itself. It didn't seem possible that she was still able to stand upright.

Dan touched his cap. "Good morning, Mrs. Tattersall. I've just been giving Callum some good news."

Callum interrupted. "Let me tell her. Sybil's expecting!"

"Really!" Nuala's face burst into life, and the small spark of what was left of her lit up her beautiful blue eyes. "Well now, isn't that good news, for sure. When?"

"Within the week, I would have thought."

"Within the week!"

Dan watched Callum hug her as though she were made of the finest glass. So tenderly.

"I might just see that. Yes, I might. They must look so sweet."

"They do, Mrs. Tattersall, nothing sweeter." Dan noticed a grimace cross her face. Immediately Callum said, "I'll take you in." He picked her up as easily as he would a baby, and set off for the house, calling over his shoulder, "I'll call you when she's in labor. Can't afford to take any risks."

"Right. 'Bye, Mrs. Tattersall."

"Bye, Dan. My love to your Rose." Her feeble voice just reached Dan, and he was glad she couldn't see his face, because he felt so distressed. He looked at Sybil and said quietly, "You'd better hurry up or she won't see that kid of yours. Do you hear me?" Sybil, however, had other things to think about, as Callum had left the goats some tidbits in the feed trough, and she was concentrating on getting the major share.

Dan was almost home when he decided to ring the practice to see if there were any more calls for him, but found he must have left his mobile in the goat pen. One—nil to the goats. He just hoped Rose hadn't been trying to ring him. He drove all the way back to Tattersall's Cop, parked his Land Rover, intending to knock at the farmhouse door, but saw a doctor from the medical practice in Barleybridge just going in. So he went quietly to the goat pen to find his mobile laid abandoned and unharmed in the long grass by the fencing.

It had a text message on it from Rose. "Baby started."

Also by Rebecca Shaw

WELCOME TO BARLEYBRIDGE!

A Country Affair
1-4000-9820-3
$12.95 paper

YOUNG, inexperienced, and somewhat shy, Kate Howard arrives in Barleybridge to begin a job as a receptionist at the Barleybridge Veterinary Hospital. As Kate learns the ins and outs of her job, handsome Australian vet Scott Spencer takes an interest in her and encourages Kate to pursue her dreams to become a vet herself. His advice is solid, and his charm is intoxicating, but Kate is well aware that she is hardly the only woman to fall under the dashing doctor's spell. Add to this the pressure of her longtime but rather dull boyfriend, Adam, who is not at all happy about her newfound aspirations to return to school, and Kate has some decisions to make, decisions that are growing more complex at every turn.

Tender, funny, and full of warmth and simple joys, *A Country Affair* is the perfect introduction to a delightful place and its witty and lovable inhabitants.

Available from Three Rivers Press wherever books are sold.

THREE RIVERS PRESS · NEW YORK